Broken Songs
An Adolescent in War-Torn Vienna

Studies in Austrian Literature, Culture, and Thought

Translation Series

General Editors:

Jorun B. Johns
Richard H. Lawson

Graziella Hlawaty

Broken Songs
An Adolescent in War-Torn
Vienna

Afterword by Rainer Lendl

Translated by
Pamela S. Saur

ARIADNE PRESS
Riverside, California

Ariadne Press would like to express its appreciation to the Bundeskanzleramt –
Sektion Kunst, Vienna for assistance in publishing this book.

KUNST

Translated from the German *Die Stadt der Lieder*
© 1995 Paul Zsolnay Verlag, Wien

Library of Congress Cataloging-in-Publication Data

Hlawaty, Graziella, 1929-
 [Stadt der Lieder. English]
 Broken songs : an adolescent in war-torn Vienna / Graziella Hlawaty ;
 afterword by Rainer Lendl ; translated by Pamela S. Saur.
   p.   cm. – (Studies in Austrian literature, culture, and thought.
 Translation series)
 ISBN 1-57241-132-5 (pbk.)
  1. World War, 1939-1945—Austria—Vienna—Fiction. 2. Vienna
 (Austria)—History—Fiction. I. Saur, Pamela S. II. Title
 PT2668.L38S713 2005
 833'.914--dc22
                                              2005041039

Cover Design
Art Director: George McGinnis
Photo: Institut für Zeitgeschichte, Vienna

Copyright © 2005
by Ariadne Press
270 Goins Court
Riverside, CA 92507

All rights reserved.
No part of this publication may be reproduced or transmitted
in any form or by any means without formal permission.
Printed in the United States of America.
ISBN 1-57241-132-5
(original trade paperback)

Table of Contents

Prologue 1
Chapter One: The Smile 4
Chapter Two: Smoke Signals 18
Chapter Three: German Oaks Stand Tall 21
Chapter Four: Ring-a-Round the Rosie 27
Chapter Five: Farewell, My Darling 38
Chapter Six: Easter, 1945 61
Chapter Seven: The Fortress 74
Chapter Eight: In the Spring 82
Chapter Nine: Easter Bells 88
Chapter Ten: The Hiding Place 102
Chapter Eleven: Necessity is the Mother of Invention 108
Chapter Twelve: Stories from the Vienna Woods 127
Chapter Thirteen: The Bliss of Wine 133
Chapter Fourteen: A Movie Visit in a Red Blouse 144
Chapter Fifteen: Flight 157
Afterword 175

Acknowledgment

The translator of this book, Pamela S. Saur, wishes to express sincere gratitude for the generous support of this publication by Dr. Brenda Nichols, Dean, College of Arts and Sciences, and Dr. Jerry Bradley, Associate Vice President for Research and Graduate Studies, Lamar University, Beaumont, Texas.

Prologue

Herr Pospischil belonged to that class of people who always knock too softly and as a result all too often have to be satisfied with locked doors. And so it is not surprising that in time he got out of the habit of knocking at all and even gave up hoping and expecting. Expecting: expecting what?

People around him recognized right away that he was a nice, insignificant person, and his modesty was generally beloved. His thirty years of service with the police, partly on the street, partly in the precinct behind an old ink-stained desk, had done nothing to change his fundamental character. His colleagues were sure of him: sure he would never rival them for a promotion, decoration or advantage — such a thing simply wasn't in his nature.

Approximately once every four weeks Herr Pospischil was overtaken by a terrible migraine that lasted two or three days. There was a lot of mockery of his periodic illness, but nevertheless, if Pospischil didn't have outside duty, the men in the guardroom made adjustments when he had his "critical days." During breaks they played chess instead of cards, because the game was quieter, and no one was compelled to cry out, "Ace" or "Trump" and see a look of reproach on Pospischil's pale face, distorted with pain.

The decades passed quite uneventfully for Pospischil. Walks, migraines, police office, bachelor apartment: his routine conformed to the quiet heroic life of the masses. Looked at from the outside, nothing in particular seems to happen. And so the fates of the masses are not written about in history books, for no historically significant deeds accompany them. One lives: more is not required, more is not done.

Isn't it almost a miracle that the masses are satisfied with their lives? They live, they simply live from day to day! But must there not be, somehow, somewhere, a secret way out, some kind of trick that makes it possible to endure a life lived in this way? Some kind of illusion that distorts the truth and grants the strange tenacious ability to be able to close one's eyes and not see the emptiness of all one's days? A faith? Or a love?

But perhaps the word "trick" is too harsh. Should one say: a "medicine"? A medicine that we all use, each in our own way, to help us along through this life?

Herr Pospischil took early retirement. He had an old heart ailment, along with the cursed migraines. And for a lonely bachelor to be retired, that meant having time to be alone. Plenty of time, perhaps far too much time? No wonder, that Pospischil started to think a lot, to think about all kinds of things, more intensely than ever before. Now, as a civilian, he often retraced his old patrol rounds, but he saw life on the streets from a new angle, and soon his excursions stretched far past the borders of his old precinct.

Herr Pospischil's most important walks tended to lead to the small paper goods store opposite the school. They already knew him by name there. He was greeted with the words, "Oh, good day, Herr Pospischil, what would you like today?"

He was happy every time someone knew him, addressed him by name! And, a little embarrassed over his joy, he stammered out his order, took the writing paper, paid for it, and left.

All at once the whole world was changed for him: the chestnut trees on Maroltinger Street wore their first buds, quite clearly it could be seen that they would soon blossom; in the park the children were building an especially beautiful castle in the sandbox; the people standing in line in front of the dairy lady's store were chatting with each other in a more friendly manner than usual. Thalia Street, leading out from the end of the perfectly straight tracks of the number 46 streetcar line, stretched in these happy moments out to a very open, very free road, upward, outward, to the Liebhart Valley, to Gallitzinberg.

Oh, it wasn't half bad, this life. Wars, love and death marked the major or minor stations along the way; one had to take them as they came. In the trees the blackbirds sang untroubled, chirping away and composing their songs. One strolled through the streets, greeted acquaintances with the old local expressions, "Honored," "I kiss your hand, gracious madame," "Servus, servus!" There was so much expectation in the air. From Gallitzinberg St. Stephen's Cathedral could be seen, the whole city of Vienna with her towers, houses, gardens, shining in the sunlight, surrounded by hills, forests and the green of springtime. One lived, one was, one *is*. One is — *now.* That was the most essential thing, the most important, wasn't it? Yes, the blackbirds were singing, there was really something meaningful and eternal in the air. Spring, music.

Music and fresh new paper — they were indeed a kind of medicine. Even in the war year of 1945 they seemed to hold a promise of reconciliation and healing.

Chapter One: The Smile

In the morning hours the streetcars were always over-crowded. The women conductors stood helplessly hemmed in somewhere in the cars' interiors and had to make an effort to reach the leather straps to sound the departure signal at each stop. On every footboard the passengers hung like grapes on the vine, some in acrobatic contortions with one leg on the step, and held onto the strap or onto other passengers.

For a while now, Ilse had stopped bothering with the monthly student passes. She had been brought to that point by the feeling that there was no order in the system any more, and also by the fact that she could save money. People could always ride for free on the running-boards, and if by chance an overzealous conductor should appear, this was no great misfortune. All one needed to do was shift to a different place as fast as possible at the next stop.

Besides, the trip on the running-board was a lot more suspenseful and eventful than it was inside the car. At every stop, one had to climb down to make room for the passengers getting in and out, and at the same time to maintain the place one had fought for. During these breaks it was good to shake one's cramped fingers a little and relax one's leg muscles. Afterwards came the fast ride again, with wind in one's hair and tears in one's eyes, the curves, the sudden emergency braking with sand; the gravel that crunched and shrieked under the wheels; the clouds of dust that billowed up between the wheels and the tracks.

These suspenseful minutes on the narrow running-boards — what an adventure for those who dared it! Such dangerous rides had long been a part of Ilse's usual daily routine; she was tolerated by the authorities, hardly ever forbidden to ride. There wasn't enough room for all the passengers anyway, for since the last big bomb attacks there were even fewer streetcars than before, many lines had been completely discontinued, and the trams ran less and less frequently.

Ilse had just fought for a place on the running-board. Her bookbag prevented her from holding on with both hands, but that didn't matter, she had plenty of experience with one-handed running-board rides. With just one hand on the strap the illegal ride was even more exciting.

And today we'll write compositions in German class, thought Ilse, as the streetcar began to move. She looked forward to it. There was nothing she loved more than this subject: addressing a new, surprising theme, a theme she could express something about and develop, a subject she could use to prove her ability at last. And the more that Ilse immersed herself in the assigned task, the more clearly previously vague material began to take shape, formed itself into a coherent whole, into a meaning that was hers alone, very personal, but carefully thought out. A meaning that often surprised her with its definiteness. When the essays came back corrected, they were discussed, and Ilse was almost always asked to read hers aloud. But beforehand, she always sat on her bench, ready, as if for a death sentence, to have to hear decimating criticism, but at the same time filled with an obstinate longing, perhaps once again to have turned in the best paper.

It'll soon be eleven, I'm running late, Ilse realized. But always, when the first classes were canceled, or the whole schedule was turned around — and that had happened a lot lately — it was somehow difficult to be punctual. Today, however, it would be good for her to be on time because German class and the writing assignment were first. A good start! She could see the beloved themebook in front of her, the blue lines, the red correction border. At the upper right side of the paper, on the new, empty page, her pen would ceremoniously write the date: March 12, 1945. And after 1945 should be a period, as the professor had just recently preached about.

In the wharf park the branches already had their first buds; the trees gave off a light green shimmer. It occurred to Ilse that Else had promised to bring the newest Heinz Woester picture to school. Else, just as enthusiastic a Burg Theater fan as Ilse was, already had an autograph of "Heinzi," her favorite actor. Ilse didn't even want to start to think about the many Fred Liewehr autographs that Else was hoarding. Anyway, in the case of Ewald Balser photos, Else was behind; Ilse owned two more autographed pictures than she did. They were even in regard to Maria Eis and Raoul Aslan. Werner Krauß belonged to Else's special collector's interest, while Ilse had specialized in Maria Holst and Alexander Trojan.

Yes, life looked good, seen from the vantage point of the running-board of the streetcar, with wind in her hair and the prospect of an approaching German composition in class and a photograph exchange during the breaks — but now, suddenly, the streetcar braked, again came the great interruption: the sirens howl, howl — howl in three long blasts: first warning — air raid warning!

Alternately building up and dying down, the ear-deafening noise thunders over houses, streets, piles of rubble and ruins on the street, and the "golden" Viennese hearts, (not really made out of metal), beat faster and faster, more and more fearfully. After the sirens are silenced the ticking of the radio clock sets in, echoing loudly through the streets. The eerie sound of the ghostly ticking fills the pauses between the enemy flight announcements over the radio wires. Whoever usually plays the radio "cuckoo" calls that announce the first alarm seems not to have heard. Now he has, now he too has learned of the danger from the howling of the sirens and from the ticking of the clocks.

The picture of the street changes with every beat; the whole city is seized with disquiet. All the streetcars have come to a stop. Window blinds are clattering shut. A gigantic pair of scissors is setting about cutting through the thread of life in the city. People are streaming in all directions; nothing will be carried out that was planned. Now there is only "chance" determining everything: the chance moment at which a container of bombs is opened; the press of a button, carried out one second earlier or later; the planned actions or the mood of a bomber pilot; the thickness of the wall of a building; the amount of supporting strength of the vault of a cellar.

Tomorrow is math day at school, Ilse thought. Then there will probably be no air raid warning. Such luck! Today, the day of the easy German composition class, today of all days, "it" happens.

Annoyed, Ilse looks over at the Schwedenplatz, just at the moment that an O car is coming out into the curve on the embankment to avoid being stuck on the Schweden Bridge during the bomb attack.

There was no use. She couldn't possibly make it all the way to school. Radetzky Street was too far away. Now the air raid wardens had taken charge. They were marshaling the crowds of moving people into the bomb shelters, driving all the pedestrians off the street.

She had to forget about schoolwork, about school period. Okay, then the only thing to do was to head toward the Rudolfsplatz, to go back home. She had been so happy to set off this morning, and now she had to turn around and go back to the same place she had started from. What a pity!

Walter, age five, had already put on his air raid backpack. Her little brother always looked very proud to have his own backpack. Peter was lying in a clothes basket that his father had mounted onto a carrying harness during his last leave. Peter was in a good mood. When Ilse met her mother and her half-brothers in the stairwell, he cried, "Lala! Lili!"— which meant the same as, "Here, you're here, Ilse!"— and he stretched his tiny, fat baby fingers out toward her.

"Good, you're here," said her mother. She had a lot to carry: a backpack on her back, Peter in the clothes basket and besides that their important documents — and a bag of groceries.

"Our German composition class is down the drain," Ilse moped. "And I was really looking forward to it!"

Her mother put the clothes basket with Peter in it on the window-sill and Ilse took the backpack from her. Just as she had it strapped on, the sirens started howling again. General alarm! The stairwell was filled with the short blasts, swelling and receding, the ear-deafening sound seemed like it would never end, that it would stay in their house forever.

Ilse looked over at the hall window. Through the darkened, blue-painted panes, she saw a small stripe of sky and the inner courtyard looked strangely near. Then the windowpanes began to rattle softly.

"Hurry, hurry!" Frau Rainer from the fourth floor hurried by. Taking two steps at a time, she was running in the direction of the cellar. "Hurry, hurry!" she gasped. "The Augarden Flak has already begun to shoot."

"Flak" was short for "*F*lieger*a*bwehr*k*anonen" Ilse thought to herself. Abbreviations were one of her favorite subjects; whenever she heard one she immediately thought about whether she could identify the original phrase. If not, she looked it up as soon as she could. Doing so seemed immensely important to Ilse, although if asked why, she wouldn't have been able to say. But, she told herself, it could only be an advantage to know a little more than necessary.

"The flak always starts half an hour before the bombers come," Ilse called out after Frau Rainer.

"I wouldn't count on that!" cried a shrill female voice up from the cellar door — Frau Zirkelbach's voice. And Frau Zirkelbach, the building superintendent, gasped for air, as Ilse, then her brothers and mother, went past her and past the cellar door and toward the entrance to the building.

"You're crazy!" Frau Zirkelbach, who had been serving as air raid warden for a good while now, was beside herself. "Crazy! The flak has already started. You must go into the cellar. You can't be on the street anymore! It's forbidden."

"I can. I can!" declared the mother in a decisive tone. "You won't forbid me to do anything. I'm going to find myself and my children a better shelter than this dilapidated basement here. It's much safer in the catacombs."

"There you're safe from bombs," added Ilse with the bold and careless certainty of a fifteen-year-old.

"Irresponsible!" Frau Zirkelbach's voice was filled with indignation. "Irresponsible, this mother! And listen to the nonsense the girl is spouting too."

They ran across the Rudolfsplatz. Besides them, no one else seemed to be on the street. Ilse was on the lookout for Robert, a boy her age who lived in one of the neighboring buildings. As a matter of fact, the two hadn't really gotten acquainted until one of these air raids. Ilse had just come out of the catacombs after her mother had told her to return to their apartment to cook some hot cereal because Peter had nothing to eat and was screaming with hunger.

In the middle of the park, right on the path of Ilse's short-cut, Robert had been standing, just standing there and looking up at the sky. He had looked like a statue, and as she came near him, he had pointed up and said, "Look! Those are Americans! The first bomb squadrons. Don't they look magnificent?"

Yes, they had looked "magnificent." A cloudless, blue sky, streaming sunlight, and high above, high, high above their heads, blinking and gleaming, small and silver-white, were the well-ordered formations of the bomber squadrons. They were flying forward so slowly and quietly that it almost looked as if they weren't going to

move from the spot.
"If that isn't a sight!" cried Robert.
"You're not afraid," said Ilse.
"No. Are you?"
"No." Ilse was still looking up. No, she wasn't afraid. Not at this moment, not next to this boy. Actually, it occurred to her for the first time, she had never really been afraid of the bombs.

She said so to Robert. Why shouldn't she say it? It wasn't really boasting or exaggerating. In fact, she was amazed herself that she had no fear of the bombs and that she had just this moment noticed that she didn't.

Robert told her that it was exactly the same with him. "I really don't know why," he said. "I can't explain why I'm not afraid. Ordinarily, I'm not especially courageous. Maybe it's because you and I don't have anything to lose yet. Today is today— and tomorrow is tomorrow."

They kept looking up, hidden in some bushes so that no zealous air raid warden would discover them.

"Of course, we have our lives," said Robert after a while. "We do have something to lose, our lives. But, you know, I don't care if I die. So what if I do?"

"You too?" cried Ilse. As they set off running home, she thought, "He must not have a very good home life, or he wouldn't talk like that."

After this encounter Ilse was always on the lookout for Robert when they ran through the park during an alarm. Now and then she saw him on her way to school, but his streetcar went in the opposite direction. She had no idea what school he attended. "I'll ask him sometime," she planned, but the idea remained just a plan. Everytime they saw each other from afar, they waved at each other like old friends, but it seemed to her that the only time they would be able to really talk would be during an alarm.

A few young men were standing on the fishermen's steps in front of the entrance to the catacombs. "Come on, hurry, everybody inside!" ordered an air raid warden. "Don't stand around in front of the entrance. The Americans take pictures of everything, and the next time will be our turn."

"Nonsense," said one of the youths who was sitting on a step in the sun. "Nothing but hysteria! Nothin' is gonna happen to us in the first district."

"Inside, inside!" cried the warden. He pointed to Ilse's mother. "You, there, ma'am, with the children! Hurry, hurry. Go straight into the shelter now!"

Ilse and her mother took the clothes basket with Peter by its handles and forced it into the narrow hallway. It smelled damp and musty; as they started to climb down the worn, narrow stone steps Peter began to lose his good mood and cry.

"Oh no, kids again," muttered a woman.

They were on their way to their usual place, groping forward through narrow corridors, through a many-cornered maze, pressing quickly forward through tiny rooms in which the shelter seekers were pouring onto wooden benches. The passages had no doors. They were only faintly lit by the dull glow of light bulbs set in recesses on the walls.

"Today the whole Floridsdorf is here again," someone said.

Many inhabitants of Vienna's outer districts, especially residents of Floridsdorf, who had already experienced several heavy bombings, made the trek to the catacombs in the mornings, because here, so far, nothing had "happened." The inner city had thus far been spared and so was viewed as relatively safe. If the "cuckoo, cuckoo" sound was heard on the radio in the morning, that was the first warning; next came the first alarm; next the clock began ticking and then a voice announced the arrival of enemy aircraft in Carinthia or Styria; then the emigration of Floridsdorf residents began in earnest: women with baby carriages, carrying backpacks, thermos bottles and groceries, filled the streets and streamed over the Franz Josef Quay toward the inner city. They dragged sedan chairs and camp chairs, and the older people especially were equipped with plenty of blankets and pillows.

Ilse's mother steered toward her usual place. The bench next to the wall was still vacant. Places by the wall were dangerous, according to popular belief. Walls could collapse.

Peter had quieted down again and stopped screaming. Walter had discovered two boys he knew in the opposite corner. They were the sons of Frau Renz, a musician in the neighboring building. He wanted to run over to them, but his mother held him back. "Stay here," she commanded. "The catacombs aren't playgrounds. And besides that we have to be careful not to use up too much air."

Frau Kerschbaum, the physician, and her ninety-year-old mother were already sitting in their places. "Go on, Frau Renz," said the elderly woman, "play us somethin' on the accordion to give us somethin' nice to think about."

The woman musician looked Spanish and her two children like Italian street urchins. She was single. "Yeah, that's jus' how they are, those artist folks," the dairy store lady always said when people were gossiping about Frau Renz and speculating about her children's father. "He's gotta be some kind of 'arteest' too," a lady from house number five had said when she picked up her milk ration. Ilse, who was in line with her milk bottles, laughed out loud. "I'd like t' know what there is ta laugh about," said the cashier. "Well," answered Ilse, "because then the two boys will surely be 'arteests' also." Then the dairy lady had to laugh, but the Bohemian woman from house number five didn't think that was funny at all.

"If you want me to, Frau Kerschbaum, I'll play. That is, if the others have nothing against it?" Frau Renz looked questioningly around and reached for her accordion.

Frau Doctor Kerschbaum, ear, nose and throat specialist, was "someone" in the neighborhood. Of course no one had any objections.

And so Frau Renz, the "artist," began to play. And because she was in Vienna, surrounded by only "genuine" Viennese people sitting together: Novaks, Dvoraks, Navratils, Blazeks and Birnhubers — "solid folks" and "upstanding, honest workers" — the whole familiar and beloved mixture was there, with their sweet decadent reminiscences of the certainly not always golden age of the monarchy, and because around her was a genuine Viennese mood ("Now they're about to attack. The outside doors are already locked shut — to save oxygen," grumbled the skinny, dried up old air raid warden); for all these reasons, Frau Renz, herself a genuine Viennese as well, began playing her special music for this occasion and for the ninety-year-old Frau Kerschbaum. And she sang as well. She had a soft, pleasant alto voice that needed only a little oxygen. "If I C'd Jus' Return to Grinzing," she sang, and "My Ma, She Was a Viennese," "Vienna, Vienna, Only You," "In Prater Park the Trees are Bloomin' Again," and "Oh, When Y' Run Out — of Music or Wine."

Old Frau Kerschbaum was content, and, thank God, a little deaf, so she was spared hearing a few unpleasant interrupting sounds: dull rumbling, then a strange rolling and chopping, as if nearby someone was chopping up the soil with a pickaxe. And this chopping sound was getting nearer and nearer.

"Quiet! Shut off that damn accordion," cried a shrill woman's voice from the next room.

"Psst!" The old air raid warden put his finger to his lips. "Now, let's not have no panic. At the moment they're right above us, but soon they'll be gone!"

The warden was the highest authority there, and people were accustomed to listening to him. Today, at this moment, the "highest authority" had tears in his eyes.

Frau Renz, the "artist" — whose name had never appeared in big letters on a kiosk — on this particular twelfth of March was a great and influential entertainer — Frau Renz kept on playing. Was it for the old lady? Was it to please the elderly, trembling air raid warden? She kept on playing and she kept on singing " There's a Ol' Nut Tree in Heiligenstadt," "That's a Piece a' Heaven: Vienna an' Wine."

Little Walter grabbed Ilse's hand. Under them the ground began to move; it shook, swayed; seemed to be pushed up by an enormous powerful machine. After that it was suddenly still again; no chopping, no rumbling; the only sound heard was Frau Renz's accordion music. Her fingers danced over the ivory keys; quickly from one refrain to the next. Nothing could make her stop. It was as if she was begging for her life, playing for her life, begging and playing for the lives of everyone around her.

"They're gone now," said Ilse's mother.

Peter lay in his basket and slept. Now and then a broad, contented smile passed over his chubby baby face. "Only children can smile so happily in their sleep," thought Ilse. And with the unburdened and uncompromising philosophizing of a searching adolescent, she asked herself, "Do we all live through so many bad experiences that we lose the ability to smile like that in our sleep?" She couldn't imagine that a sleeping adult could possibly smile so blissfully.

Ilse fished her brown notebook out of her coat pocket. She brought it along to the cellar every time there was an alarm. She had written down all kinds of things in it: poems by Friedrich Hölderlin, Josef von Eichendorff, Martin Greif and Friedrich Nietzsche, titles of musical pieces she especially liked; films that had impressed her. Lately she had added something new: round postal cancellation marks with faces of famous men. She had bought the whole "cultural series" for only ten cents and glued in the wonderful, brightly colored portraits: Nietzsche, over the poem, "To the Unknown God," with his black, glittering eyes and long bushy moustache; Schubert, with his gleaming eyeglasses and red cheeks, and next to him, in Ilse's best handwriting, "Unfinished Symphony in B-Minor;" and Richard Wagner, with his violet velvet cap and haughty aristocratic nose. Next to his picture Ilse had written simply "Ring." On the next page there was a handsome picture of Beethoven with his thick black curly hair, and the words "The Ninth, Ode to Joy, the Heiligenstadt Testament, Fidelio," written with elaborate flourishes.

"Don't start your silly scribbling," Ilse heard her mother say. But she began writing anyway, putting down her thoughts about smiling on the page, "Personal Notes."

Frau Renz was still playing Viennese folk songs. A woman from Floridsdorf was holding up her baby to Frau Doktor Kerschbaum. The infant was wrapped in oversized swaddling clothes. "Take her a minute, Frau Doktor," she asked. "Y'know, my poor kid has something wrong with 'is hip, he does. Poor l'il thing is all wrapped up in a plaster cast." The doctor took the heavy bundle. "Oh my, that's a pity! You have a pretty good weight to carry around!"

"Yes, true, a pretty good face, that's for sure," nodded the doctor's old mother, who hadn't really understood the nearby bomb attack and didn't quite comprehend what was being said now. "Really a perdy l'il kiddo." Then she slipped back into the Viennese melodies and — look! — something like a smile crept over her wrinkled old face.

"They're coming back," said the air raid warden and looked up at the cellar ceiling, as if he could read there the route the bomb squadron was taking.

Ilse had finished her entry about babies' smiles and was just about to put her pencil and notebook back in her pocket when old Frau Kerschbaum started to smile. An old lady, a very old lady was smiling now! Strange, how quickly a thought written down needed to be revised! She hesitated, took the pencil in her hand, looked at it, a small wooden object with four edges, wanted to write some more, but found no words and no continuation of her thoughts. She shook herself and finally put away the pencil and paper.

"High time you stopped dreaming and started taking life seriously." Her mother's voice reached her as if from a long distance away. And only much later, years later, would Ilse comprehend the direction her thoughts were taking; back then, when she couldn't think of the words she wanted to write down: when paper, pencil, and the words she had just written weren't so important in themselves, but first and foremost, the important thing was to perceive the surprising and unexpected things in life. Because while you're writing, while you're thinking, just when you think you recognize things and know things, the course of events runs, flows, streams past you; when you want to hold something still it pulses forth through the veins of life, it has already been changed or confirmed. Insignificant things can become important and apparently inconsequential things can be meaningful. Is that what Mother calls "taking life seriously?" But, then, why did she say, "silly scribbling?" Is it really "nonsense," when a person starts to think?

"Oh — too bad!" cries out old Frau Kerschbaum, because the accordion is suddenly silent. "What's the matter?" she asks, bewildered. And why is Frau Renz suddenly so strangely thoughtful? She seems strangely suspended in the air, waiting for something, something behind the wall and about to appear.

And it comes, it comes, it comes; the enormous, merciless pickaxe, it's coming nearer and nearer. Rumbling, echoing, pounding, rolling, come the loud blasts, shaking everything. In a monstrous, unrelenting rhythm they plow speedily through buildings, walls, iron and concrete; the bomb attack seems to be simultaneously everywhere; a carpet of bombs descending piece by piece, laid over the entire city.

The first terror comes so fast, second by second — and after that time seems to stand still. Everyone sits still, bent over, eyes wide open, as if to see whatever comes with open eyes. Ilse discovers that she has begun to count: twenty-one, twenty-two, twenty-three . . . , the way one begins to count when lightning strikes to see how far away the storm is. And it seems to her as if the whole cellar is full of intent counting machines, all counting with their eyes wide open: twenty-one— twenty-two—. Hunched over, sitting fearful counting machines — twenty-three: that was how many buildings away? Twenty-one, twenty-two; the chopping is more to the right — twenty-one, twenty-two: in the front, now way over to the left — twenty-one, twenty-two; the great pickaxe is rumbling in the direction of the entrance door— twenty-one: the light flickers — twenty-one: the ground rumbles, wumm! Dust everywhere, wumm! Sand everywhere.

"Now I hear it too, I hear it clearly!" cries old Frau Kerschbaum almost happily— wumm! The ground, the walls are askew, the bench is being lifted up, the light goes out, women scream, children cry. "Just don't panic!" (the air raid warden) "It's us! It's us! Now they've hit us!" (a woman in the next room). For a fraction of a second everyone is suspended in the room, feeling: the earth turning, "Yes, it's really turning!" (Ilse) "Quiet, quiet, take a deep breath!" (the doctor). "Are they over us now?" (old Frau Kerschbaum)

The light sputters back on, goes out again, comes back on. There is dust everywhere. The air is grayish white, a strange air, one can see it, taste it, feel it between the teeth, in the eyes. Frau Renz still has the strap of the accordion on her shoulders, and she's pressing her two sons with both arms close against herself.

The pickaxe is fading away and all of a sudden a great silence falls, for a tenth — a hundredth — of a second — how long is this second? How long has this great silence lasted?

And then, many voices, sounds, sobs, crying. "Let us out! We want out!" "My boy has run off… Where is my boy?" Suddenly most people are speaking High German, without knowing it.

"There hasn't been an all-clear," announces the air raid warden. "We still have to wait. Just don't panic now. The worst is certainly behind us."

"So much dust!" complains old Frau Kerschbaum. "But we're still alive, Mother! We're alive!" the doctor shouts into her ear.

"I'll go ask what's going on," says the air raid warden. "Maybe I can get through to a radio." He gropes his way out of the dark corridor.

It is still silent, no detonations, no defense alarms. Silent as a grave. Somewhere a couple of children start to cry, to scream, and

Peter joins in. Ilse's mother gets the thermos bottle out of her backpack and pours some cereal into the baby bottle. Ilse fits the nipple onto the glass bottle. Peter begins to suck loudly. Everyone around looks at him, and thinks for a moment, "Ah, listen to the child enjoy his nourishment!"

The air raid warden comes back. "They're retreating. The all-clear will be any minute!" Everyone sighs with relief. (Later they would recall that they were happy and thought they were out of the woods. But that was years later. *At the time* this feeling that they had "dodged the bullet one more time" had no reality, no substance — it meant nothing because the very next movement with all its lurking uncertainty and dangers could turn that "dodged the bullet one more time" into its opposite. No, at the time people didn't think ahead; they existed from moment to moment; they were robots, who automatically played the accordion, automatically stroked children's hair with their fingers, or automatically pulled bodies out of ruins with their hands. No one was a hero, no one a martyr. Everyone was thrown onto center stage, pushed into the inescapable course of events, allowed no free will and no decisions of one's own, at the mercy of chance each second.)

A sigh of relief, yes. "We were lucky," reported the air raid warden. He took his helmet off and ran his fingers through his hair. "Because around here — ," he hesitated and then continued, speaking quickly, "Well, the exits are destroyed, we're closed in. Now we need to be quiet and wait."

Be quiet and wait; give no expression to one's own uncertainty. Let the hours pass. Only soft conversations here and there; important topics, unimportant. Fears pop up: "Will they find us? What does it look like outside? Is our building still standing?"

When the entrance is finally shoveled out, one after the other climbs into the daylight. In a daze, almost mechanically they move forward, climbing over beams, pieces of walls, bricks, and rubble. Ilse registers what her eyes see, but her eyes can't take in the whole picture. Like the small, modest circle of light of a flashlight that gropes its way forward in the darkest night, she makes out only the nearest, the very closest things: shreds of curtains on a ruined house, pots and pans on an iron circular staircase leading nowhere. Something that looked like a human foot — without a shoe. A woman sitting on a wooden board and crying. A startled cat springing up from reclining on some men's suits from a clothing wholesaler's. A tin sign, dented and bent: "Müller & Sons Clothier." A truck on which a crew of Hitler Youth are heaving lifeless corpses and stacking them up. They are twelve- to fourteen-year-old boys, Wolf Cubs. Short black corduroy pants, brown uniform shirts. Triangular unit badges and swastika patches on their sleeves. Triangular scarves with woven leather knots firmly tied around their necks. They are working quickly, skillfully, as if they had plenty of experience in this kind of transporting.

Chapter Two: Smoke Signals

Every now and then, at appropriate intervals, Herr Pospischil was invited over by the old widow Frau Kreidl. For decades the two had lived on Maroltinger Street, both on the third floor. They were almost next-door neighbors; only the apartments of the dressmaker Frau Weissenböck and the family Brunnhuber were between them. Their two dwellings resembled each other, and because there was no elevator, Frau Kreidl and Herr Pospischil had often climbed the stairs together, chatting as they went.

On this particular day Frau Kreidl had only dark wheat rolls and malt coffee to serve her guest, and she was very upset about it. "I've used all my bread rations up," she explained. "And I don't have any more flour or I would have been able to bake something myself."

"But that's no reason to be sad," said Herr Pospischil. "Irritating things happen. And I don't come over just because I want something to eat."

"Irritating — that's for sure!" She looked at him with tears welling up in her eyes.

"What's the matter, Frau Kreidl? Why are you crying?" Herr Pospischil asked.

"Right there, at the window; I was standing there and I saw it plain as day..." Frau Kreidl pointed to the window. "As plain as day I saw it, the way the clouds of smoke rose up, there, over the inner city. The whole first district is nothing but a pile of rubble. Hadn't you heard?"

No, Herr Pospischil didn't know anything specific about the bomb attack that morning. No bombs had fallen in their immediate area; everyone was saying that this time the outer districts had been spared, and instead the inner city had been "bombed out." The 46ers and most of the other streetcar lines in the inner city were out of commission, they said. But who was saying so? The people he had met on his way to the stationery store. Because since the attack there had been no electricity and no news could be heard on the radio. Of course the radio newscasts didn't ever give very precise information anyway, mostly just local events that had nothing to do with the "final victory." The special broadcasts of the army's high command still announced — after the fanfares from Les Préludes by Liszt — only reports of victories: strategic advantages and victorious front straightening in the East and successful orderly and victorious retreats in the West.

"A pile of rubble? The first district? Who says so?" Herr Pospischil bit into his roll and tried to reassure Frau Kreidl: "You know yourself how people talk. Not half of what they say is true!"

"But I have it on good authority that the catacombs are destroyed. And that's where they always go, my daughter and grandchildren. All three grandchildren. I know that for sure."

Herr Pospischil had learned the art of comforting people from his service with the police. Except when he had a bad migraine, he had always been a real master at it. "Frau Kreidl," he said, "the catacombs are enormous, they have many, many branches, and they're deep underground! I wouldn't worry."

In reality, however, Herr Pospischil was worried. He thought about Ilse. Since he had heard that the whole Kreidl family had sought shelter in the catacombs, a few minutes ago, he really had started to worry. About Ilse.

"Little Ilse," he said involuntarily (he always called her "little"), "wasn't Ilse at school during the alarm?" he asked. And it would have comforted him if old Frau Kreidl had said "Of course, of course, she must have been at school. And from school they don't go to the catacombs. No doubt they have their own air raid shelter."

But old Frau Kreidl remained standing at the window, saying nothing of the kind. Did she perhaps expect to get new information, hopeful messages, from the fact that plumes of smoke were rising or not rising in the sky?

"Dear little Ilse," thought Herr Pospischil silently. Over forty years difference in age between us! And that was as it should be. The little Ilse, whom he had brought chocolate when she visited her grandmother, Frau Kreidl. The bigger Ilse with her first report card. Her eyes — he always remembered her eyes. Big, dark eyes that reminded him of Irene, his first love! That's kitsch, he told himself. Forget about it! You've forgotten everything before her and everything after her, like you've forgotten your violin on its place on the wall, the violin you never take down anymore.

But to spoil Ilse — to spoil her a little — to keep giving her presents; no one could stop him from doing that. Her home life wasn't "so good"; he had heard that often enough from Frau Kreidl. Her mother's second marriage, the little stepbrothers she had to take care of; the nervous, short-tempered mother, to whom Ilse meant nothing more than a bad memory of her first unhappy marriage. No, all that couldn't have provided Ilse with a very good home life.

To spoil her a little, yes, that was what he wanted. He always had a few presents ready when she came to visit her grandmother. He always popped in with his "trifles" (goodies he had paid dearly for on the black market, little books of poems that she could easily hide from her mother): "Here, Ilse, I happened to come across this recently. Just a trifle..."

Old Herr Pospischil; he didn't know any better: sympathy can be as dangerous as love. Hadn't he planned to go his way in peace? Not to worry about anything or anyone? What was he getting involved in? He was getting involved in life, in the midst of life itself. Could life still touch him?

His eyes started to flutter; it was the first sign of an impending headache coming suddenly upon him. He stood up, thanked Frau Kreidl for her hospitality, and took his leave quickly (hastily offering a few words of comfort: "Nothing is as bad as it seems on first glance!"), and hurried across the hall to the door of his apartment.

Chapter Three: German Oaks Stand Tall

Torn up — the whole textile district around the fishermen's staircase had been torn up by the bomb squadrons as they plowed through the sky, gleaming in the sun.

The way back to the apartment required detours around mountains of rubble, ruined buildings and lonely fire walls looming up into the sky. The green Spring Park wasn't there any more; no one could get past the bomb trenches and piles of rubble to enter the park.

The familiar streets had become strange. Were they really streets? This climbing over piles of bricks, this inching forward through beams, pieces of walls, iron crossbeams; this groping through a gray world that no one could recognize any more — no, this wasn't walking through streets to get somewhere, it was searching, asking: Where are we, where were we, where is our home?

Ilse was astonished to find that her building was still there. Oh yes, it was still standing in its place! The first and second stories, up to her apartment, were just as before. The fourth and fifth story of the side of the building with the right-hand staircase had been blown away; all that was left of the third story was pieces of walls; the ceilings of her apartment had become the roof, and in the outer wall of Ilse's room there was a big gaping hole — the bomb had hit right next to it.

It was like a miracle: the front gate of the building was standing open, the entrance and the left-hand staircase were still standing.

In the front hall, between rubble and shards of glass, the tenants were scurrying around armed with brooms and shovels. The next miracle was something to celebrate: "You, you are alive!" cried Frau Zirkelbach as the "catacomb family" emerged. There was a general embracing between the neighbors and her mother. Everyone gave her a hug, even those who Ilse knew all too well would have preferred to have her mother out of the way. They all greeted her warmly. In the cellar, it had been "horrible," the neighbors were reporting. "Like the end of the world! We were sure it was our last hour! Our last hour!"

— Yes, they had been convinced of it.

"And you are still alive!" cried Frau Zirkelbach again and again.

Then she started hugging Peter and Ilse. "They said everything was destroyed in the catacombs. One direct hit after another — no two stones left standing on top of each other, they said."

"And they said no one survived," added Frau Rainer, formerly of the fourth floor. "These rumors! That proves it again: you can't trust all these rumors."

"Enemy propaganda!" muttered Herr Kaufmann, a resident of the side of the building with the left-hand staircase. Herr Kaufmann came from Berlin. In 1938 he had taken over the Jewish family's apartment on the third floor. He had also taken over their little umbrella store on the square, "Arianized" it, as it was so nicely put, like the expression "Annexation of the Ostmark by the Great German Reich." He was a so-called "Marmeladinger," one of the "Reichsgermans," who had suddenly turned up at this time; one of the men who, for unexplained reasons, didn't have to join the military, even though Herr Kaufmann was quite obviously of an age and fitness level that seemed "service worthy."

"Enemy propaganda!" Herr Kaufmann repeated. "It's supposed to destroy the German people's will to fight."

No one contradicted him. First of all, they had long ago learned that it was best to greet remarks of this kind with silence, and certainly not to contradict them. People could sense, whether or not they had learned it from experience, that only unpleasantness could come from arguing. And secondly, at this moment they all had more pressing concerns than military morale. Besides, it was easy for Herr Kaufmann to talk; his apartment was still there, his wife and children had long been safely settled in Vorarlberg in a "bomb secure" area. But everyone who was now standing there without an apartment really had more important concerns than the "will to fight" of a people they had never really felt that they belonged to.

"We have to go upstairs," said Ilse's mother. "Up to the second story. Let's go see what is left up there."

"Well, you ain't never livin' up there again," said Frau Zirkelbach.

"How could you know that? I need to go up and see for myself and think it over."

"There's a danger that the building will collapse," reported the building superintendent. "I already looked. You're not allowed to go up."

"You're lucky," said Frau Rainer to Ilse's mother. "Look at me. I don't need to think anything over. There's nothing left of my apartment."

Frau Zirkelbach, in her authority as building superintendent and air raid warden, barred Ilse's mother's path. "You're not allowed to go up," she repeated. "Danger of collapse!"

Ilse knew from experience that her mother always tried to impose her will. And she was right. "I'm not letting anyone forbid me from entering my own apartment!" she cried. She pushed Frau Zirkelbach aside and went over to the stairs.

"That's it with the chumminess," thought Ilse. Quarrels between the superintendent and her mother were a daily occurrence; even the events of this day couldn't change that.

"I assume no responsibility," cried Frau Zirkelbach after her mother. "For such an ill-considered action I assume no responsibility. There is a grave danger of collapse here."

The climb up did prove to be dangerous. A large part of the landing was missing, the stairs, covered with dust and debris, seemed more a steep mountain than a staircase. Peter began to cry. Walter clung to Ilse. "I don't want to go up!" he cried, but his mother paid no attention. "Keep going, just keep going!" she said. "Just don't carry on like that!"

"Carry on" — that was a catch phrase for Ilse. For her, everything was material, material for her next theme at school. "You should write about your own lives!" the German professor always tried to impress upon them. "In our Thousand Years' Reich no one needs to fantasize. We are a people of *action*. We're leading the German race toward the final victory. We can leave the fantasizing to the less intellectually prepared peoples. We're living in a *great* time!"

By this time, almost no one really believed in the "final victory" anymore. It was just a word, but a word that belonged to a vocabulary that one was best off not to speak against. But the part about the "*great* time" was true — at least in terms of extraordinary experiences that at the same time had come to seem almost ordinary. "Great" above all in what everyone had to learn to tolerate: people buried under buildings, families that suddenly were "missing," soldiers who didn't come back from the front. That had happened to her school friend Liesl's father. An SS-man had come to Liesl's mother, saluted and given her the death notice with the words; "Your husband has fallen on the battlefield for the honor of Führer and Fatherland. His hero's death will fill you with pride." Liesl had had to hold her mother back, she had told Ilse. She had gone after the SS-man, scolded him, and said some rather dangerous things. "Like what, for example?" Ilse had asked and Liesl had said, "That she didn't give a hoot for this so-called honor — that was one of the mildest things. It's better that I don't repeat it all. You never know who might be listening. It could have bad consequences for my mother."

Ilse resolved to keep her eyes and ears open. There really was a lot of personal experience to report on in this "great" time! At the same time she was aware that she couldn't really lay out everything for her German teacher. That was the thing: it was an unwritten rule that you had to hold a lot back. Maybe, later, it would be different with a different teacher? Or would that always be the rule, that one *never* said everything, *never* wrote down everything. Would there always be some lurking danger?

But pieces of the truth, pieces of what had happened could certainly be put into the next essay. In this way I can be somehow rid of it — and everything will be easier to take if I look at it from the beginning as material for a theme, Ilse realized. Material that requires no more of me than writing about it.

Her mother had now reached the apartment door. The door didn't need to be unlocked; the air pressure had taken care of that. Ilse quietly took note of the path through the front room over debris and shards of glass: glass on the floor, fallen from the high entryway window, Grandmother's winter pears from the garden patch stuck on the foyer wall, cracks in the walls, broken windows, burst window casements and frames, glass, glass, splinters of glass everywhere. And pieces of windowpane strewn across the floor, some still held together by the glue on the brown paper strips that had been put on the windows in crisscross patterns to protect them. The admonition crossed her mind, "German housewives! Secure your window panes against the air pressure!" On the rubble pile in the light-shaft Ilse discovered her grandmother's Christmas present, a decorative hand-crocheted blanket with a slogan in blue cross-stitches, "Beloved home — True happiness!"

Peter lay in the laundry basket, sleeping through his mother's inventory report, "We'll take the silverware with us. And what's left of the porcelain service. And the groceries. Everything of value. The apartment door doesn't close anymore; anyone can come in, so we'll have to go to grandmother's. We really can't stay here anymore."

Walter looked for his remaining toys. Why wasn't he crying? His favorite toy, the rocking horse, was dead. He showed it to them: the head, the black mane, the red saddle, but the rocking part was in splinters. No, he wasn't crying because he was a brave boy. He had been told often enough that he had to be a brave boy.

In Ilse's room the next scene of devastation awaited them: a large part of the neighbor's apartment on the other side of her wall had fallen in. It was as if the apartment had been blown away — it simply wasn't there any more. Looking through the gigantic hole Ilse could see directly down to the vaulted ceiling of the entryway to the building. Down there she could see towers of bricks, rubble, beams and pieces of walls in a tangled pile.

But Ilse's big bedroom chest was still standing in its place as if the building had never been bombed. The imposing chest, an enormous piece of furniture made of German oak, an antique left her by her great-great aunt, was virtually intact. It had several small scratches on one side, and there were a few pieces missing in its decorative border, but otherwise it was unscathed. There it stood, with the same imposing glory it had always had. And with one wall of the room missing, the chest looked like it was hovering in the air, a defiant monument in the middle of chaos and destruction.

According to Ilse's grandmother, her aunt had called the piece a "portable chest." When the word "portable" was quoted, of course it always brought a laugh. No one understood why she called such a large, weighty monstrosity "portable." Movers had to strain themselves half to death just to budge it! Why on earth did her great-great-aunt always ascribe this quality, which suggested that it was lightweight, to the sturdy chest? No one in the family took the idea that it was portable seriously — until one year when the time came for the next round of spring cleaning and Ilse and her grandmother had to try to move the thing. Grandmother braced it on one side; Ilse stood in front. It was her job to push on the chest while making sure that the tall heavy doors on the upper part didn't fall open. But suddenly, in the middle of all their valiant bracing and pushing, the upper part of the over two-and-a-half meter high chest slowly began to lean forward. It started very slowly, very slowly and very inevitably. There was nothing that could stop the movement of the upper part of the chest. And then it all happened very fast and there was absolutely no possibility of doing anything. The doors of the chest couldn't be kept shut. They flew wide open. The chest tumbled down all around Ilse. With a single blow, the back wall hit Ilse's head. Then all the wooden shelves crashed down to the floor with an enormous clatter. Ilse stood there, surrounded by pieces of German oak, framed by the single remaining outer wall of the chest, framed like a picture.

Aha, now they knew what portable meant, portable in the sense that it could be dismantled. That was what her aunt had meant. Because, in spite of the chest's sudden and almost instantaneous collapse, which made such a loud noise that it sounded like it was being completely destroyed, it turned out that the thing could actually be put together and no special expertise was required to do so. In fact, it could be so perfectly re-assembled that it would look as if its many pieces had never been separated from each other.

This single adventure had been enough to make Ilse love the chest. The chest had a history, a history in which she and her grandmother had played a role. Besides, it was *her* chest, the only object in the apartment that belonged to her alone. And the inside of the chest was a special place to keep things, to keep all the things that she didn't want to share with anyone.

She made a brief check, now, in the middle of the rubble in her room. There was dust and sand everywhere, but nothing in the chest was affected. The stamp album, the movie book, the folder with the Burg Theater program, the books, the puppets from her old puppet theater; all were undamaged. The king had his throne and crown; Mephisto's red velvet cape was free of dust; the princess, huntsman, forest fairy, cook — they were all just fine, every one of them. Just fine, even though a bomb had hit next door!

Yes, this was a worthy subject for an essay, without a doubt. And she also knew the concluding sentence that would appease and impress her German composition teacher after she had described all the events, sights, and experiences of this day: "German oaks stand tall. And if they fall, they fall with dignity."

Chapter Four: Ring-a-Round the Rosie

"*Ring-a-Round, Ring-a-Round, Ring-a-Round Ring,
fun to play, all the day, and it doesn't cost a thing!*"
Why in the world was Ilse singing this cheerful song so exuberantly? Cheerful songs didn't fit a day like this at all. Everywhere one looked there were bomb craters and ruined buildings. Many people had been killed, and it was feared and expected that many more were still buried and hadn't been discovered yet. Even the usual news reports, which always minimized the bad news, couldn't reach the public by radio or newspaper because after the bombing nothing, absolutely nothing, was functioning normally — no gas, no electricity, no streetcars — so the extent of the destruction was being passed quickly by word of mouth: countless dead in the inner city and in the catacombs (ironically, mostly refugees from the outer districts that had been spared this time); St. Stephen's Cathedral had been hit; the Burg Theater bombed, the State Opera House was on fire; multitudes were homeless.

However, the full extent of these terrible realities was hardly comprehensible. These events had happened; they were inevitable, overwhelming, impossible to foresee — they touched the realm of the absurd; they left behind them a sense of unreality. How could such "unreal" realities, against which there was no defense, actually come to pass? They happened far away; they happened nearby; they came closer and closer; they were a matter of life and death. No one could escape them, but because they happened again and again, day in, day out, in the end they became ordinary, something one got used to. One got used to them, one didn't look around or look back, one didn't think about being afraid of what was coming. From moment to moment one moved about, one stayed still, one operated only in the narrowest personal realm of the self. Only in this way could one survive the realities of this war: as something unreal, that had to be grasped as *real* when it affected you personally.

And so, it was even permitted to sing a happy song, especially while contemplating the nice prospect of moving in with one's grandmother. At her place everything would be better, of that Ilse was certain. If they all lived with Grandmother, then . . . yes, then everything would be different. Mother wouldn't disappear every evening to go to her "adult education courses" (really the movies or some other outing, she suspected) and leave Ilse alone, alone with her fear of night air raids, alone with her two half-brothers, whom she might have to lead down into the basement. She would be spared these excursions with Walter and Peter, spared all the packing and carrying, lugging all the baskets and backpacks down into the cellar; spared too, the looks of sympathy from the neighbors, as well as Frau Zirkelbach's curious, malicious questions, "Where is your mother this time? Why does she always leave you children by yourselves?"

At Grandmother's Mother always behaved quite differently; she didn't slap or hit Ilse when she forgot something ("Every time I send you to buy three things, you forget two of them. Your head is full of nothing but nonsense."); or if Ilse was "sloppy" when she washed dishes, or if she didn't wash the diapers long enough or hot enough. And these endless scoldings, accusations that she used her homework and need to study as an excuse to "avoid housework out of pure laziness." None of this would happen when they moved in with Grandmother. In her presence her mother always controlled her behavior.

No wonder, then, that Ilse was singing a cheerful song. And the Ring-a-Round song; it came unbidden to her lips. For her it did fit this day, this March 12. She would have to make the trek between the inner city and the outlying districts, between her bombed-out building and her grandmother's apartment, several times, on foot of course, for no streetcars were running. It was a good hour's walk, if not longer, at least on this first Ring-a-Round trip with her full backpack, with Peter in his baby carriage and Walter in tow.

"*Time and time, we all take off, yet turn around on th' same ol' spot . . .*" Along the straight, endless expanse of Thalia Street Walter and Ilse were singing a duet. By this time, he has learned the song by heart. Singing together, it was easier to keep walking and walking, following the street car tracks, with many other pedestrians taking the same route. "Hey, I know, we're all streetcars now. And now we are the 46 car ourselves," Walter suggested. "Ra ra ra ra rarara ra ra ra ra rararara, *I don' care what you say, Ring-a-Round is fun to play.*"

Grandmother opened the door right away as if she had been waiting right behind it. "Did you know we were coming?" asked Ilse.

"If only I had," complained Grandmother. "I didn't know anything! You're alive! You're still alive!" she cried and began to sob.

"Why are you crying now?" said Ilse. "After all, we're here now."

"*Ring-a-Round, Ring-a-Round, Ring-a-Round Ring, fun to play, all the day, and it doesn't cost a thing!*" Walter did his best at singing his newly-learned song.

"The baby carriage is in the entry-way," reported Ilse. "Mother is at our apartment seeing what is left there to salvage. We were bombed out, and the door won't close. We can't live there anymore."

Little Peter was laid on the bed. Grandmother kept hugging Ilse and Walter. Again and again she pressed them against herself. "I was afraid you were dead! I had to endure the fear that you were dead. Why did you wait till now to show up? I thought if you were alive you would surely send me a message. After such a massive attack you should have gotten in touch with me right away. This isn't the right way to settle things!"

"We were shut up in the catacombs," said Ilse, trying to explain the delay in getting in touch. But she knew that her mother didn't care all that much about "the right way to settle things." "Grandmother will find out soon enough, you don't need to keep reminding me over and over," she had said today when Ilse had urged her to let them leave earlier.

Anyway— settle things? How many times had her mother failed to "settle things," Ilse thought. Even things she had promised! For example: "Tomorrow you may go to Bräuner Street and order a ticket to the Burg Theater." And Ilse, full of anticipation, had set her alarm clock for four thirty so she could be one of the first in line for the best cheap seats. But then a few hours later she heard, "You forgot to get coal from the cellar. And you didn't even wash the front room floor. So, forget about going to Bräuner Street. Duty and responsibility— that's what I need to teach you. Later in your life you'll be very grateful that I did."

"I have to go right back," Ilse suddenly remembered. "Don't waste time at Grandmother's!" her mother had said sharply.

"At least have a bite to eat first," said Grandmother firmly. "And tell me a little more about what exactly happened today."

"Bombed out," repeated Ilse. She couldn't bring herself to give a detailed report.

"Well, well, you're still alive, and that's the main thing. So, you'll move in with me? It will be cramped."

Cramped? Ilse hadn't even thought of that. Grandmother's "closet with kitchen" apartment as she liked to call her modest dwelling — would have to house five people!

"But, is it okay if we move in?" asked Ilse.

"Where else?" laughed Grandmother. "Don't look so shocked; of course you'll have to move in with me. We'll work it out real nice. We'll push things against the kitchen credenza; Walter will sleep on the sofa, Peter in his carriage, and you, your mother and I will all sleep in the big bed. It will all work out, if we try."

Grandmother looked from her small kitchen into her small main room. Her blue eyes looked trustworthy and content; to Ilse it seemed like the apartment had suddenly grown considerably bigger.

"We'll work it out real nice," promised Grandmother.

Ilse was there a good half an hour longer. First, she carried the baby carriage with thermos bottle, baby cereal, and baby bottle up to the third floor. Grandmother gave Peter his "widdle boddle," and then she served Ilse and Walter her famous malt coffee and the dark wheat rolls Ilse was so fond of. And for the trek back she gave them some breakfast rolls that smelled a little like the breadbox. Ilse did start to tell a little more about the catacombs and the bombed out apartment after all; why was it so hard for her?

Grandmother soon gave up asking for many details. "I know you're uneasy; you're afraid to stay away too long," she finally said. "But you can just tell your mother that I wouldn't let you go back right away."

But no, fear of staying away too long wasn't the reason Ilse didn't say much. It was something else — but what? It's as if I want to keep it all inside, just for myself, she thought. Maybe because I haven't finished experiencing it all myself? And maybe I can't come to terms with my experiences if I talk about them too soon? Because my memories might be distorted if I talk about things in bits and pieces right after they happen?

"Grandmother, you know what, I completely forgot that I

promised to come right back, " said Ilse. "Your place is so peaceful and comfortable. But now I really do need to get back."

She took her leave quickly. Ilse could already hear her mother's reproaches in advance. She started to run through the hall. She really had to hurry! But then — who should appear and stop her in her tracks, right before she reached the stairs? Herr Pospischil! Funny old Herr Pospischil was standing there, barring her way.

"It's you!" he cried, beaming with joy. "Thank God! Your grandmother was so worried about you!"

Of course, this statement was only partly true. Frau Kreidl had actually expressed worry only about the *whole* family; that's all she would say, as Herr Pospischil knew. The truth was that Herr Pospischil was talking about himself. If anyone had been worried to death about Ilse, who else would it be? Only Herr Pospischil himself, and he admitted it to himself.

"Yes, here I am," said Ilse. "But I'm in a big hurry. I have to go back to the first district right away. And then I'll come back here. And I'll have to keep going back and forth. On foot," she explained to emphasize how long her trip would be and how long it would take. Not only was her mother waiting for her, but it was already late afternoon, and with all her treks back and forth she would still be out in the evening, the evening and maybe the night, with the streets in complete darkness, without streetlights or lights of any kind.

With such time pressure, of course Herr Pospischil had no opportunity to ask Ilse about her experiences. No doubt something had happened in the bomb attack; otherwise, Ilse wouldn't have brought her half-brothers to her grandmother's. And yet, he had definitely heard her singing in the hall. Singing! That would be like her. She was always singing — why not, even on a day like today?

"Wait just a little moment," said Herr Pospischil. "I have something for you. For the walk." Before Ilse could stop him he had disappeared into his apartment.

Ilse liked Herr Pospischil. He was kind of an odd bird, not like anyone else; to her he seemed clumsy and always a little confused. "That's because he's been alone so much," her grandmother always said. "He has no one in the whole world." It was hard for Ilse to believe that he had been a policeman. He didn't seem like one. Had anyone ever been afraid of hm?

Now, however, Herr Pospischil was really trying her patience, because the "little moment" lasted and lasted — Ilse could hear her mother's reproaches getting louder and clearer. But she couldn't bring herself to just take off down the stairs instead of waiting for him; it wouldn't be right. She began to call his name, "Herr Pospischil! Herr Pospischil!"

No Herr Pospischil appeared; only rustling sounds and noises of things being moved around were coming out of his apartment. Frau Weissenböck, curious as always, stuck her head out her door to see what was going on.

Ilse pushed the door open, which was ajar, and because she didn't see Herr Pospischil in the kitchen she knocked on the door, also ajar, to his main room and called, "Herr Pospischil, I have to go!"

The door opened up and Herr Pospischil popped up behind an ancient desk. "I don't know why my things keep hiding from me," he lamented.

He probably wants to give me some more poems to take along, thought Ilse. But poems were the last thing on her mind at that moment. Maybe he was looking for chocolate? He used to give me chocolate all the time — where on earth did he get it? And look at his apartment! Papers strewn around everywhere, books scattered in all directions, and a violin on the wall. Ilse wondered if he ever played it. Probably not, it looked untouched; it was covered in dust.

For the first time Ilse was standing in front of Herr Pospischil's holy treasures. She could sense that they were holy treasures to him by the ceremonial way he picked them up, the way he lifted a book and stroked the leather binding. . . . He must have forgotten that he is looking for something and that — as I told him! — I'm in a big hurry. "What are you looking for, Herr Pospischil?" she asked half seriously.

But at this moment Herr Pospischil found what had been "hiding" from him. Triumphantly he held a thick bar of chocolate toward her. "Genuine Swiss quality. Milk chocolate with hazelnuts," he read on the blue bow. "I bought it on the black market. This should be a good provision for your journey, don't you think?"

"Thank you, thank you," Ilse tried to show as much visible joy as possible over the present. "Thank you. But I really need to take off now."

The "provision" for her journey tasted wonderful. Actually it was a good idea, and so nice of him, she realized. And, when she reached her goal, with the good taste in her mouth, it would be easier to endure all of her mother's harsh words over her lateness.

Her second Ring-a-Round-trip went fast. Her mother had borrowed a hand truck from the coal dealer and packed it full. Together they pulled it all the way to Grandmother's. Then Ilse made the trip once again back into the inner city very rapidly, and some of the time she rode, sitting on the hand truck, especially down the slightly inclined Kopp Street. She braked with her feet, and she could steer very well with the truck hand controls. It was a good idea. Riding along up the sparsely populated Kopp Street put her in a good mood. And besides: now she was alone! Alone and out from under her mother's thumb! That meant freedom, freedom that she meant to make use of. But first she had to go to the coal dealer's. "He is waiting for his truck; hurry up this once!" her mother had said in a downright threatening tone.

But then — and at this point she needed to go even faster, to make up time — for Ilse had taken some detours, detours her mother never would have allowed.

Previously, back in their apartment on the second floor, Ilse had stood in front of the "portable" chest and realized that the sun was already starting to set. The missing wall gave her a clear view of the sky; up above the chest the first pale stars were starting to appear.

"Just take the things that are necessary!" her mother had commanded. "Don't drag all your stuff over to Grandmother's. She doesn't have much room. The looters will only look for valuables."

What things were the most "necessary?" Well, her school satchel and her most important books and notebooks. Her geography atlas, for example. She hoped there would be school again. Thank God, school had kept going after every bomb attack. Ilse was always happy to go to school, because being at school meant not having to be at home.

Writing utensils, notebooks and books, she would definitely take. She would have been able to find her books in the dark. The one with the thick, hard cover and frayed back — that was her English book. Yes, that was important to her. She couldn't get by in English without it. Doctor Melanie was very systematic, requiring a few paragraphs to memorize for each homework assignment. This book had many pictures, portraits of historical figures, photographs of London, of English landscapes and harbor cities. When the class complained, "Memorize so much — a page and a half?" the teacher's gray eyes always lit up as she said, "Yes, but you don't need to memorize the pictures!"

A book with a crack in its back — that was her geography book. Also "necessary" to take along! It was impossible to write down the material from Frau Rietsch's lectures, with their hundreds and thousands of details. To be sure, learning from the textbook had its challenges too. You read it and learned the assigned chapters, and then came to the test and were tempted to fall into the broad narrative tone of the book: "The road leaves the rugged rocky gorges of the ... mountain range and stretches to ... the fruitful plains, acre upon acre. Shepherds in picturesque local garb travel through expanses of green hill country with their herds of sheep."

Her school satchel was soon full; it took Ilse considerable effort to snap the lock shut. Next she turned to the "valuables." What would qualify as a "valuable?" Ilse looked over her treasures and all at once they really were treasures to her: the Burg Theater programs, the movie magazine with photographs of the stars, the autographs, the stamp album, the poems by Hölderlin. And then the puppets from her old puppet theater: the king, the velvet Mephisto, the forest fairy, the princess, the hunter, the cook. Yes, they all seemed valuable to Ilse and therefore also desirable to others. How could you predict the taste and favorite things of plunderers? By chance, they could be the same as hers!

Ilse looked at the bombed-out wall. The stars appeared above the ruined wall; they were getting brighter, the sky darker; it was so still in the room, so still between the piles of bricks, the shards of glass and the piles of debris. She'll be angry if I take all my favorite things, she thought. And will it help any if I tell my mother that these things are *really* valuable to me? She could guess her mother's reply: "Useless junk," she would say, "useless junk that no one else would want and no one will steal."

Oh yes — a thought occurred to Ilse — there is someone who will steal these things from me, namely my mother! She had already confiscated some of them, once the movie magazine, another time a theater program, another the poems or the autographs. That was one of her punishments that hurt Ilse more than blows because she never said how long she would keep these things or if she would ever give them back. This confiscation for punishment — isn't it a proof that the things had value? She recognized that my treasures had value! Taking away worthless things would never be an effective pain-producing punishment! So these things are "valuable" not just for me, but also for my mother!

Not a bad insight, thought Ilse defiantly, and she began stuffing her treasures into her backpack. If the reproaches came raining down on her, then she would express this insight aloud, even if it brought worse punishment for impudence and even if it brought the immediate loss of the salvaged objects. But it would be better for her mother to take away these things than if a stranger took them away forever.

At last she finished her task. Now she could finally turn to what she really wanted to do. Ilse left the apartment, step by step, walking gingerly along the wall, and peering down into the stairwell. Debris and broken glass crunched under her feet. The stairwell was completely dark, pitch black. The blue-painted windowpanes let in no light at all. Not even a glimmer of the light from the searchlights looking for airplanes could be seen, but she knew that they were out there, shining out from the flak towers, casting fingers of light up into the sky. At this time there were always searchlights beaming across the night sky.

And I'm all alone, thought Ilse. Completely on my own. What an exciting adventure! Now I can finally take my own little detours.

An adventure indeed. Now I'll be a reporter, Ilse resolved. Too bad I don't have a camera, but that doesn't matter. I'll photograph everything with my own eyes, my own senses, everything that happened on this day. Because it was a unique, historical day, wasn't it? I have my history book with me, but it just tells about faraway events that don't affect me personally. Maybe they will affect me more from now on, though. Maybe I'll gain a deeper understanding of all the wars we've had to learn the dates of?

Yes, it is an historical day. Only now was she starting to really "experience" this day. Only now, in retrospect and from a distance, was it all becoming real to her: the catacombs, the experience of being shut in, the buried people, the carpet bombs, the bombed-out buildings, the trucks carrying the victims, the Hitler Youth stacking up corpses — only now was it all becoming real to her.

The Ring-a-Round song had faded away. Ilse walked through the landscape of ruins, climbing over piles of debris, pressing forward in the direction of St. Stephen's Cathedral. A fire was burning somewhere, and there, in the direction of the State Opera House, there was a glow of fire. She hurried on, on and on, past the droning motors of the sweeping machines, past the flashlights of the digging teams. Everywhere there were shadows of people using their bare hands to dig through bricks and rubble looking for human beings.

Now it was all real, here and now; this was history. It is terribly real and yet so absurd! How could human beings inflict this kind of "history" on each other? How could they provoke this? she wondered. And how could people endure such misery? This "historical" mass killing — how was it possible? Why couldn't such cruel slaughters ever come to an end? Slaughters, accompanied on one side by fanfares of victory, and on the other side by experiencing an apocalypse! Who wants this murder? Who orders it? It happens. It simply happens; it is reported in the history books, discussed, taught and passed on, as if it were a completely natural and acceptable thing to happen, that has always happened and always will. The causes are explained, the dates required to be memorized, and this knowledge becomes part of one's general education, but this knowledge never leads to understanding or insight.

She went past the burning opera house, the Goethe statue. All the objects that she encountered in the dark had a glow of phosphorous, faintly glowing spots that were supposed to help people not to run into them. Lights, will-of-the-wisp lights. She went past the Heroes' Gate — it was undamaged. Why hadn't it been hit by a bomb? A few heroes, thought Ilse, and so much misery, so much suffering. The heroes should not be celebrated at all; their names should be taken out of the history books, obliterated. They shouldn't be held up to imitate! No laurel wreaths. The great victories, the laurel wreaths aren't for the people most directly affected. And the ordinary people don't get any laurel wreaths; there could never be enough of them. And don't laurel wreaths signify reconciliation and acceptance?

After the ceremonial ritual, one more bloody chapter is complete. Another battle is over and becomes ordinary. The suffering is forgotten, until the next time.

Smoke and the smell of burning were coming from the Burg Theater. Now her mother would no longer be able to punish her by withholding Burg Theater tickets. The opportunity of purchasing them on Bräuner Street had been eliminated, literally taken away from above.

Her school bag was heavy. Ilse suddenly realized how heavy it was. But her backpack didn't seem to have any weight. Are treasures easier to carry? Could the puppet king suffer, see the piles of rubble, hear the knocking sounds made by those buried alive, see the dead, experience the despair of the survivors? The Mephisto puppet, the red devil, he would certainly laugh maliciously and quote himself, "Everything that exists is worthy of being destroyed."

I shall keep Mephisto, Ilse decided. All of this will be easier to put on the stage with him.

She marched toward Thalia Street, taking great, strong strides. Her thoughts about the puppet theater put her into a better mood. I can shake this all off, she told herself. Yes, after all, I am still alive, alive.

But she knew that she would never forget this day. And she could laugh no defiant laugher. All laughter belonged to the velvet puppet in her backpack.

Chapter Five: Farewell, My Darling

Frau Doktor Rietsch was standing behind the podium, her right arm stretched out stiffly into the air, her hand flat, her fingers straight, raised up like spear points as she gave the salute. The girls had filed in stiffly and were standing in their places behind the school benches, their arms and hands raised in the same position.

The professor placed great value on proper salutes. If the director ever decided to surprise his classes with a control inspection, she would be ready to display a disciplined squadron of girls. After all, Herr Direktor Wimberger demanded that the slogan of the Hitler Youth, "Fast as a greyhound, tenacious as leather, hard as Krupp steel," should be followed in his girls' school. "German girls must carry out the same duties as German boys!" was the slogan he impressed on the teachers as well as the students. And he never missed an opportunity to add the explanation, "Because we, the Ostmark, in these times, have to serve as the first and most exemplary bulwark against Bolshevism."

A desk cover slammed shut, breaking the silence. It was Irmi Ziegler's loose desk cover that often came down loudly just at the stillest moment of the "German salute," because Irmi, her head always in the clouds, kept forgetting to hold onto the cover during these important moments. And her bench partner Gerti Mildner, right in the middle of the clattering, couldn't help but laugh every time. Gerti was small, pale, and thin; she seemed to be made of skin and bones. When she laughed, her thick blonde braids bounced up and down.

Frau Rietsch's spectacles gleamed severely in the direction of Ziegler-Mildner; then she stretched her hand even more stiffly and pointedly upward and cried, "Heil Hitler!" Her voice always cracked on the "Hitler; the "Heil Hit-" sounded like the shot of a cannonball, but the "ler" followed weakly, and came out a good octave higher.

The class looked forward to this event, because it was so funny, and they found it even funnier, when they then, like a well-drilled chorus, with one voice exactly mimicked the teacher's, "Heil Hitler!" Once again, the final syllable "ler" slid into a fine falsetto, reaching the upper notes at least as beautifully as did the professor's. The class had not planned this type of salute beforehand, but their imitation always functioned perfectly.

This time the imitation had succeeded especially well. The chopped off last syllable "ler" was all too clearly uttered, the shrill, air-cutting "-ler" hovered disturbingly long in the room. The aping of the teacher's voice could hardly be ignored. But no one dared to giggle, although everyone was close to doing so, because the echo had succeeded better than ever. At the same time the class knew that there were things that shouldn't be joked about. They knew that instinctively, and they knew that this greeting was one of those things. Such knowledge didn't need to be taught; even the most distracted and scatter-brained of the thirteen- fourteen- and fifteen-year-olds had picked such knowledge up through experience and without effort.

Moreover, Frau Doktor Rietsch was the type of faculty member who commanded respect. Strict, but just, even capable of brief, ironic jokes, she had her class under control. Always in a brown work jacket, her dark hair pulled into a tight bun, she had something Spanish about her. She demanded achievement, wasn't stingy with recognition when it occurred, but also not with brief but shaming rebuke when it didn't. In a word, Frau Rietsch possessed authority; no one dared act impudently toward her or joke with her. The girls could do so with impunity toward the physics and biology professors. From the beginning, both of them had missed their chance to defend themselves against bad behavior. They were vulnerable to whatever moods or practical jokes the students wanted to dish out.

The imitation of her Hitler salute was, in fact, the only breach of discipline the class dared in Frau Rietsch's class. It seemed like a miracle that she tolerated this exception, but maybe it was because she liked the echo of her own voice. In any case, Frau Rietsch didn't seem to find it necessary to concern herself with the echo. "Sit down!" she commanded, sending a stern look at the class from behind her black-rimmed glasses, in order to size up the class for a moment before turning to the lesson material.

Frau Rietsch taught geography — it was called earth science in those days — and, despite her dry demeanor, she understood how to make the lessons interesting and vivid.

"The bubbling lava from the eruption of a volcano — now can you imagine what that looks like?" she asked. And as the entire class was silent, because not one of them had looked into the crater of an active volcano, she answered herself, "Well, take a look when your mothers cook spinach; when the thick liquid begins to boil and throws out bubbles."

"Spinach," said Lotte Buhl, impertinent and off the track as usual. "Can you still get that at all?" Lotte's mouth was always ahead of her brain, but Frau Rietsch was prepared to answer, secure in her belief in the final victory.

"It is understandable," she began, "that in our times victorious self-defense and the heroic will to survive require food limitations. You must realize that the German folk has always been a folk without room; now we are surrounded and blocked by imperialist Jews and subhuman Bolsheviks. But endurance, courage, the rights and the superiority of the German race will conquer all evil and injustice. Our wonder weapons will prevail, despite the overwhelming numbers of enemies. It may be that during this decisive phase of battle we do have to put up with the temporary lack of a few kinds of foods. Babies and small children will always be taken care of, of course, and none of our fellow Germans will suffer hunger. — And now that we've established that Fräulein Buhl is eager to speak, let's give her the opportunity to speak up some more and inform us about her knowledge of Italy."

An audible sigh of relief went through the rows of benches. No one had prepared for a test. Lotte hadn't prepared either, but now that was her problem and no one else's.

Behind Ilse sat Inge — called "Longlegs" because she was tall, 1 meter 82. She was the best student in the class and the only one who studied even when no test was coming up. Inge had not only gotten "Very Good" in all her classes, the highest grade on a 6-point scale, she was also friendly to everyone, even the ones who called her "stuck up." Right now Inge was trying to tell Lotte a few Italian harbor cities and rivers, but it was a difficult undertaking because Frau Rietsch had darn good hearing and a watchful eye for whatever was going on in the classroom. "Poledna, you're too helpful," remarked the professor. "We know that you can answer every question."

In the meantime, Hansi was shoving a package of raisins over the benches in the direction of Ilse. Hansi's parents owned a delicatessen, and so she could sometimes supply her bench neighbor with some treats unavailable to the general public. So while Lotte was struggling with details about the height of the Apennine Mountains, Ilse and Hansi were quietly and carefully enjoying wonderful Greek raisins.

The two also got a lot of enjoyment from the "arrow." The arrow was a light signal on the streetcar line that could only be seen from the window next to Hansi's and Ilse's bench. The signal lit up only when a streetcar turned and made a loop past the school building. Sometimes they forgot to watch and missed the light, but the special fun of their "arrow" game was discovering the light effect by chance. When it happened, the one who saw it nudged the other with her elbow and whispered, "arrow." The game became a little conspiracy between them, and the arrow was also the reason that Hansi and Ilse were often chided and asked to "pay attention to their lessons."

Once in math class, for example, the strict Frau Doktor Lauter drew a half-arc on the blackboard and Hansi and Ilse were reminded of the arrow and their observation of it. No, it wasn't gleaming at this moment; but the professor had noticed that both girls had been looking away. She demanded that Hansi tell her what she had just drawn on the board.

Hansi didn't know; Ilse didn't know. They hadn't heard the word "half-arc." They both stared hard at the board. Hansi suggested, "A *straight line?*"

"No, that isn't it," cried Frau Lauter bluntly. "Johanna, you weren't paying attention. What is this, please?"

Ilse realized that the chalk image didn't look like a straight line at all. "It's a *slanted line*," she whispered timidly.

Hansi, however, believing that she had heard the right answer, said it loudly, "It's a *slanted line.*"

At this point the class broke out into loud laughter. Frau Doktor Lauter defended her artwork with the loud assertion, "Its a *half-arc.* A *half-arc!*" Then she got out her grade book to write "Impudent during lessons" after Hansi's name.

The school class, the "old class" as it was later called, later, after the end of the war, when many of them were gone, were missing, in other classes or other schools, or had simply disappeared — to places unknown and perhaps gone forever? A few were never heard from again.

The class, at this time, in March, 1945, was still sitting together in the comfort of a community they had been with for four high school years. They sat now in their "earth science" class and tried earnestly to answer a question directed at the whole class. Frau Doktor Rietsch had appealed to their ambition, to all of their "healthy human understanding" and their "gifts of observation." She was asking an "intelligence question" that wasn't in any textbook or on any worksheet. She was enriching her instruction with more and more of these questions. She emphasized the slogans "work together" and "think together" along with all her other slogans, such as "pillars of the coming generation," and "the rising intellectual foundation of the chosen Aryan race."

The question was, "What cloth color is used the most in our time?"

Greeted by a general pensive silence, Frau Rietsch, who had hoped for a quicker response, tried to explain more precisely. "Well, you just need to think logically; this is a very simple question. Think about it, what garments are worn the most by our German folk? And what color are those garments? You will, yes, you *must* arrive at the correct answer." It was unmistakable that Frau Rietsch had grown quite animated over the thought of this color.

The answer to this question was apparently of the utmost importance to the teacher. And there they sat, "the supporting pillars of the chosen Aryan race," and racked their brains for the answer she was so eager to hear. Ilse and Hansi, distracted as they were by the arrows of light, were already puzzled by the teacher's leap from Lotte and the Apennines; perhaps she would land on German industry, on aniline dye. They started to discuss the question softly. "Brown," occurred to them both at the same moment, and Hansi called out, impulsively as usual, "Brown!"

But no, to everyone's surprise, Frau Rietsch shook her head. "No, no. Not brown!"

The class was astonished to hear her utter these words, united in their amazement.

"Maybe we don't have all that many SS-men," whispered Hansi

softly, very softly; this time she had the right sense of what was appropriate to say aloud and what was not.

"It wouldn't be red either," Ilse said.

"No, not red," agreed Hansi. "I'm certain it isn't red." They had all heard about the "red danger." No, no, red could never be the favorite color of the German folk.

"Gray?" they asked, again speaking at the same time.

"Gray!" cried out Else as well; for once, she wasn't daydreaming about Heinz Woester, but about her father, from whom there had been no news since the invasion at Normandy.

"Yes, gray!" cried several others. "Field gray."

"We are a folk at war and defending ourselves," stated Frau Rietsch. "You are right on this point. But gray, no, gray is not our most common color." The teacher looked displeased as she spoke.

Now there were not many colors left to answer. Yellow? Hardly. Who wore yellow? What about blue and green? The class thought of blue skies, green meadows and forests, natural associations with these colors in the truest sense of the word.

"Black!" Several thought of this possibility. "Black" cried out a majority of the class at last.

Once again Frau Rietsch shook her head, accompanying the gesture with a frown. Was she upset at the class's lacking powers of observation? Or was she perhaps thinking about what had made the girls come to this conclusion? The "future supporting pillars," the future German wives and mothers: had their instincts led them to choose this color? There was a lack of soap, a lack of washing powder; on the basis of these shortages, one could say that black was a prominent color and would be for the foreseeable future.

Or did Frau Rietsch's frown perhaps signify that she had thoughts, suspicions that she could hardly dare to think through, because they bordered on betrayal, treason against the "Thousand Year Reich?" If the answer were black, it could be meant sarcastically and critically; this choice could be understood as veiled hostility. Was it possible that she was standing in front of a class whose parents had doubts about the "final victory," and that they had passed these doubts on to their children, doubts justified by the results of the heroic battles so far? Black — the color of mourning: the professional garb of the whole German nation! An innumerable throng of black clad soldiers' widows, black clad mothers and orphans, suddenly appeared in Frau Rietsch's mind's eye. She shuddered. Terrible, terrible, how was it possible? How could it happen, that it was *she*, she herself, who was thinking such pessimistic and distrustful thoughts?

Frau Rietsch shook off these wayward thoughts. No, these brats here, their heads were full of nonsense, but when the time came, they did show that they had learned to stand up straight and give the Heil Hitler as forcefully and convincingly as she could! And what could they know about clothing colors, these pale girls in their shabby, mended dresses — after so many years of war there was a shortage of cloth too. In a twinge of sympathy, Frau Rietsch thought it understandable that they couldn't answer the question; how could they be expected to have a broad understanding of the whole German people?

"You really don't know what color? The color worn the most by our people?" she asked again, because it was time to bring this discussion to an end. Her voice, she heard it herself, had taken on a milder, almost pleading tone.

"No, no, we don't know the answer," confirmed the class. A few of the pupils looked genuinely distressed. They were interested in cooperating with her, she realized, relieved. At any rate, they liked questions that challenged their intelligence. They led to a kind of competition to determine who was the most clever.

"Well then, I'll just have to tell you!" The professor's face and voice were full of confidence once again. "*Blue!*" she cried, and now her voice was full of enthusiasm. "Blue!" she repeated. "Blue is the color worn by our industrious, capable folk, undefeatable by any enemies. Blue — it is the color of work. The garments of the workers, the guarantors of the future of the German folk — their garments are blue. Our army of heroic workers keep the wheels turning — for our victory. Theirs is a great army, because we are a great people of workers. Yes, my dear children, this blue is the color worn the most in the German Reich!"

"We could have thought of that ourselves," whispered Hansi. "That's the way it always goes."

"That's true; that's true," nodded Frau Rietsch. "You could have arrived at this answer yourselves." Fortunately, she had heard only a part of Hansi's impertinent comment.

The "emerging intellectual foundation of the chosen Aryan race" had failed this intelligence test. But by the afternoon, during a bomb attack on the meadow in the fourth district, on Neu Street, they all proved to be eminently useful and in fine form. During the "brick pitching," as the activity was generally called by the people, they had a chance to show what they were worth. Actually, there wasn't much opportunity to literally pitch bricks, but there were plenty of chances to dig out whatever was under the piles of debris and rubble. For the most part, they used their bare hands to bring the buried objects to light. They scrambled over pieces of walls, rubble, and piles of sand, and climbed up mounds of ruins, like mountain climbers, only without picks or ropes. They climbed up to the second and third stories of buildings whose staircases were forever buried, always succeeding perfectly, conscious of their athletic ability. Their lessons were paying off. Gymnastics — during the days of the Thousand Year Reich called "bodily education" — took up more school hours than any other subject; after all, there was no place for weak young people among the people who needed their "Lebensraum."

On this particular afternoon Ilse and Else were guests in the apartment of Frau Gerstinger.

"Are you really not dizzy at all?" Frau Gerstinger had greeted her visitors with this question.

"Yes, of course we aren't dizzy. That wasn't our first bomb attack. We've had practice before!" Else assured her.

And Ilse reported that they had climbed up high before, even up to the fourth story, not long ago, in a building without any walls at all. "And this time we were only on the second floor. And we even had a fire wall to lean on," she asserted expertly.

Frau Gerstinger, a small, thin woman about forty years old, didn't seem to be dizzy either. She moved quickly and nimbly on the high plateau that had been her apartment, and as befits a good hostess, she showed the girls all her rooms. "This is the kitchen here," she said. "And this is the living room. This we call our cozy nook. And over there – that's the bedroom. And the little store room," she pointed down below, "it's in the basement."

An unusual woman! She kept saying "is," about things that didn't exist anymore. And all these rooms that could no longer be identified were filled with debris, bricks, pieces of wall, and just a few traces of her earlier life there: fragments of furniture, splintered wood, household objects, strips of curtains, here a lampshade, there a stove pipe, an exploded tea kettle. The whole "apartment" was made of air, surrounded by nothing but air. There were no doors, no walls, only the tall firewall loomed up into the empty, pale sky above them, lonesome as a tower in the desert.

"And now," said Frau Gerstinger suddenly, "let's get to work. I've looked around enough."

Ilse and Else had experienced this situation many times. There was no lamenting; everyone simply said, "Let's get to work." "I didn't lose anyone under the rubble," one woman had said, "and so I'm among the lucky ones." "Things, things," another had said. "What do things matter anyway? Things can be replaced. But — people?"

Frau Gerstinger had indeed already "looked around" and had actually done a little preliminary work. "We can forget the kitchen," she decided. "there's nothing left there. But here, under the clothes cabinet; here, I think, are a few things of value."

This clothes chest had not been built of German oak; it hadn't been able to withstand the bomb or the air pressure. But its wood, and especially its shelf boards, were to some extent still usable as makeshift pry-bars and shovels. So they dug carefully into the depths of the rubble, making openings between beams and pieces of wall and finally reaching the contents of the cupboard compartments. They pulled ties, shirts, garments out of the ruins; more and more. They rejoiced over everything, even the smallest garment they unearthed. They pulled up single shoes, and when they dug up the mates, they cried out with joy.

A practical division of labor had emerged right away, as if by itself. While Ilse and Else worked exclusively on what they called "archeological" excavations, Frau Gerstinger examined, dusted, and sorted all the possessions recovered from the bomb ruins. "Terrific. Not damaged at all. Wonderful, this just has to be washed. This is still a good shirt. My husband will be glad to see it when he comes back."

In the "cozy nook," Frau Gerstinger pulled a framed picture out of the rubble. She removed the shards of glass and came to the girls with the picture. "This is *him!*" she cried and blew the rest of the

particles of glass and the dust off the black and white photograph.
    The three of them looked at the face a man in a Wehrmacht uniform, looking helpless and embarrassed.
    "He doesn't like to be photographed," Frau Gerstinger explained. "That's why he's smiling like that. He's not a real warrior. He's been at the front for four years already and has never been promoted or honored. He doesn't care about all that." Frau Gerstinger added that her husband was on the Eastern Front and that she hadn't heard any news of him for weeks. "But I think they have a news blackout. No doubt they're on their way back home already." She stroked the warped picture smooth and laid it with the other objects she had collected.
    Ilse had the feeling that she wanted to say something else, but Frau Gerstinger had turned away abruptly and resumed dusting off the articles of clothing.
    "Now we know what the owner of this suit looks like," said Else softly. Their careful removal of some bricks and many splintered pieces of wood had just revealed the first corner of a dark men's jacket, and soon thereafter the matching pair of pants had been dug up as well.
    Ilse took the jacket, Else the pants; as far as they could tell on first inspection the suit hadn't been damaged at all. Ceremoniously, in outstretched arms, they carried the two garments to the sorting pile.
    Frau Gerstinger broke out in jubilation, "His best suit!" And after vigorous pounding, shaking, and smoothing, she stated, "No damage at all. It just needs to be cleaned." Beaming with joy, she pointed to a board where two folded shirts lay. "I never would have believed that we would find so much. And undamaged, most of it undamaged! Just look, girls, this is the way shirts should be folded!" She draped the suit over a pile of bricks and lectured the girls, "Order in a clothes cabinet, that is important. Folding lengthwise and crosswise, keeping the collars smooth, putting them all in an orderly pile. Good order, good marriage."
    In fact, the order really was apparent. The shirts were precisely arranged, each perfectly straight and folded in exactly the same way. They looked like soldiers, soldiers in formation on a pile of rubble, answering their last roll call.

Next Frau Gerstinger lifted up the suit jacket, grasped the fabric on the sleeve tops and held the jacket out toward Ilse and Else. "Look at it. I want to say something else to you about this," she began in a friendly, but lecturing tone, and then added more confidingly, "Because after all you'll get married someday, and then you'll be glad to know something about managing a household."

Frau Gerstinger paused and stroked the collar of the suit with her fingers. "Right here, see," she continued, "here, the lapel. The lapels are, except for the creases, the most important feature of a suit. It is very important to men that the lapels are smooth and without creases. The cleaners are often sloppy. Sometimes they send suits back with creases in the lapels — that will never do. Watch out when you get married. Always iron the lapels so that they're perfectly smooth!"

"If all that's true, I'd rather not get married," announced Else, when she was once again kneeling at the digging-out area with Ilse. "I never realized you had to worry about so much ironing and picky stuff."

This confession didn't surprise Ilse. Else usually resisted all kinds of bourgeois ideas. After all, she had inherited an artistic streak from her father, an academic painter. In addition, her worshipful devotion to the actor Heinz Woester blocked all immediate and long-term thoughts of marriage, even though her love for him was completely unrealistic and hopeless.

"Anyway," said Ilse, "we just got a free homemaking lesson, here on a rubble heap, at the summit of a ruin."

"Even though this housewife doesn't even know if her husband is still alive. She still rejoices because he'll be so happy to see his shirts and suit." Else shook her head. "I don't know; I don't know; I don't know what to think. I think all adults are strange."

"No blue again," said Ilse. They were freeing Frau Gerstinger's red and white checked Dirndl costume from under some debris. "So many different fabrics and none of them blue. Frau Rietsch wouldn't be pleased!"

"At our house there is plenty of blue. We have every color. My father always starts working in a nice new white jacket and in a few days it's full of colors, a rainbow."

"As is suitable for a painter." Ilse threw a few bricks in the direction of the kitchen. Then she looked at Else, who was also digging down to a layer of bricks. They seemed to have reached the bottom of the wardrobe. Else had an idea. "What would you think," she asked, "about taking our leave of Frau Gerstinger and walking over to the *Paradise*? Isn't that a good idea?"

"It is a very good idea. Can you read minds? I was just about to make the same suggestion."

Really a good idea, especially because the "Paradise" was nearby, right around the corner and a few blocks away from the bombed-out ruin. Frau Gerstinger didn't object at all. She shook their hands and expressed her thanks. "You've been a big help," she said warmly. "Now, go straight home. There might be more air raids. They come all the time now."

The girls had absolutely no intention of going home, especially Ilse. The air raids provided her the best opportunities to be on her own and do things her mother wouldn't allow. And that meant anything besides housework or taking her step-brothers for a walk: movies, excursions, spending time with her girlfriends. "Gadding about? Running around?" her mother called it. "A useless waste of time."

The "Paradise" was really close by. It was located in the Hotel Stadt Triest on the Wiedner Main Street. They went past the friendly porter, who always waved them in, past the reception area, as far as the glass door leading to the back courtyard, and up to a brown wooden door. Else's key was large, as befits a key to a heavenly place. She unlocked the door and locked it again from the inside. Now no one else could enter. They came to a vestibule, and opened and closed another door. The rest of the world had to stay out.

They stood before a broad stairway carpeted in red. They climbed it solemnly, up toward the glass roof. They entered a vast room without doors, opposite the sky, and saw the familiar scaffolds, unfinished paintings, the polar bear rug, shelves of books, the Chinese floor vase, paints, brushes, canvases, watercolors, plaster busts, this was Else's father's workplace — his studio.

Yes, it was a paradise to them. No one could disturb them here, or chase them away, because no one knew about their excursions here. Else had the key; it was entrusted to no one else. She had promised her father before he left for the front to come here from time to time and dust things off, air out the place, and see if everything was all right. He had asked her, "to bring some life into the place."

They aired out the room, wiped away the dust, hurrying because they were looking forward to more enjoyable pastimes. They didn't need to spend much time cleaning up; everything looked very clean and orderly compared to the rubble on Neu Street.

"We don't have anything to eat," said Else. "Not even a breakfast roll. I forgot to bring my bread ration stamps."

"I don't have any to forget. I don't ever get any at our house," sighed Ilse.

A little hunger and nothing to eat in Paradise — that didn't bother them. In the next moments they forgot such banal situations and desires. Higher, less humdrum aspirations were waiting to be fulfilled! Else had brought most of her "treasures" to the studio. Her idol Heinz Woester was everywhere, in pictures, programs, newspaper clippings.

Surrounded by an atmosphere of art and theater, Else began to orate. Else — the quiet, redheaded, freckled, round-eyed Else — she suddenly acquired serious features, shrewd eyes; she became Zanga in Grillparzer's "Life as a Dream," or Marquis Posa in Schiller's "Don Carlos." With the sheer power of her voice she took control of the upper hall, the whole studio, the world itself, and her friend Ilse. "Arm in arm with you, I'll conquer the whole century!" And soon thereafter followed the next quotation, so perfectly suited to the room they were in, "One moment, lived in Paradise, is not paid too dearly with one's death!"

Ilse had nothing against conquering the century. One century, one day, or only a few hours — they weren't interested in measuring exact intervals of time. But the conquering, the challenges, the defiance! That was what it was about, what was right and important, and worth taking seriously in all eras.

Ilse had settled into the "music corner." There, at the phonograph, was her special kingdom, the part of Paradise that she liked the best. Where else was there a record player? She didn't know anyone who possessed such a miraculous device and had never seen one anywhere else. In the middle of the wildest rhythms of the Hungarian Rhapsody Ilse had discovered a slumbering talent in herself and an unbridled desire to use it: directing! She was transformed into a Knappertbusch, a Furtwängler — her raised hands were spellbinding, her arms moving as passionately as these greats. Loud, louder, she let the music stream out of the loudspeaker, and yes, the orchestra was obeying her, but she needed a baton; she had to have a baton! She ran to the majestic door to the stairway and removed a brass stick from the carpet runner, and now the studio air was cut through and shaped by her passionate rhythmic direction.

Else, who was preparing herself spiritually to play the role of Saint Joan of Arc on the stake, was moved by the wild, overly loud tones; she began to dance the Czardas; transported, she cried, "Look! I can dance the Czardas!"

Something unique and special seemed to be present in the room. Had it been left behind by Else's father along with his oil paintings and watercolors? Had Else and Ilse with every trip to Paradise brought along something of this indescribably, airy feeling of freedom? Here everything was so completely different, within the walls of the studio there seemed to be no restraints on courage, daring, flights of fancy and self-expression; in fact, this seemed to be the only place that demanded these feelings. They didn't need to do anything; the tumult, the joy, the wildness — it all came on its own. They had nothing to eat; they needed no alcoholic drinks; they were far from thinking of themselves as artists despite the artistic atmosphere — what art could they have created anyway — but, nevertheless, they were in another world where they could be as they wanted, without having to ask permission, or offer excuses or explanations, even to themselves.

Yes, Else was dancing a dance that looked like the Czardas, and she was moving so wildly that she almost ran into the valuable Chinese floor vase. Ilse's heavy, overlong brass baton had come dangerously close to hitting several objects as well. No wonder that both of them collapsed, completely exhausted, on the polar bear rug as soon as the Hungarian Rhapsody came to an end.

"And that concludes our rhapsody," said Else, out of breath. In a sudden flash of soul-searching, she asked seriously, "What will become of us in the end?"

Whenever this question arose, silence followed. They weren't used to thinking about the future, to making concrete plans for the blank white no-man's land ahead, even though they sang countless songs about the future, songs specifically aimed at young people. They knew these songs by heart, down to the last word – whether they tried to memorize them or not – because they heard them at every ceremony, every meeting; there was no way to avoid these songs, and it would have been unthinkable not to sing them along during roll call in the schoolyard. The eyes of the teacher, the director, yes the "whole German folk" were upon them, whether it was on April 30, the "Führer's birthday" or November 9, fallen heroes' day, or some other of the many National Socialist memorial days.

Serious consequences would also have resulted if they ever forgot to put on their uniforms on one of those days. Unthinkable! Everyone was proud of belonging to the Hitler Youth, the Jungmädchen, or the Bund Deutscher Mädchen, and proud to wear the corresponding uniforms. When it came to songs, they were expected to show enthusiasm while singing. "Forward! Forward!" The bright fanfares were sounded: "Forward! Forward! Forward! We youth fear no dangers. Germany, you will go on after us all, gleaming in glory, if we fall. Our flag leads us on. We march on, man for man, march on for Hitler through night and day, come what may. Yes, our flag is stronger than death!"

What prospects for the future did these songs hold forth? None at all, or at least no good ones. And the songs had no happy prospects for their future career plans: "A young folk stands up, ready for the storm! Hoist the flags higher, comrades! Our time draws near, have no fear, the time for all of us young soldiers!" No, Ilse and Else didn't feel the spirit of "man for man," nor did they want, now or at any time, to join the ranks of the soldiers.

After the silence that followed the question, "What will become of us in the end?" Ilse and Else always gave the peculiar answer, "We'll be shoe shine girls in front of the opera building!" They always say you have to start at the bottom, so they would begin with shoes. And at least be near the great cultural events! But, then they thought of the problem of dividing the labor. They couldn't both be working there at the same time because there wouldn't be enough business for them both. Then it occurred to both of them that the opera building didn't exist any more; it had been demolished by a bomb — and at that moment their fun stopped. And they didn't go on with their amusing fantasy as before and talk about switching shifts between the Burg Theater and the opera building. Before, they had both thought that shining shoes in front of the Burg Theater would have been fun, especially in front of the stage door where they might get some precious autographs. But the Burg Theater had been bombed too, so both of them had been deprived of these future prospects on the very same day. It was for the best to put this once funny subject aside.

"Let's play a Zarah Leander record," suggested Else after another somber silence. Both loved Zarah and her dark, powerful voice. "The wind sang me a song" was her big hit that they could both imitate and at times sound almost like Zarah herself. Luckily, Else's father had the same musical taste as Else and Ilse, at least regarding Zarah. "Almost all of her records are here in Paradise," Else had once remarked off-handedly. And it was true, to the great joy of her friend Ilse.

Zarah brought back their good mood. To begin, more or less as a romantic transition, Ilse laid the record "Fatma" on the player. Zarah's dark melancholy voice requested, "Fatma tell me a story, about good fortune, that doesn't really exist. . . " But right afterward Ilse had Zarah proclaim loudly, "Even if the sky is gray, the world won't come to an end." Next, for variety, Ilse played Jan Kiepura, whose fiery tenor voice resounded into the studio with the words, "I sing my song today, only for you . . ." The girls felt personally addressed by the flattering words, " . . . if you love me, ask to hear a waltz." Dreamy anticipation floated through the studio, and they played the song a second time.

It the middle of Jan Kiepura's seductive song there was a sudden howl over all the roofs. "Wuu — wuu — wuu." Air raid! No matter how loud Kiepura sang, the sirens couldn't be drowned out.

The two paradise dwellers looked at each other. Then they ran over to the studio window and stared out at the sky. It had started to get dark; pale stars blinked at them; they couldn't see any searchlights or hear any flak. The trees in the back courtyard stood like silent shadows; the forsythias greeted them with their first tender yellow . . . everything looked so peaceful and quiet; and if there had been no deafening, rising and falling howling of sirens up above — the world would have been — at least on this spot of the world —

for the two girls completely in order.

"Should we act as if we hadn't heard the sirens?" suggested Else softly. "And stay here?"

Ilse finished her thought, " — you mean, *not* go down to the basement? Or — maybe you're scared?" she asked carefully.

"Scared?" Ilse smiled her superior smile. "Do I look scared?"

No, she didn't. Else was accustomed, no matter what happened, both in school and outside, to maintain a stoical calm. And Ilse, who felt obligated to support her friend in her lack of fear, told her how she was accustomed, even during the air raids, to be sent by her mother out of the catacombs right across the Rudolfsplatz. "She does that when it goes on too long and she runs out of baby food. Then I go back to our apartment and light the oven, because they turn off the gas during the air raids. That way I can heat up some baby cereal on the oven plate. And it takes a while to cook, you can believe me."

"Go out of the basement! And light the oven!" Else gasped for breath. "You're doing two things that are forbidden. What if you get caught by the air raid warden? You know what they say, when a bomb hits, there's a great danger of fire!"

"Well, what do I care?" Ilse's laugh sounded quite indifferent.

"I would care," protested Else. "But you're right, if you're going to have bad luck, you're going to have it. It could hit you anywhere, down in the basement or above in your apartment. And afterwards no one knows what people were doing."

Without exchanging another word, the pair knew that they had decided not to go downstairs, but to stay "up above," to take advantage of their beautiful time in the studio.

"If it really gets dangerous, we can still go down in the basement," asserted Else.

"At this time of day it hasn't been really dangerous yet." This statement sounded like Ilse's last word on the subject.

They both knew exactly how they had to act now. Above all, they had to make sure that no one knew that they were in the studio. That meant that the music had to be played very softly. It also meant that they couldn't have any lights on that could be seen in the upper or lower hall. If the alarm lasted a long time, they planned to light some candles when it got dark. The main thing, however, was to be completely quiet; that was crucial. They could not betray their presence there, at any cost. Their only real worry was the porter who had seen them come in. But they put this concern aside quickly; during the air raid the porter no doubt had greater concerns than making sure that the hotel had been completely evacuated.

A single lit candle in the most remote corner of the studio. Soft record music. Else took the role of Joan of Arc again. Ilse rummaged through the book collection and made a great discovery: Klabund's history of literature. She paged through it and said, "Look — really: what a find!" The whole world was collected in the volume. Right in the beginning a portrait of Nietzsche sprang out. It looked like the picture on the postage cancellation stamp in her notebook. Unkempt moustache, wild gleaming eyes. And how dramatically this Klabund presented literature — not at all like her dull textbooks! For example, it said about Nietzsche, "When he became Zarathustra, he sang a *drunken* song:"

O Man! Pay attention!
What says the deepest midnight?
I slept; I slept, —
I awake out of a deep dream!
The world is deep
Deeper than the day, in thought.
Deep is her pain —,
Desire — deeper yet than pain of heart!
Pain speaks: Disappear!
But all desire wishes eternity —
Wishes deep, deep eternity!

And then, paging further, she encountered for the first time Mal Villon, the greatest lyricist of medieval France, "a vagrant and vagabond, a thief, scoundrel and (perhaps even a murderer)." He had written:

Ulcers have eaten the body
The sun I have wasted —
Over everything, unforgotten
Hovers the soul that feels.

Let the air raid last a long time, prayed Ilse to herself, so I can keep on reading this wonderful book. And she had another joy — during the air raid she didn't need to have any fear of her mother — what better excuse for not coming home before dark to be home during night bombing.

They heard muffled flak noises. They didn't listen and soon didn't hear them anymore.

These were quiet, wonderful hours! Was there anything more beautiful than strolling around in the worlds they loved? And at the same time the bracing aura of suspense, the unacknowledged but present uncertainty. Suspense would hang in the air until the sirens gave the all clear signal.

"It could have been our last hour on earth," they said later. Years later, when they remembered that day. But they were special, unforgettable hours!

The gymnasium in the Radetzky School was located one story under the ground floor. Only the upper parts of the windows with their iron bars allowed a view of the street. All sorts of legs went walking by, clothed differently, in different stockings or bare, and wearing all kinds of shoes: boots, wooden sandals, high heeled shoes, athletic, elegant, shabby or polished to a shine. For future shoemakers, this ground view perspective offered untold possibilities to learn the trade. Also for shoe shine girls, as Ilse and Else realized at one point.

The lights were on all the time; the school superintendent, who was in charge of the equipment room, liked to call the gymnasium a "dark prison" and "an underground dungeon." Nevertheless, the class loved the gym. It was a spacious room, filled with all kinds of equipment: a climbing wall, wooden sawhorse to practice jumps, ladders, horizontal bars, a trapeze, a rope and rings. There were even basketball hoops; plenty of equipment to keep the students busy for their many hours of "bodily education." And they were happy times, hours spent without fear of schoolwork, vocabulary tests or pressure to recite.

Most of all, the class looked forward to the last quarter hour of "bodily education," because that was their chance to play "folk ball." This game had become a kind of class obsession. They divided into two teams, one marked with red ribbons and one with white. When they started throwing the ball at each other, the competition got so intense that their teacher, Frau Serndatzky, had to keep blowing her whistle "so no one had to be transported to the hospital," as she put it. They ran and jumped in all directions on the playing field; the ball flew back and forth. Small, fat Ingrid Cugel was easy to "shoot down," Gerti Mildner, "The Streak," impossible; Lotte Buhl could catch the hardest balls and hold them the longest, and whoever succeeded in keeping the ball away from mighty Fräulein Bauernberger showed the achievement for several hours afterwards with red marks on her arms, chest, and neck. Inge "Longlegs" was a master at dodging, and, when necessary, at catching as well. Erika Berghofer, in black pants and a black vest, stayed in the background. She wasn't shot down until the end when she was discovered, always one of the last players on the field. Ilse and Else tried, whenever they could, to be on the same team so that they didn't have to shoot each other down.

The love of folk ball went so far that the class pooled their money to buy their own leather ball. They soon collected enough to buy one and after that they played folk ball almost every day after school in the Arenberg Park, not far from the flak tower. They also took the ball along on school excursions, found the best field to play, and grumbled when they had to move on. If the ground was wet, they all bore the traces of battle on their blouses and dresses when they went home.

Once they had the misfortune of "shooting down" a man who happened to be walking by. Unfortunately it happened on one of the days when the ground was wet, and the very elegantly dressed gentleman was wearing a light gray flannel suit. What a disaster! They anticipated bad consequences, for his flannel suit had undoubtedly gotten dirty. But the man actually laughed and tossed the ball back. It was a laugh they knew from the silver screen. They had "shot down" Carl Raddatz, the famous film star! A few days later the school superintendent brought them a big brown envelope with a photograph inscribed with the words, "To the folk ball class, from your fellow player Carl Raddatz." In the following weeks his hit song, "Someday you'll be with me again; someday you'll be true to me again," was elevated to the class hymn, and from then on they all went to his films wherever they were playing.

The class! They had lived through so much together, and created so much wonderful mischief! They had "singing hours" in the big auditorium because there was a piano there. They always had fun there with the temperamental music teacher, Professor Edlitschek, who let them laugh and make jokes. One day the strict Director Wimberger who for some reason didn't get along with Professor Edlitschek, burst into the singing lesson, red in the face with anger, and scolded her, "It is too loud, dear colleague, please do me the favor of holding the noise level of your lessons down to a reasonable level!" The door had barely shut behind the director when the music teacher sat down at the piano and said, "All right, children, and now we'll practice *wild* singing!" For the rest of the hour the class sang the scales, up and down, as loud as possible, and so shrilly that they made their own skin crawl: "DO RE MI!! FA SOL LA!!!"

Another time Irmi Ziegler and Gerti Mildner crawled behind the high swastika-draped middle wall of the auditorium. From their hiding place they howled such disturbing boo-hoo cries that the startled professor, who hadn't noticed their absence, hit a five six chord instead of a seventh chord. After this incident the superintendent had to make sure that order and cleanliness were maintained behind the swastika flag walls, because when Irmi and Gerti came out of their dark hiding place they were so dirty that Frau Edlitschek had to send them straight to the washroom. And the silver laurel wreaths that the two had borrowed from plaster statues of Beethoven and Wagner to wear during their performance also had to be cleaned.

The class! They loved folk ball, and on one particular day, a special one, they were allowed to play their favorite game all hour. A special day, yes. They knew that it was their last bodily education class together; tomorrow the school would be closed. What would come after that was unknown, like so much at that time. The news accounts, all coming from the same propaganda mill, still contained the same familiar slogans, "Never give up," "Wonder weapons," "Final victory," "Stay the course," but the real situation could be read on maps and it contradicted all the heroic sounding reports of the Wehrmacht High Command. The Red Army was marching forward; the Red Army was already getting close to the Eastern and Southern borders of Austria; more exact news wasn't provided to the people, only talk about the "atrocities of the murderous Bolshevik hordes."

It was high time to evacuate the women and children, high time to close the schools.

Folk ball! There stood the class, now at the end of their last game together, hot, out of breath, sweating. They had competed especially hard, and when, long after the usual time, their professor had blown the final whistle, they all resisted. "What? So soon? Couldn't we play five more minutes?"

Professor Serndatzky waved at them, ordering them into a circle formation instead of in squads as she usually did at the end of the hour.

In the middle of the circle stood Frau Doktor Serndatzky, a strict but beloved teacher, an excellent coach, young, tall and thin, with ash blonde hair and blue eyes. "I believe we should sing a good-bye song. What do you suggest?"

They were all accustomed to breaking into the prescribed songs at all ceremonial occasions, and they were all songs belonging to "National Socialist Culture," from the Horst-Wessel-song to the England Song, which began: "Now we'll sing a little song, as cool, refreshing wine we'll drink; and our glasses we will clink, for it's time to say good-bye. Give me your hand, your fair, white hand, farewell, sweetheart, farewell, sweetheart, farewell, farewell, for we're setting off, setting off, against England, England, ahoy!" This England song would have been most appropriate, because it was a good-bye song. Its melody also was catchy, warm, and lively.

In addition, earlier, the song had brought the class a stern reprimand from the Director, who had scolded, "Why are you laughing? That is completely inappropriate." They couldn't explain well why they were laughing so "stupidly," but the song's lyrics, combined with its jaunty melody, had seemed funny, especially the words of the third stanza, "If the news comes, that I've fallen, that I sleep beneath the sea, do not, my dear, don't cry for me, for my blood was shed for the Fatherland. Give me your hand, your fair white hand. . . . " The white hand, sleeping, blood, and sea water . . . it had all been too much for the thoughts and imagination of the class — they hadn't been able to help it, they simply had to giggle.

Strange; as they now stood in a circle, no one suggested songs of that kind. Without thinking, quite impulsively, the class decided quickly and unanimously on an Austrian folk song, "When I Pass Through the Valley." A few could sing the second voice, a few the third, and in the end they showed that they had retained the good instruction in singing received from Professor Edlitschek. "When I pass through, pass through the valley — Hey, Boy, holler ag'in! Let me hear you once more! This may be the end."

It was a simple song, as only genuine folk songs can be. It sounded beautiful — they could hear that themselves. The song was melancholy: "I don't hear no whispers; I don't hear no shouts — me boy is long gone, gone to the granite stone . . ."

Shining eyes. As they stood there in the circle, their eyes began to shine with tears. Only now, during the singing, did they truly realize that this really was a farewell. It really was.

They kept standing together, stealing glances at one another. No, no one was alone with glistening eyes. They were all still together, but tomorrow this class would not exist anymore. Tomorrow they would all go their separate ways.

"When I pass through, pass through the valley . . . " They repeated the first stanza, as if they could delay facing the uncertainty before them if they kept singing.

In the dressing room, as they changed their clothes they asked each other, "What will you do?" "Will your family evacuate?" "Are you staying in Vienna?"

They were asking these questions for the first time, and only a few knew exactly what to answer.

Chapter Six: Easter 1945

The Easter Bunny brings the little children Easter eggs. The Easter Bunny laid the eggs herself and then painted them with her own paws, in blue, red and green, in cheerful colors, because Easter is a joyful holiday, and the Easter Bunny knows that it is.

It is good that there still is an Easter Bunny, from one generation of children to another: the Easter Bunny never dies. But what can be done, when there are no more eggs? Perhaps tell the children that the Easter Bunny has taken sick? Or that she ran away? Or laid her eggs somewhere else this time? But where would this "somewhere else" be?

In the "Golden West," in Salzburg, for example, the Easter Bunny still exists. And she brought colorful, gleaming Easter eggs to the families who evacuated the city, and even hid them in the grass — as is appropriate for a proper Easter Bunny.

From the stone terrace of the spa hotel where the "bomb refugees" are being housed, Ilse looks out at the children. How they run and tumble around on the meadow! How loud and joyfully they shout when they find another egg between the bushes and the flowers. Walter just found his first one, of course; no wonder, when he always runs after the other children and comes so late that the area has been cleared out. Ilse would love to help him look, but, "You aren't allowed to," says her mother. "How would that look? You are much too big for Easter egg hunts."

So Ilse sits with the "grown-ups" on the wooden benches of the terrace. When the weather is nice, the guests of the spa hotel that has opened its doors to "all families with children from the city of Vienna, endangered by bombs and warfare" can take their meals here.

There is still time before lunch; the last Easter eggs have been found; the Easter Bunny has done her duty — and so they are just waiting for their next meal. The group is a mixed one; supposedly all are "families with children," one big happy family, lucky and privileged enough to have been accepted in this "remote valley of peace," as Senior Instructor Professor Doktor Ohlers always called the place, his voice dripping with sentiment. But, if one looked more closely, only a few such families were here. There were also other people, such as the bachelor Herr Ohlers himself, who systematically forgot, after two days, to put on the party insignia that when he arrived he had always displayed so prominently on his lapel. Or Fräulein Alwine von Rauenstein, of noble birth, as she often mentioned, a pale, aging lady, made visibly nervous by the children's noise. "We've all had a strain on our nerves," she excused herself once, after she couldn't help but reveal her irritation at the loud, grating street dialect of some Florisdorf boys. And there were a few childless families, the women quiet and ill at ease in this place, the men neither old nor sick and yet in civilian clothes. They were people, who, as Frau Winkler, mother of four, put it, "had had important positions in the hinterlands," or, according to Frau Winternitz, whose husband had been missing since the Battle of Stalingrad, were either "party bigwigs" or "shirkers." Frau Winternitz, also the mother of several boys and holder of the mother's cross, had become quite outspoken since Stalingrad, at least on this subject.

The mood in the spa hotel, located in a beautiful Alpine area, quite apart from world events, was not one of a united group, brought together by fate, of comrades facing an uncertain future together and forging bonds of friendship. They didn't know what protection or compulsion had brought the others here to the "valley of peace." They all felt uncertain and insecure, a state in which people are easily irritated and prone to exaggeration.

However, the times were not especially appropriate for irritability or exaggeration, for even the expression of reasonable ideas could "still" or "once again" during this Easter season, prove dangerous. In the moment when Herr Ohlers took off his golden party insignia, after decades of honest ideological commitment, he ceased to think it important to tell about his "highly positioned friends" in the Culture and Propaganda Ministry. Likewise, Frau Nowotny— already "bombed out" twice — instinctively felt that it could possibly be very dangerous to tell about the activities of her husband, a committed Communist and active in the resistance movement. Frau Winternitz was also silent about the fact that her husband had taken over an Aryanized textile store in March. It was hard for everyone to speak about the situation and events of the day. Most of the people, at least at first, gave only objective sounding, carefully worded remarks. The term "final victory," rashly, and yet hopefully, uttered by Frau Winkler just once, met only with awkward silence.

So, the group sat, watching the children play, and tried to converse with harmless platitudes, but behind the scenes they were all waiting to join in a great card game. The cards, dealt beforehand by the unpredictable, whimsical forces of world history, lay in everyone's hands. But no one dared to start the game because none of them had any idea if their cards would be trump cards or make them guilty of "high treason against the German people." And so no one started the game; instead they talked about the weather or the Easter Bunny.

The children, however, played their own quite informative games. Frau Nowotny almost slid under the table when she heard her boy say, "I's a Russky, fierce, fierce! You all gotta run!" Swinging his fists toward his playmates, he jumped around wildly and bumped into whoever got in his way, now the Winkler boy, another time young Winternitz.

"We're gonna hide," suggested Walter.

That was just like him — such a coward! thought Ilse and looked at the other spectators on the terrace. Should she intervene and try to stop the fighting? No, everyone was sitting there in stony silence.

"Us are da Hitler Youth," cried Frau Winkler's sons. "Watch out! We're making a storm attack!"

At that point the Winternitz boys, true sons of their father, owner of the Aryanized textile business, showed their ability to put the current geographic and military situation to their advantage. They yelled, "And we is da Americans! OK, boys, get goin,' march!" They got down behind some ornamental bushes and then stormed out, ducking down, toward the battlefield. Then, face to face with the "enemy forces," they stopped and stood still a moment, overwhelmed by uncertainty as to *whom* they should attack: the Winkler-Hitler Youth, armed with big sticks and shooting into the air, or the wild Nowotny-Russian flailing about in all directions? "Get goin,' OK, git Ivan!" they finally decided and thereby confused the real course of world events.

Now they all began to fight wildly, with machine guns made of big sticks and with gravel hand grenades. It came to hand-to-hand combat: the Winternitz boys threw themselves on the Nowotny-

Russian; locked together they rolled over the sloping blue-green meadow. Then suddenly the Winkler-Hitler Youth stormed forward and joined the attack with violent machine gun salvos, yelling "Grttattatta-Grttattatta" together with their comrades struggling on the ground. "We hit ya! Y're dead! Y're dead!" they insisted. At that point both "Ivan" Nowotny and the "American" Winternitz, pretending to be severely wounded, displaying their final, most heroic battle efforts, dramatically pulled out their last hand grenades and, as if posing for the weekly newscast, lobbed them off with a defiant, "This is fer you!"

On the terrace the horrified parents and other spectators gradually recovered from their state of silent shock, and smiled wanly at each other. "Where do these kids get such ideas?" they asked each other in amazement. "These boys can't get enough of these dumb war games!"

"Come up here right now!" Ilse's mother called to the "warriors." "Dinner is almost ready!"

"Hurry up; wash your hands!" commanded Frau Winkler.

"You too," said Frau Nowotny.

"But I'm a Russky," asserted her boy.

"So?" said the teacher. "Do you think the Russians never wash their hands?"

He looked around smiling, the tall, gray-haired senior teacher, as he had once looked at his pupils, understanding, benevolent, wise. "Humanity," he said then to Frau von Rauenstein, whom he usually sat next to at the dining table. "Humanity is a word that we must never forget. Yes, my dear madam, I see this word written large in the school lessons of the future."

"I would be so glad to share that hope, Herr Senior Instructor," answered Frau von Rauenstein.

Ilse, who was sitting at the next table, listened to the quiet continuation of this conversation. "Yes," the teacher said softly, "Humanity is at least a word that serves one well in transitional historical eras."

"Until other, more up-to-date slogans come to the fore once again," sighed Frau von Rauenstein.

"But, madam, what do you expect from the world? As far as we're concerned, *we* have made our contribution, don't you think? It could be that we've made mistakes, but haven't we always acted with the best intentions and in good faith? As far as I'm concerned, I have loved my profession with all my heart." The teacher pointed to the meadow which had just been the scene of the unruly children's battle. "These rascals!" he cried out, laughing. "What about those war games? Don't they touch your heart? Aren't they the best?"

"The best? But what have we taught them? They almost beat each other to a pulp."

"Nonsense! Rascals, true blue boys they are, Frau von Rauenstein. They can't wait to start their scuffling. Give the blows and take them, and survive; that's the name of the game."

"There are other more positive values we ought to cherish...."

Ilse couldn't hear the rest of the conversation because there was a new outbreak of noise from the freshly cleaned up young warriors as they took their places at the lunch table with their mothers. Behind them Resi, the waitress, popped up and brought out a cart laden with steaming soup bowls. Lunch could begin.

It happened during the main course — between the wiener schnitzel and the potato salad. Soft waltz music on the radio was suddenly interrupted. The ceremonious fanfares that always introduced each special announcement came thundering through the dining room, silencing every conversation and stopping the diners as they chewed.

The voice of the announcer reported: "The Wehrmacht High Command has announced: A few formations of Russian troops have penetrated into the area of Wiener Neustadt. Our troop units have already undertaken several successful counter-attacks and front straightenings. Vienna itself is in no danger."

Brisk march music followed. But the lunch guests had lost their appetites. Deeply disturbed and amazed, they stared at each other numbly.

"Wiener Neustadt?" asked Herr Ohlers at last. "Did I hear correctly?" He laid his napkin on the table and looked questioningly around.

"How can that be possible?" marveled Frau Winternitz and poked around in her salad with her fork. "When a few days ago they were still deep in the interior of Hungary?"

"That's right," said Frau Nowotny, "and not long ago they said the danger had passed; that the Russians had once and for all been beaten back from our borders."

The senior teacher cleared his throat. "The famous Russian steam-roller — who can hold it back? I can remember so well, in the First World War it was the same story. The Russian steam-roller — pfiff — unstoppable! It was back then that . . . "

"Oh, please, spare us these terrible war stories!" pleaded Frau von Rauenstein. "We all hear our fill of them nowadays."

"What happened to the Americans?" whined Frau Winternitz. "The Americans! They were supposed to be our last salvation! Our culture, our traditions — and so on —," she interrupted herself in embarrassment.

"Last salvation?" Herr Ohlers turned around to face Frau Winternitz, who was sitting in the row of tables behind him. "What do you mean by that?"

"Well, I mean — the Russians have penetrated deep into our country already. . . . "

"The Russians will never take over Vienna!" Frau Winkler pushed her empty plate into the middle of the table. "That can't be possible . . . I think, we must have some military reserves, saved for the final decisive battle. And what about the new secret weapon! The wonder weapon that we've heard so much about for so long. They'll finally put it to use!"

"Yes," joined in Ilse's mother, "if the situation were really so hopeless, our Wehrmacht would long ago have stopped fighting and surrendered! They must still have something up their sleeves to use to turn things around. I can't imagine anything otherwise!"

Frau Winkler nodded. Then she looked at Frau Nowotny and said in a very decisive tone, "Otherwise all the victims and all our sacrifices would have been in vain. Just think about our soldiers' heroic fight in Stalingrad."

"If only the Americans were faster!" lamented Frau Winternitz.

"Do you expect something special from the Americans, dear madam?" Herr Ohlers smiled disdainfully. "I don't think you should. They are our enemies too, after all."

"Absolutely," seconded Frau Nowotny and looked thankfully at the senior teacher. "This one-sided demonization of the Russians — " She broke off her sentence when she realized that she had been the one to sing the praises of the communist ideology. It's too early for that, she told herself. That is still dangerous to talk about.

"If worst comes to worst, only the Americans will be able to save us from the Bolshevik barbarians," insisted Frau Winternitz, holding her ground. "Bolshevism will mean the end of our culture."

"The Americans?" Frau Nowotny clasped her hands togther in agitation. "The Americans are the ones who will save our culture? They bombed our Opera House, and St. Stephen's Cathedral...."

"By mistake!" interjected Frau Winternitz. "Those attacks were aiming at military targets, barracks and train stations."

"C'mon, that's crazy!" cried Frau Nowotny. "Mixing up the State Opera House with the South Train Station — that would be pretty dumb of the American flyers! The few meager streetcar tracks leading out from the Ring Street and line 66. They thought those were the tracks at the train station? Don't make me laugh! And all the apartments, all the innocent civilians, the women and children, all killed by bomb attacks? I suppose they were military targets too?"

Frau von Rauenstein pushed her chair further and further from the table. She hated squabbles like this and thought it would be best to distance herself visibly from the dispute.

But now Ilse's mother turned toward her. She seemed to be the only one who shared her concerns and whom she could ask for advice. And so she told Frau von Rauenstein that she had been bombed out; that was the only reason she had had a chance at a place in the evacuation camp. But she had heard that "more important" people had higher priority. It had been made clear that this place was only temporarily granted to her and her children, unless she could produce a document — written proof that she had been bombed out.

"It's always about papers," sighed Frau von Rauenstein. "It's terrible. More and more our lives depend on papers. If you don't have the right papers, apparently you have no right to breathe, no right to exist."

"But I have the document! I got it right away!"

"You do? Then you should be all right. Then there's no way they can kick you out of here." Frau von Rauenstein, who had been listening sympathetically, gave a sigh of relief.

Ilse's mother sighed. "I have a document certifying that my home was destroyed by bombs. But imagine, what a misfortune! The document is still back in Vienna, along with all my other papers. I had no way of knowing that I would need that paper here."

"That's terrible!" said Frau von Rauenstein. "What are you going to do?"

"There may be a way out," began Ilse's mother. "But I would like to ask your advice. What would you think of the idea of trying to get the papers?"

Ilse had been half-listening to the beginning of the conversation. Bomb documents, what of them? What is all this useless talk? My mother is not easily defeated; she always survives. But when she heard her mother mention a "way out," a quiet hopeful feeling suddenly began to well up in her. A way out? she wondered. Someone her mother could send to retrieve the papers? Someone who could, so to speak, pull the chestnuts out of the fire? Finding "a way out" for her mother — that had always been *her* job. And, even before her mother developed a plan, before she asked Frau von Rauenstein tentatively, "My daughter, she could still pick up the documents?" — before this idea was formulated in words, a warm stream of hope and expectation had already gone through Ilse's entire body, from her elbows to her finger tips, over her neck, circled her head. A fearful suspense, an excited, happy expectation: Is this *my* chance? Will it actually happen that she will send me? Alone? Away from here, from her — toward freedom?

Ilse pretended that she didn't hear the women's conversation. She bent over the baby carriage, played with Peter's fingers, and told herself, "Don't give yourself away! Give absolutely no indication that you want to go. If you do, she certainly won't send you."

"Oh, what should I do?" Ilse heard her mother say. "Without this paper something terrible may happen to me."

"I understand what you mean," replied Frau von Rauenstein. "I needed all kinds of papers to get this far. Thank God I brought everything along: doctor's and hospital records, proof of my disability and heart problem. Our permission to stay here actually depended on such a ridiculous pile of papers. Yes, I can understand why you're worried. I've heard they intend to take over this spa hotel and make it into a military hospital. Then every room will be needed for wounded soldiers."

Ilse wanted to hug Frau von Rauenstein for every word. And

then, she finally heard her mother actually say, "My daughter, could she go back and get the document? What do you think — would it be too dangerous? The front is getting closer and closer to Vienna . . ." When her mother said these words, Ilse knew that the "way out" had been all but settled in her mother's mind; but still, the final decision would depend on her own reaction. She warned herself again that it would be dangerous to show eagerness. Whatever she had shown enthusiasm or joy over, that was always the very thing her mother had taken away or forbidden, she recalled bitterly. There was another possible "way out:" that her mother would be the one to return to Vienna while Ilse stayed with the children. Ilse silently hoped that this idea would not occur to her mother. Staying here with the children would offer Ilse much less freedom. Then she would be constantly busy taking care of the two boys, as usual.

Involuntarily, Ilse looked at her mother. To the question, "Well, Ilse, what do you say?" she had to answer positively or negatively. I can't act as if I don't know what she's talking about, she thought. Besides, I don't want to hear the whole story again.

"Well," her mother asked impatiently, "tell us your opinion!"

"I don't know," she began hesitantly, trying to sound as doubtful as she could. "I don't know. Do you really think the bomb document is very important to have?"

"Of course it is!" her mother answered. "Of course these papers are important. They are extremely important. But you wouldn't understand that; you don't have much insight. You need to leave these decisions about what to do or not do to me."

"Terrible, terrible," chimed in Frau von Rauenstein sympathetically, "it is hard to believe how vulnerable we all are. And if they turn this place into a military hospital — we may all have to leave. Without proper documents your mother will surely have a hard time."

Frau von Rauenstein was saying exactly the right things! Ilse wanted to hug her again.

"Would you be scared?" her mother asked. "To travel back to Vienna under these circumstances — it may not be easy."

"No, I'm not scared," said Ilse matter-of-factly and truthfully.

"To go back to Vienna; that shouldn't be too hard. But I'm not sure about the way back out?" Frau von Rauenstein was thinking out loud. "It's a question of time: the Russians are in Wiener Neustadt, but from Wiener Neustadt to Vienna . . . that's still quite a ways."

"You'll need to leave as soon as possible," decided her mother. "Otherwise you won't get through."

Ilse rejoiced inwardly. "As soon as possible" — that meant that the matter was decided. There would be no more maddening discussion back and forth that could lead to giving up the idea.

"You need to get information about the trains," suggested Frau von Rauenstein. "Find out if the normal schedule is being followed." She turned to Ilse and asked, " And you really aren't afraid to go?"

Ilse reassured her again that she was not. She was close to saying that she would go back to Vienna on foot if she had to.

"The girl is a gem," said Ilse's mother. "I think this is really the best solution, to send Ilse back for the documents."

"Listen to that," thought Ilse, hearing such unaccustomed praise. "All of a sudden I'm a gem? That's a new one!"

Ilse's mother made inquiries and received encouraging information about the trains: yes, there were still enough trains traveling to Vienna, she was assured. The trains were almost empty, however; who would want to travel back to Vienna? Travel nearer and nearer to the front!

"You won't have any trouble getting a seat on a train going into the city," said the spa hotel director. "I don't know about the other way, though."

"Trouble getting a seat? That might happen?" asked Ilse's mother.

"Now, what do you think, madam? You know how it was coming here. The trains all full! But organization's always good in the great German Reich. Trains'll keep running, right up to the last minute, I guarantee it. It's just a matter of timing, that's the thing. But I think your daughter can make it back before the Russians attack. But one thing is sure! There'll be a battle for Vienna, a hard battle, Vienna is one of the last bastions." The director struck a determined pose — suddenly he stood upright in his gray loden garments. And then, imitating the victorious High German of the Wehrmacht reports, he concluded solemnly, "Vienna will be declared a fortress; I know that; I know it in my bones. Vienna may not fall, and Vienna *will* not fall. We owe that to our Führer. As for your daughter, my opinion is that she'll come out in time, back out of the fortress, that is, out of the city."

Her mother looked a bit uncertain when she reported on the director's remarks.

"Vienna will be declared a fortress. Do you still want to go?" she asked. "You must hurry, understand? Otherwise, you won't be able to get back out of the city. Remember, I have to be able to rely on you. Don't get lost in your dreams, Ilse! You simply cannot dawdle around!"

"Of course you can trust me! Why not?" answered Ilse sincerely. "And I promise to hurry." In the park she heard Walter's war cries and the loud voices of the other boys. The Winkler, Nowotny, and Winternitz progeny were staging another battle.

"And give my love to your grandmother. And don't forget: at her place, in the bookcase, in the brown case, in a big white envelope..."

Peter was sleeping on a little sofa, surrounded by chairs so he couldn't roll off.

"... this envelope has all the papers..."

Peter was sleeping soundly. His face looked sweaty; his cheeks shone like red apples, and his blonde shock of hair, that his mother always combed straight, had fallen over to the side and was sticking to his head. As he lay there, he looked like a little girl in captivity, she thought. "Would her mother at least be nicer to my half-brothers than she has been to me?" wondered Ilse.

"... the bomb document, the medical certificates, everything is in that envelope. And if not, then right by it. Bring the envelope and all the useful papers you can find..."

And on the other side of the park there is the forest. And behind it the mountains — steep, rugged peaks. Glaciers ... blinding white snow in the sunlight. The world is beautiful if only somewhere you can find an open gate. A way out. A path to freedom.

"Are you daydreaming again? Are you even listening to me?" Her mother's voice sounded uncertain. "I'm not completely sure if I should send you to Vienna after all. With your constant thoughtlessness! You forget half of what I tell you!"

Ilse began to repeat what her mother had just said: "Give your love to Grandma. In the book case, in the brown case, in a big white envelope: the bomb document, the medical certificates. Bring the envelope. Also all the papers that are by it and useful. — Of course I've been listening. You can rely on me."

"Really?"

"Absolutely."

"All right. I'll depend on you then."

Now Ilse was almost sorry for her mother. How was it possible that her mother couldn't see through her at all? Her mother really didn't have the tiniest clue how much she wanted to get away from her! Ilse tried to push aside a wish that kept coming to her more and more insistently: the wish not to come back to "the valley of peace," but to stay in Vienna. Then her mother would be as she was now, *without* papers, and the whole trip back to Vienna would be senseless and unnecessary. No, she didn't dare do that. That would be a complete swindle.

But why sympathy? — she asked herself. And why am I ashamed to wish that the "fortress of Vienna" would close behind me, sealed so tightly shut that coming out and returning would be impossible!

"And pray tell, how does my mother dare so suddenly to place such faith in me?" She wondered, as she packed her backpack with supplies. In me, whom she has never before called "a gem," but "sloppy," "rebellious," "disobedient," and totally "unreliable?"

Does my mother have such a poor memory? Ilse recalled a time, when she, once again, received such hard blows for coming home late that she blacked out and saw stars, and her mother spat in her face and called her a "whore." "You are not my mother anymore," she had thought then, as she washed the spittle from her face in disgust. And in the middle of the blows she became indifferent to whether she had said that aloud or just thought it. She had said it aloud. She had said, calmly and clearly, "You are not my mother anymore." And she thought that her face had showed how sincerely she had meant this sentence.

At any rate she had resolved to stand by these words, to act as if this statement was a valid pronouncement. Because her mother never believed her when she spoke the truth, namely that she had been with Else, that she had gone to Else's and then accompanied Else to school to take her final leave of her; and it had been impossible to explain to her mother what they had talked about on the way, about

Wallenstein, Woester, and the Burg Theater, even about Socrates and Plato... If her mother had labeled all that excuses and lies, then she, the girl, beaten and punished for lying, never would have had to listen to her mother again. And the blows were always followed by the words, "Let's make up now; tell me we've made up." Those were just words, nothing but words. Words, that one could hear, could say — but they did not reflect the truth. If her mother placed no importance on these incidents, well, that was her business. She, Ilse, counted from the time she was spat upon all the other scoldings and blows after that as a great mound of injustices. No, *she* would not forget, and she would never again "make up." So, why did she feel sympathy? And why shame?

"I hope you can come through quickly," said her mother. "Promise me you'll hurry. Don't dawdle around!"

Ilse looked at the park, then peered over the treetops toward the mountains. Between the gray cliff walls some white snowflakes shimmered in the sky.

"Yes, I promise," she said. She pointed out the window. "Look, the weather has gotten nice. Everything will work out. The whole thing will be a little Easter excursion for me."

Chapter Seven: The Fortress

"Like I don't have enough work," lamented Frau Weissenböck. "Now even Frau Swoboda from next door has given me her flag to repair. What am I supposed to do, Frau Binder? Me, I can't just say no! I'm just afraid that in the end the whole Maroltinger Street is going to come to me with jobs!"

"Neighbors are supposed to stick together. And especially in times of need, don't you know?" Frau Binder, the building superintendent, a woman in her forties, still rather corpulent despite the privation of the war years, sat down at Frau Weissenböck's sewing table. Ceremoniously, she fished around in her shopping bag and pulled out a little package, whose contents were hidden in the wide pages of a copy of the *Folk Observer*. "I gotta job for you too," she said and laid the package on the table. "A flag that belongs to Frau Vojtisek on the first floor. She asks would you please be so kind as to fix it when you can get to it."

"Now look here, of all things, the Vojtiseks went and used the *Folk Observer* for packing," protested the old seamstress. "That's a dangerous thing. And I got no stove to burn it in. If the Russkies find this paper in my place — then God help me!"

"I'll just go and take it back to her then."

"Okay, do that if you'd be so good. Because I really don't know what I'm supposed to do with a Nazi paper."

Frau Weissenböck, who was already white-haired and bent, stood up with effort and went over to the big cutting table. She bent over the cloth spread out there and smoothed it out. "Too bad," she said. On the wide side she had sewn a new seam. Her small, yellowish fingers felt the opening. "Do you think this is wide enough, Frau Binder?" she asked. "I only took an approximate measurement."

"Oh yes, that's big enough," the building superintendent assured her. "Our flag pole can easily fit in there. But do you know what I'd suggest? That we dye the cloth red."

"Red?!" cried the seamstress, looking quite shocked.

"Of course — red! What else?"

"But . . . we're not Communists!" Old Frau Weissenböck, paler than usual, gasped for breath. "No, Frau Binder, that I just can't find it in me to do! The nice white linen! You couldn't use it for nothing else after that. No, I won't go that far!"

Frau Binder sighted: "Need knows no rules! Heindl, our air raid warden, he agrees with me: a red flag would be better than a white one."

"Well, *I* won't dye it at any rate, no not me." Frau Weissenböck shook her head energetically. "Look here, remember, I was the seamstress for the Lady Baroness Furtenback. And Frau von Lichtenberg. I cut the clothes for the fine ladies my own self, and gave them advice, I did, as to what colors went with their complexion, what flower arrangement looked best and what tablecloth with it. And more than once the honorable Frau von Lichtenberg, God rest her soul, said to me, 'You have good taste, dear Frau Weissenböck, a lady can always just follow your advice to the letter!' — You know, Frau Binder, I've never been one for the garish loud colors. I got good taste! And I won't ever give it up!"

"I believe you, I do, everything you said," the superintendent said reassuringly to the agitated seamstress. "But this is something else altogether now. We gotta think of the Russkies. If they see red shining out from the rooftops they'll surely be friendlier disposed. It'll look just like a regular message of welcome."

"I think a lot of little flags is enough." The seamstress pointed to the many piles of small flags in her workroom. "Look, just about everyone in the building wants to display one. Well, anyway, we're used to it; we've practiced enough in recent years. No one wants to draw no negative attention to themselves! We had flag days on May 1, on April 20, on March 13, on April 10, on November 9, on January 31 — with all that we could've left flags in our windows the whole year over. Do you know, I'll be glad when all this stops once and for all, and when . . . "

Frau Binder broke in. "Do you hear it?" she asked and pointed to the wall of the room. "A violin. Somebody's torturing a violin!"

"Herr Pospischil! Of all times, he chooses this moment to start playing his violin again? It's been forever since the last time he played it!"

"How can he play the violin at such a time as this?" Frau Binder was amazed. "What a nerve people have!" she cried. "But then

Pospischil he's always been a strange one. I hope he doesn't crack up completely!"

"No, no, he's just a quiet guy. One of those confirmed bachelors — they're always kind of odd. But he always greets me politely. And in the winter he always asks, he does, if he can lug the coal up from the cellar for me. He's helpful. And at one time he was one of the friendliest guys on the police force."

"Okay, then, well, it takes all kinds," philosophized Frau Binder. "But, I gotta go now. I got a heap of work myself!" She shook hands with Frau Weissenböck, turned around once more on her way out, and said: "For all I care Heindl can dye the cloth, if he's dead set on it. He puffs himself up since he's been air raid warden. I don't give a damn one way or the other."

The door closed behind the superintendent. Frau Weissenböck went to the newly arrived flag and put a tag on it, "Vojtisek, Apartment 14."

It looks like a flag store in here, she noted as she looked over all her work. But, as always, she had arranged everything in an orderly way: here one order, here another, all carefully labeled with names and apartment numbers. The sunbleached, light red flags, with their very clearly recognizable red circles, lay on the table in the pile "just finished." On the left side of the door, however, on the top of the dresser, were the unfinished ones, the "dangerous" flags. The white flags with the thick black swastikas in the middle lay waiting for Frau Weissenböck, and for a hasty and urgently needed removal.

The seamstress touched the dark red circle of the already "finished" flags. "It looks downright treasonous," she thought. "You can still see exactly what was underneath. But from a distance the Russians won't notice." With a soft sigh she picked up the next flag. "Two windows, two flags. Right!" she murmured. "But does everyone have to come to me? Yeah, to me, probably because they want to get these things out of the apartment as fast as possible. No one cares about *me*, what I'm supposed to do with all these swastikas!"

Frau Weissenböck, with another sigh, picked up her razor blade and began to cut the white circle off the red material of the first flag in the waiting pile. At that moment, a good idea occurred to her. She remembered the big heating kettle in the laundry room; there, in the stove, she would burn all the swastikas. They would give off a bad odor, she thought, but she assured herself that there was nothing she could do about it.

Quite by chance Ilse encountered Frau Navratil and Frau Zimmermann at the end station of streetcar line 46. There was a wall there, covered with posters, right next to the entrance of the Wilhelminen Hospital. On the poster wall was displayed an appeal to the Viennese people. The appeal was everywhere; they had read it before, and because they had seen it so often on every lamp post and building, they took no notice of it.

Frau Zimmermann had just come from the Flötzersteig, from her garden plot. She had something to do in her apartment. Frau Navratil, on the other hand, had just been at the butcher's and was on her way to do some more shopping.

Both lived on Maroltinger Street. Both were about fifty, and they lived in the same building as Herr Pospischil, Frau Binder, the seamstress Weissenböck and Frau Kreidl. To be sure, Frau Zimmermann didn't live in the apartment all year. When spring came she always moved into the cottage at her garden plot and stayed there, except for short visits back to her city apartment, until it got cold again. Frau Navratil visited her from time to time, especially in the autumn when the rhubarb and the big plum trees, apple, and pear trees bore fruit. Frau Navratil — married to a man more than twenty years her senior who avoided the long journey to the Flötzersteig garden plots — used to help Frau Zimmermann harvest her crops; on her way back to Maroltinger Street she was laden down, but satisfied over the fruits of their labor.

They were good friends, although their friendship was sometimes strained, especially by gossip that made its rounds in their building. When Frau Navratil heard from Frau Ruzicka that Frau Resch had said that Frau Zimmermann had confided in her that Herr Navratil got drunk every night, then Frau Navratil was quite offended.

When Frau Zimmermann heard that Frau Navratil had said to three or four others that she, almost fifty years old and still unmarried, had had "sooo" many relationships with men — Frau Zimmermann was wounded by these "attacks on her honor." When the two women tried to ferret out the sources of these stories, and find out *who* had actually said *what*, they never came to a conclusive result. Suddenly no one could remember exactly; no one had actually heard a certain story or spread it further, and everyone claimed to have been falsely quoted or said that the story in question was completely false.

Their innumerable enjoyable conversations, the fruit trees and harvest days and even the experiences of "malicious gossip" — everything they shared bound them together and their friendship endured as if it had never been strained. The strength of their friendship was shown in the fact that Frau Navratil knew a very dangerous secret about Frau Zimmermann — and she had known it for many years — but never would she have dreamed of saying a word about it to anyone. Frau Zimmermann was a committed Communist — a fact that was hard for Frau Navratil to understand. Not only was "being a Communist" strictly forbidden and therefore dangerous, but to Frau Navratil the very word sounded so disreputable and offensive that she wanted nothing at all to do with it. "I don't understand anything about politics," Frau Navratil was in the habit of saying, and the statement was true. She wasn't ashamed of the fact, but in fact proud of it.

But one autumn evening in the garden plot, while drinking rhubarb wine, Frau Zimmermann finally explained her philosophy to Frau Navratil, as a kind of comfort, but also to share the weight of their common fate. They had just heard that Herr Navratil, the day before, had come out of the tavern and returned home the next morning very "radicalized." "Now, listen here," Frau Zimmermann had begun, after drinking three or four glasses of her homemade rhubarb wine, "Listen, I have a worry. I'm a Communist, but no one can know it. I've got involved with one or two things that could be real dangerous. You know, every time a guy in a uniform comes near my garden, I think it's to snap me up. Please don't tell anybody! It would be over for me."

So, they were standing under the "Appeal" poster. The appeal was signed by the Reich official and Gauleiter Baldur von Schirach and addressed to the men and women of Vienna. Thick black letters announced the fact that the enemy stood at the gates of the city. Vienna, the announcement continued, had over the course of history often proven to be an undefeatable fortress. One had only to think of the Turkish invasions. Mindful of their unique and historical responsibility, the inhabitants of Vienna were called on to show courage and to take on the duty of holding back the enemy. VIENNA IS DECLARED A FORTRESS! said the thick letters. Vienna must not fall at this decisive hour of history. Enemy propaganda brochures are not to be given any credence; they are intended to instill panic and contain pure falsehoods and propaganda lies.

Frau Navratil and Frau Zimmermann had, however, at this moment other things to do than think about the Turks, enemy brochures, or Baldur von Schirach.

"Have you bought some meat already?" asked Frau Navratil.

"Yes, right when they opened this morning," reported Frau Zimmermann. "It took just about all my bread rations. You gotta grab what's there when you can."

"Three quarters of a kilo of meat instead of half a kilo of bread!" cried Frau Navratil enthusiastically. "You gotta take advantage of that. Besides, my husband's such a meat lover."

"They're supposed to slaughter only when needed," reported Frau Zimmermann.

"I hope the cow wasn't dead yet, before he got stuck!" said Frau Navratil. The shopping bag in her hand suddenly felt a few kilos heavier.

"Ah, nothing will happen to us," comforted Frau Zimmermann. "Who knows what all we ate last time we were together. And we're still kicking."

Frau Navratil came a step closer to Frau Zimmermann and whispered in her ear: "They say it was really terrible! I got it from a reliable source."

"What was terrible?" asked Frau Zimmermann. She looked happy; she was unmistakably getting more cheerful with each passing day.

"You know, the Russkies!" Frau Navratil reached for Frau Zimmermann's coat button and held onto her coat for dear life. "They kill everything big and little, rob, take away, whatever. And imagine: out there in Pressbaum they shot all my brother-in-law's chickens, they did."

"That's war for you. Nothing can be done," replied Frau

Zimmermann. "Besides, you shouldn't believe everything you hear," she said, trying to console her friend. "Lots of exaggeration goes on, you know."

"But they say it's all true!" Frau Navratil let go of her friend's coat. She wasn't easy to console.

"Those are just the ones who go to excess. The Red Army doesn't allow that stuff. They don't go and attack anyone who's friendly toward them."

"How can they tell so quickly who is?"

"They can. The Russian people, they are a good-hearted folk. They like children, after all. Surely you've heard that, right?"

Frau Navratil nodded. "I've heard it, I have. They even give the little ones bread and sugar they say."

"Well then. And he who likes children, he is not a bad person!" Frau Zimmerman issued this pronouncement in her deepest, most convinced tone of voice.

"But, they say it's gotten real bad out there, out in the country!" protested Frau Navratil. From the bottom of her heart she wanted to believe the best of the Red Army, but unfortunately she had heard a different story, complete with terrible details, from her brother-in-law who had just barely escaped Pressbaum and made it to Vienna at the last minute. "And the women," she lamented, "They chase down all the women, the Russkies, even the sixty- and seventy-year-old women they rape."

"I'm telling you, that is war. And among the soldiers there are good and there are bad. And the excesses, are you telling me that there haven't been any on our side too? In Russia, in Poland, and wherever else our armies have been."

"*We* are not Bolshevik barbarians," said Frau Navratil, trying to defend the honor of the German Wehrmacht.

"No, barbarians we're not. But war can make human beings into barbarians. That's why the proletariat of all countries should unite, and nevermore let itself be provoked to fight against each other by the rich who just get richer by the wars. Look, that's what Marx said. And that is the communist ideal."

"If it only were all over," sighed Frau Navratil. "I'm so afraid. My grandkid is with me because her mother was called up, away from Vienna, to help with the information service. If I weren't around, she'd be all alone, the poor girl. Twelve years old! But looks fifteen. If the Russians'd do something to her, I wouldn't survive it."

"Get on, don't make yourself go gray! It's much safer in the city than in the country," Frau Zimmermann comforted her. "Besides," — Frau Zimmermann took a step back and opened her arms so invitingly that her gesture could not be misinterpreted. "Besides, you can send all the Russkies here to me; I'll take care of 'em."

Frau Navratil couldn't believe her ears. "All the Russkies? To you?" she stammered dully.

"Yes, right." Now Frau Zimmermann was laughing. "All the Russians," she confirmed. "I'll lift my apron up, for one after the other! But now," she gave Frau Navratil her hand to take her leave, "now I gotta go. I got a couple of important things to take care of."

"Jesus!" said Frau Navratil, as she watched her friend hurry away. "For every Russian her apron . . . I knew she was a Communist, but this . . . "

Completely confused, Frau Navratil tried to find the right words. "This, well . . ." she finally was able to say, "this is being a Communist with heart and soul." And deeply shaken by the immoral depths to which her friend's political stance had brought her, she continued her shopping, vigorously shaking her head.

Chapter Eight: In the Spring

> In the spring, the spring so nice,
> My Vienna turns to Paradise.
> A force so strong I cannot halt,
> Draws me to the forest, Wienerwald,
> To the lovely forest Wienerwald!
> A force so strong I cannot halt.

The bright tips of the shovels gleamed in the sunlight. Shouldering spades, the Hitler Youth marched along the edge of the forest. Hans, the Wolf Cub Führer, commanded: "Left, two, three, four, left, two, three, four!" and then led the song:

> We march along the streets
> Quiet and firm step our feet.
> And above our heads so high,
> Waves the flag up in the sky.

But they weren't actually "marching along the streets," but walking along a forest path. And there was no "flag waving up in the sky," over their heads were only the tips of the firs and pines, mild sunlight and spring air.

The work troop consisted of twenty "men," none of them older than sixteen, the youngest twelve. Hans, himself not many days over sixteen, had been allowed to pick out his own boys and of course he had chosen only the strongest, most diligent and reliable. It was not the first time that they had followed orders together; Hans knew every single youth from the "home evenings." They were capable, disciplined young men, now marching up the gradually steeper incline. They began to sing the second stanza of the song:

> Forward the drummer boy
> He beats his drum all day.
> Too young to know of love,
> Or pain when love goes away.

Robert realized that they didn't have a drum. "Hey, Hans, where is our drum?" he cried.

Hans turned around to him. "You want a drum?" he asked, laughing. "I'm just glad that each of us has a spade, that we don't have to dig with our hands."

Bernd, marching next to Robert, asked scornfully: "Hey, Robert? Since when did you start making a stink about the song lyrics?"

"Oh, maybe I listen to them once in a while," said Robert, who had no desire to continue the discussion.

At this point the path narrowed and they found themselves climbing up a steep slope. They stopped singing and no longer kept up a march rhythm. The troop trudged along behind Hans, breathing heavily.

"It's not much further," called Hans to the youths.

No, it was not much farther to the place where the ramparts and foxholes had to be dug out. And if anyone had asked the boys if they were tired from the long march, none of them would have admitted it. Too often had their duties been compared with those of the soldiers on the front. At every roll call it had been hammered away at them that the continued existence of their homeland, the fate of women and children, the welfare and woes of the entire civilian population, all was now resting on their shoulders; that they now had to do their part to prevent the "red hordes of Bolsheviks" from entering the gates of the city. It had long been self-evident to them all that in all areas of life they had to be fit and strong, and true to their slogan, "Swift as a greyhound, tenacious as leather, hard as Krupp steel!"

During the last weeks and months they had had ample opportunity to demonstrate the qualities in this slogan. They had dug out bodies from ruined buildings, searched for the missing, transported the wounded and the dead, carried munitions to the platforms of the flak towers and rendered first aid in the air raid shelters. In the last few days they had had a crash course in all types of weapons they might be using; short, theoretical exercises about machine guns, side-arms, cannons, hand grenades, and bazookas.

In the meantime the "mental and spiritual well-being" of the boys was also quickly addressed. At roll call, pointed, slogan-laden addresses told them again and again that failure to hold back the

"Bolshevik flood of terror" or the "Mongolian hordes" would mean the end of the German race and the Aryan culture, in other words, the "end of the world." Songs were provided to help steel their nerves, and even though their lyrics didn't correspond exactly to the actual military situation, the songs had a persistent and undefeatable life of their own:

> The dry bones they tremble
> of the world before the red war.
> We have broken their terror
> and we have settled the score.
> We will march on to glory
> our flag o're all we'll unfurl,
> now belongs to us Deutschland
> and tomorrow the whole wide world.

When the boys sang the song with these words, they were always corrected by Hans. The correction was one single word, but Hans had been corrected himself on the same point when he had learned the song as a small ten-year-old boy. His group leader had asked angrily, "What are you singing? We can't sing the song that way."

Hans, skillful and precise when he memorized pieces, had been wounded by the correction because he was used to making no mistake.

"But that's the way the song goes," he had dared to protest, whereupon he received a stern lecture from the group leader, who informed him that while singing one must always be aware of *what* the song was saying, because even the smallest syllables had their meaning, and, if sung wrongly, could lead to very serious misunderstandings.

"It doesn't say that Germany 'belongs to us' today and 'tomorrow the whole wide world,' but that today Germany 'listens to us,' and 'tomorrow the whole wide world.' My boy, that is an enormous difference!"

In the year 1938 Hans didn't fully understand this "enormous" difference, but he had been raised to be obedient. A few years later Hans began to understand the meaning of the difference better, and he took a slightly malicious pleasure in instructing the boys under his command not only on the original text but also impressing on them the importance of being aware of the meaning of song lyrics, and on the two words in question. Because why — he thought — why did everyone sing "belongs to us" instead of "listens to us?" It wasn't by chance! Somehow he sensed that the instinctive replacement of words stemmed from the fact that the error was closer to reality than the more harmless original text. Nevertheless, he told himself that a text should be sung as it was composed. The author must have had his reasons for every syllable included or omitted — and that principle justified his insistence on the correction.

The boys were digging at the edge of the forest at the places marked by stakes. The soil was not hard, for it had rained the day before, not heavily, but just enough to soften the ground, without making the soil heavy.

At the beginning of the shoveling the boys had no connection to work required of them. The sloping meadow lay in front of them, looking just as it should, composed of grass and earth. It seemed to Robert as if the meadow was resisting being changed; but the longer the troop kept digging, deeper and deeper into the earth, the more determined they became, and the trenches began to dominate the boys and the section of the landscape; in contrast, the meadow and the edge of the forest faded in their dominance and significance.

They dug; they threw the soil up; they sweated; they didn't speak with each other — maybe none of them thought about the meaning or meaninglessness of their labor. Robert was curious to know what the others were thinking about the job, and Hans was wondering the same thing.

Maybe they were all wondering the same thing, "What are the others thinking?" And maybe that was the only thing that came into the minds of the trench-digging troop, "What are the others thinking?"

It was certain that they were all accustomed to obeying, and that in this moment the only other thing they might have been doing was digging their own graves, in which they might soon lie as "heroes" and "defenders" of their city. It was possible that some, or even many, of them were afraid. Afraid of the enemy, afraid, perhaps, in the next few days to have to put to use their freshly acquired knowledge of weapons and their instruction as soldiers. They were content right now to dig and to sing songs, and somehow they knew that it was too late to think things over. It was far too late.

The work troop took their first break in front of the half finished trench. Leaning their backs against the newly formed wall of earth, their legs stretched out, covered all over with dirt, the youths reached with dirty hands for their supply kits. They took big bites of buttered bread, and passed around their tin field bottles. They were so hungry that they competed to eat the fastest; whoever ate fastest, was full first, and then no event in the world could make a full person quarrelsome.

Fritz, who finished his bread first, looked at his hands. "We're really a dirty bunch," he said to Robert.

Hans, who was just then going by with the tin water bottle, agreed with Fritz, "Yes, we're dirty," he said. "But not really dirty yet."

"You mean, we'll be really dirty tomorrow or the next day?" inserted Bernd. He was one of the really "gung-ho"; he reported for every job voluntarily, and everyone knew that he envied Hans his position as troop leader. "Is that what you mean?" he asked insistently.

Hans screwed the bottle closed, threw a quick glance at Bernd and then said abruptly, "Nice weather today." Then he went on with the bottle and poured out the rest of the tea to the others.

Bernd stood there with a red face. For a moment he looked like he wanted to go after Hans and start a fight. Then once again he picked up his spade and started digging again, even though the break wasn't over.

"He's gonna show us," laughed Fritz. "If it were up to Bernd, we'd never take a break."

Robert folded his arms behind his head and stared up at the sky. There were no airplanes up there, but whether there were or not was indifferent to him. Today is today— and tomorrow is tomorrow. He thought of the moment in the park, the gleaming silver bomb squadrons, and he thought, "And Ilse, she must be in the West. Maybe she was better off than he was? But, was there really anyplace in the world where people were actually better off?"

Further away, at the top of the highest spruce tree, he saw a blackbird sitting, singing, and composing her songs. The black body of the bird, high above, lonesome against the blue of the sky, the green needles of the trees, flooded with sunlight; in front of him, the sloping meadow, the narrow part of the valley, other hills, other valleys, the crest of the mountain in the background: what a lovely view the blackbird had!

Chapter Nine: Easter Bells

The train station was not far from the spa hotel. Ilse looked forward to the walk: past the narrow valley and farmyards, then a little forest and finally the village and the station.
Thank goodness no one had thought of accompanying her! She wanted to be alone, alone with her happiness over being allowed to leave the "valley of peace."
Her first steps toward freedom! Up until the last minute she had been afraid that her mother would think it over and not let her go after all.
And so her trip was especially nice. Meadow and forest wall, plants and flowers, every curve in the path brought new colors, new shades of green. Lizards that ran across the path; noisy birds that flew up out of the bushes; the deep blue sky dotted with cotton clouds, that came along, shifted, changed. Everything, everything was like the first day, as if never before seen, not yet really perceived, like the beginning of something unique. And the further Ilse traveled away from the "valley of peace," the more unique and beautiful the landscape seemed to her. More and more expectantly she kept going, toward the center of the adventure that awaited her, of which she had not the slightest fear.
There was much along the way that she wanted to entrust to her journal, but she had to think of the time. She had to get to the train and it was already late in the afternoon. She felt the little notebook in her coat pocket, tapped with her fingers on it. Yes, it was still there; it was going with her, not running away.
Secretly, very secretly she had stuffed the notebook into her coat pocket, as if it would betray her and reveal how much she wanted to leave and especially to distance herself from her mother.
Yes, she was taking an Easter walk, like the one in Goethe's *Faust*. Wasn't she now undertaking a very special, personally meaningful Easter walk? She came to the forest, and it seemed to her like a cathedral; the tall spruces loomed up like pillars; a wonderful fragrance came up from the ground. Quiet, quiet, one must be quiet here, walk very carefully over the brown carpet of needles, be quiet

within the quiet all around. A shadowy half darkness enveloped her; now and then single, slanted rays of sun glinted between the tree trunks — they came as if from hidden windows, as if sent to illuminate her way. The quiet of the forest began to grow, surrounded her, was audible, palpable; she felt secure inside it. If one can have this stillness in oneself and around oneself, then one is surely protected by something great, she thought. One is in a good house, and a good builder must have built it.

There were only a few people at the train station. The ticket agent explained that there were no regular departures or arrivals. "But the trains are still running," he assured her. "One just has to wait until one arrives."

The train to Vienna came right away, but the cars were almost empty. No "trouble getting a seat" going east! Inge walked through the train until she found a completely empty compartment. One jerk — the trip began. Ilse landed, before she had thought of sitting down, on the wooden bench.

And what a trip! Ilse pulled the window down so she could see the locomotive in the curve. It puffed, steamed, blew thick swirls of smoke into the air, pulled a plume of smoke behind it. The train snaked around the wild, frothy Ache; on both sides of the tracks loomed great rocky cliffs steeply upwards, blocking the view of the sky.

Some day in the future, when she had put her school and the Rudolfsplatz prison completely behind her, when she could freely govern her own life, then she would often take such journeys. "Travel makes you free," thought Ilse. "I'll try never to settle down; I will keep traveling from one freedom to another, always in motion."

She began to imagine her travel wardrobe: a big silk coat with a checked lining. Leather gloves. A light brown leather suitcase. Everything like the items in the display windows in the Michaeler Passage. There they had yellow and white speckled toothpicks, soap bowls and toothbrushes, all in the same color and material. Everything one needed to take on trips — to be free. But no one should pack too many things. No, only the most necessary things would she take along so she could always move freely. Move freely and be always underway; travel wherever she wanted, without having to deceive anyone or lie, without any promises, without a job to carry out. Then I'll stand at the train window, just like I'm doing now, roll the window down and stick my head out into the landscape, and let the wind whirl around me. And I'll remember this first practice trip, remember this first taste of freedom.

And I'll travel to Italy to see my father. That will be one of my first journeys, Ilse resolved. I would really like to get acquainted with my father at last. My father, about whom my mother says only negative things, my father whom my mother says I resemble to a tee, but only in his bad traits; this father is worth a trip! She loved him secretly; the more her mother maligned him, the more she loved him. Because she wasn't such a "bad person" herself, her role model couldn't possibly be the worst person in the world. To be sure, her father had left her and her mother in the lurch after their divorce, but wasn't she doing the same thing now, fleeing from her mother?

From a few remarks of her grandmother's, who never said anything bad about her father, Ilse had been able to put together a picture of her parents' very short marriage: the wedding, brought about by a motorcycle trip to the Semmering, an overnight stay, during which she had been conceived! Ilse had calculated the time between the wedding and her own birth: of course, they were in a big hurry; of course, everything was her fault because she had been born only four months later. The marriage was forced, a certificate acquired to be able to "give the child a name." That can't be a good way to get married; it was hardly a deep love. They quarreled the whole time, Grandmother had said. She concluded, "Your parents really weren't right for each other." All he meant to her was a fling, an adventure with an Italian with a motorcycle.

A trip to my father! Ilse resolved again. As soon as the war is over, and I can finally stand on my own two feet. I'll travel to see him and my other, my "Italian" grandmother, and old Omi. I haven't been there since I was six, but I remember how nice my visit there was. Old Omi, my great-grandmother, who used to like me so much!

And my father will say, "Hello, hello, here I am." And you, my dear father, you didn't trouble yourself about me at all? How were you able to do that? You could have easily figured out how I was getting along at mother's, namely poorly. Very poorly, because I constantly reminded her of you, and *you* she did not like! It was a riddle for me, how you both misunderstood each other so when you took that motorcycle trip to the Semmering, that you didn't know better than to sleep together. "In any case," I'll say, "I haven't seen you since I was one year old, that was the last time, so you will understand why I remember absolutely nothing about you."

I will tell him that I have secretly loved him. No, I won't; I don't want to reward him for not caring about me. I won't reveal that I often yearned for him — because we were supposed to be so similar, to have so much in common. And because the whole time I've been so lonesome, so terribly alone.

Salzburg, the Salzkammergut. Open land, mountains retreating into the background. Meadows, fields, villages, towns. The train turned toward the east; then it came to the main East-West cross-country road, ran next to it for a stretch here and there; the tracks criss-crossed the road at intervals. Did Ilse want to continue her conver-sation with her father? Try to guess what he would answer? When she first glimpsed the long road, she forgot him; he disappeared once again into faraway Italy.

Suddenly her solitary trip, alone in her own compartment, came to an end, along with her fantasy trip into the distant future. When they reached the East-West road, the present forced itself upon her, pressed against the train, kilometer after kilometer, an endless stream: the migration of refugees to the West. People on foot, ox-carts, bicycles, hand trucks, dilapidated automobiles run by wood gas, ancient-looking motorcycles with sidecars, horses pulling wagons. Everything was packed full with possessions, whatever people had been able to grab at the last moment: bundles of clothes, suitcases, blankets, cartons stuffed full, tied up tight, cooking utensils, cans, children's beds, chairs, rugs, pictures (paintings in wooden frames, wrapped in cloth) — what were the pictures of, that made them valuable enough to be taken along: Guardian angels? Saints? Enlarged photographs of loved ones, perhaps fallen soldiers who hadn't returned from the front, sons, fathers, grandsons, grandfathers? Or a landscape? A — memory?

And the endless caravan pushed forward, step by step, everything and everyone united in the same slow pace; no one went faster, even those in vehicles, who were mostly mothers, children, and elderly people. The stream moved forward quietly, following a common rhythm. It seemed to be driven forward by its own inner motor, to be a mechanical event, taking place of its own accord, rather like the workings of an ancient mill that now and then turned a hundredweight heavy wheel.

A caravan of ghosts: no sound from the stream of people reached as far as the clattering train. The tired, slowly measured forward footsteps, the slowly turning wheels, made their way along, up hill, down hill. Up hill, down hill trudged the people, the ghostly crowd had no beginning, and no end to it could be seen. If the train tracks crossed the road, the refugees waited behind the railroad gates — resigned to God's will. (This phrase occurred to Ilse, at the sight of the calm, patient and impassive faces.) There was no great distance between her train window and the people waiting behind the gate; if the train had stopped, she could have been able to ask them: "Have you been forced out? Are you fleeing on your own? Where are you coming from? Where are you going?" She could guess the simple answers she would get: a shrug of the shoulder, a crack of the whip, a sigh: "From the East, from the East. To the West, to the West."

Twilight was spreading; the stream of refugees didn't diminish, but faded into hazy contours, silhouettes, shadows that were moving, step by step, from the East, to the West, to the West. . . . The darkness of night came; the shadows kept moving forward; the stream of people had no gap, and no end.

"What do the refugees think when they see the train?" Ilse wondered. They must be amazed that a train is taking a few passengers in exactly the direction from which they, step by step, are taking such efforts to leave behind them. Perhaps they are surprised that there are still any trains running, and they wonder why they aren't going in the opposite direction, in *their* direction. Because none of them were successful in trying to storm into one of the last trains that left for the West.

But probably they didn't think anything of the kind, but just kept going, step by step, to the West, pushed by fate into the great, forward moving mass of fleeing people.

The refugee procession in the daylight; the refugee procession in the twilight . . . Deep sympathy overcame Ilse. Several times she felt a strong twinge of sympathy when she made out an individual person within the gray, fleeing mass of humanity. A frail, elderly little woman in peasant clothes stuck in her mind. How exhausted she had looked as she took hold of the crossing gate!

What circumstances, what providence, Ilse wondered, had compelled this peasant woman to flee? "Providence!" Yes, that word, somewhere, some time — Ilse didn't remember any more — she had heard used in a grandiloquent speech (was it by Hitler himself?). More precisely, *divine* providence had been the phrase; "divine providence" had singled out the German folk, and made it possible for the German folk to aspire to the Thousand Year Reich, under a "Führer" who strove day and night to provide for the welfare of this uniquely superior folk of all folks. Maybe — as mentioned, Ilse didn't exactly recall — a thousand years is a long time and this time seemed to be coming to an end already— maybe the "Führer" had been speaking quite personally, saying that he thanked divine providence for granting him his historical role? Divine providence had been mentioned, in any case! Was the simple peasant woman there, on her flight, a very devout person? Had she been especially impressed by the word "divine?" Now, to be sure, far from any "divine" realm, she had to contend with a very earthly trek: the path that providence had chosen for her began with being driven out of her home and ended in uncertainty.

In the darkness, however, the individual forms became indistinct; the stream of refugees melted into a unity, a whole, a mass, whose progress forward became a silent reproach. This mass, this human procession became something violent, a strength, out of which a message, a warning, emerged. "My generation and I," Ilse said to herself, "It is my hope that we will not believe the words and speeches from above, not believe them at all, no matter how exalted, how impressive, and 'divine' they sound. We will need to be vigilant."

No, she didn't feel any more sympathy. Here, before her eyes, unfolded the ineluctable procession of history. And hadn't Voltaire said long ago that the history of humankind was nothing but a chain of deception, crime and intrigues? Yes, we will need to be vigilant, she told herself again, because we, the ordinary people, we are the ones who have to determine the fate of a people. It's not the great people, and as long as we don't realize that we are to blame for our own misery.

As Ilse, still standing at the train window, steeled herself against sympathy, her thoughts drifted into other directions and perceptions.

She didn't notice it at first, but wasn't a feeling of happiness welling up inside her? A happiness that she was just becoming conscious of? Yes, a joy, a completely personal, completely egotistical joy? A feeling of happiness that she owed to the sad, endless column of refugees? Because, the isolated, quiet "valley of peace" — wasn't it receding, the further east the train went, into a farther and farther removed, quite undeniable distance? A wall of people, a densely crowded, majestic ghostly procession of refugees was between, thousands and thousands of people were filling the road, sealing off the way, *her* way back!

Frau Winkler, Frau Winternitz, Frau Nowrotny, the senior instructor Herr Ohlers, Frau Alwine von Rauenstein: they were just characters in a brief episode, peripheral figures, people that she could hardly expect to see ever again. The coming events would propel all the shelter-seekers in the "valley of peace" further away, or back where they came from. But her mother and half-brothers would come back again, back to Vienna, and Ilse didn't want to think about their homecoming. Until "order" was restored one again, a considerable time would elapse, and in that time, she was free — *free!* A benevolent fate had, at any rate, released her from the pressure to return right away to the "valley of peace;" there would be "difficulties obtaining a seat," wished-for and yet demonstrable "difficulties" that would make her stay in Vienna understandable and approved, even by her mother. To join the great eastward migration of refugees seemed now a hopeless, even impossible undertaking. And how much less possible would be a departure from Vienna tomorrow or the next day when she had her desired papers in her hand! Ilse thought she could count on the fact that her grandmother wouldn't let her depart.

And while Ilse leaned on the train window, still looking out into the night, another wave of happiness came over her: "I am free! I am happy! Now I can be 'myself.' I am on a kind of vacation, a wonderful vacation." And with a quick wink of her eye, — surely her father would have such a wink ready for similar situations — with a quick wink of her eye she said to herself and to him: "No, Vienna and the war and the Russians — we'll get through all of that; we'll survive all of that somehow, won't we? — Don't you think so?"

It was strange how quietly she was received in Vienna. A wonderful sparkling sky full of stars spread over the West Train Station, over Mariahilfer Street; a quiet, gleaming sky, without search lights, without lighted rockets. Now and then, from a great distance, could be heard a soft, dull rumbling, as if from a distant thunderstorm. It seemed like the growling of a faraway monster in a cave, a monster who wanted to come out but couldn't find the way.

It was one o'clock in the morning. Ilse wanted to go to her grandmother's and announce, "Here I am," but the way there was further than the way to the inner city, to her bombed-out apartment. Besides, she was supposed to go straight there — as her mother had impressed upon her right before she left — to see if the temporary lock on the apartment door was still in place, and to take any valuables she found to her grandmother's. "Whatever you think is of value," her mother had said vaguely, surpisingly leaving the judgments to her. One thing she knew she would take, Heyse's foreign word dictionary, a thick, heavy volume, but one of her favorites, and therefore "valuable."

For a while Ilse stood indecisively in front of the bomb-damaged train station, looking first in the direction of the inner city, then in the direction of grandmother's and the outer zones. Finally she decided on the bombed-out apartment. Why alarm her sleeping grandmother now, in the middle of the night? And besides, she thought, she ought to go to the Rudolfsplatz first anyway, stay overnight there, and go to grandmother's in the morning. My trip to Rudolfsplatz will take care of part of my work here. Then I'll have no need to go back there; I can stay the whole time at grandmother's after that.

Going down the straight path of Mariahilfer Street, there was not a soul to be seen; it was as if everyone in the city had died. Not until she reached the Ring Street did she see a few people straggling along, here and there a car, with a narrow strip of light showing out of the taped-over headlights, barely enough to guide the cumbersome, slowly moving vehicles along. Everything looked ghostly in the near-total darkness. The vehicles moved down the streets, hardly visible, dark, formless shapes; and the few lonely shadows of human beings groped through the stillness, in which now and then only a few muffled sounds could be heard, sounds that seemed to come from behind a wall of cotton.

At the Burg Gate, Ilse set off in the direction of the inner city, over the Heldenplatz, the Michaeler Platz, the Kohl Market, the Tuchlauben, and toward the bombed-out High Market. A familiar place — now turned into a landscape of ruins with high mountains of rubble. When she arrived there, she went past the no longer existing Nobel Club, the site of an unusual experience she still recalled vividly. It was the elegant club Ilse had entered, in her Jungmädchen uniform and carrying the collection can for the winter charity drive, before the porter in his gold braided uniform had been able to stop her.

It had been a bold entry into another world, made in defiance of the sign: "Reserved. Entry for Invited Guests Only," and it had led to an unforgettable interlude. At the end of her collection Ilse had been named the best fund raiser of the inner city district, received a gift of a book (*German Heroic Sagas*, Part I) and a certificate of thanks.

Asked, how she had raised so much money, and where she had gotten her can filled to the brim, not only with change, but ten and twenty-mark bills, she refused to answer. She didn't answer because she wanted to visit the exclusive club again, if she could, during the next fund-raising campaign, although she thought the porter might be more alert the next time. As she accepted the *German Heroic Sagas*, she said only that she had been collecting all day long and that she would be glad to collect money her whole life long. This wasn't a lie, for she enjoyed walking around with the collection can because doing so meant that she could be away from home for a few hours.

Ilse owed the courage she had mustered to enter the Nobel Club to chance. Just as she was passing by, an SS-man, in his brown uniform, had been leaving. As he pulled back the velvet curtain, piano music and the voice of a singer drifted out onto the street. "I carry my love in my heart, silent with bliss," wafted out, and as Ilse heard the line of the song, which was rarely played on the radio, she suddenly wished that she could hear the rest of the piece. Before the door could close again, she was in the lobby and soon thereafter on the other side of the thick velvet curtain. The porter ran after her and cried, "Halt, halt," but he was compelled to retreat silently by the admonishing gestures of some intently listening spectators.

What an illustrious society was there! None of the military men were wearing ordinary field gray. It was obvious from the cut and decorations of their uniforms that they were high officers, although Ilse knew nothing about the significance of their signs of rank. There were a few men in civilian clothes, almost all in smoking jackets. The singer was wearing a tuxedo. The ladies were dressed in evening gowns adorned by pearls and other jewelry. The whole scene had an aura of irreality; Ilse had the feeling that she had been transported into a movie, a movie set in the atmosphere of a strange, noble world, located planets away.

Pressed into the most remote back corner of the hall, Ilse waited for the end of the musical piece. She was not at all sure what she should do next, for she was very ill at ease in her environment. Just don't make a racket with the collection can, she told herself. And after the singer had received the appropriate amount of politely restrained applause, she turned toward the nearest table and began to peddle her wares. She offered glass medallions bearing the heads of famous Germans — Schiller, Goethe, Beethoven, Nietzsche, Richard Wagner — "Twenty cents each," she whispered as softly and modestly as she could. "Twenty cents. For the winter relief campaign, please."

Did she owe it to her quiet modesty? Collections with these coin cans were usually carried out by the Hitler Jugend in a great commotion, with loud demands for contributions! Or was it the glass images of the great men of the past, who fit so well into the enchanted mood of the music lovers — one experience of their cultural legacy followed another — was it really the beautiful images? Or perhaps was it the slumbering guilty conscience deep in the hearts of this exclusive society, about being discovered consuming champagne and fine delicacies so far removed from the bloody tumult of the war? At any rate, Ilse enjoyed unparalleled success in her sales. The glass medallions were snapped up like hot cakes, and one mark was the least anyone paid her. The guests at different tables competed with each other in their donations; bigger contributions — even mark notes, carefully rolled up and pushed through the round, hardly ever used bill slot of the can next to the coin slot — streamed as if of their own accord out of the generously opened wallets and brief cases into Ilse's collection can.

Or was it just because of the interruption, thought Ilse, as she now, at the end of the Vorlauf Street, came by the Fishermen's Steps.

Do I merely owe my success to the fact that I barged in and interrupted them? The collection can and I did cause a surprising, almost sensational interruption of the planned entertainment program of an exclusive, protected social gathering.

Ilse hurried along past the bombed-out buildings. Fishermen's Steps, Salzgries, Gölsdorf Street. Ruined walls in the moonlight, remains of house facades, empty window openings, lonesome looming fire walls: ghostly stage sets in a ghostly landscape, created by "divine providence."

Finally, the Rudolfsplatz. The park. And at the end of the park, her building. The half bombed-out and yet still inhabited building that continued to shelter its tenants in the parts not in danger of caving in. For the first time she took a good look at the remains of the building. She stared at it for a long time, as if from a great distance.

Strangely enough, the parts of the building that were missing she seemed to see more clearly than those that were still standing. The no longer existing side wall of her room, for example; the exploded section whose trench-shaped depths, widening as she looked upward, traced the path of the bomb; and finally the apartment located next to the wall of her room: an apartment that now was made of nothing but air, air and emptiness. (Decades later Ilse was to see a photograph, come across by pure chance in a monograph, a photograph that showed the balcony and facade of this neighboring apartment, whole and in the familiar old form. Hermann Broch had lived here before the "Annexation of Austria into the Great German Reich." Hermann Broch, the writer, in exile after 1938, but not yet far away from the deprivation and suffering of his homeland. In 1945, in the year before the bombing of his apartment, he had completed his great novel, *The Death of Virgil* — this rich, deep book about dying and the closeness of apocalypse at the end of an epoch.)

The uninhabited, the no longer existing places, seemed to send out stronger signals than the undamaged parts of the building. Was it so, that the lost, the removed, had greater power than all the remaining walls?

Ilse crossed the street. Right in front of her building door, immediately after she took her last steps toward it, she heard for the first time with great clarity, the sounds that she later called the

"Easter bells." The "distant storm," the soft, dull roaring that had welcomed her at the West Train Station, now she recognized again — wumm — wumm — wumm — wumm. The Easter bells: the noise of the Russian artillery.

While climbing the stairs, she met the building superintendent, who had just been trying to convince the coal dealer to try to find the basement. Frau Zirkelbach, who was wearing a brown, rather shabby-looking fur coat over her long nightgown, didn't seem in her official uniform to have the slightest bit of authority as building superintendent.

"Go down to the basement?" protested the coal dealer. "Ten horses wouldn't bring me down there! At the first puff of wind it'd fall down on our heads, it would! Nope, I'm going to my shop. I won't let myself get buried alive down there!"

Ilse wanted to go past the pair and climb up to her apartment, but the building superintendent blocked her path.

"Jeesus, it's Ilse," she cried. "Yes, it is; what on earth are you doing back here? I thought you'd gone West long ago! Your family were supposed to have evacuated to Salzburg, they said." Her hands on her hips, she stood in Ilse's path and kept her from going on.

"We did," Ilse explained. "But Mother sent me back to Vienna because she forgot something important."

"What a crazy idea," the coal dealer growled. "To send a girl back here now, with the Russkies standing in front of our door!"

"I can't allow you back into the apartment," announced the building superintendent. "Grave danger of collapse. You know that. And now besides that the Russian artillery – "

"They're just starting to shoot," interrupted the coal dealer. "Still a good piece off. Believe me, an old front soldier I am from the first war. I can hear it exactly."

"Well then, which is it?" asked Frau Zirkelbach, agitated. "Are the Russians far away or at our door?"

Alarmed by the wumm — wumm — of the Easter bells, several of the building residents came running from the other staircase, mostly in pajamas and nightgowns, with coats thrown over them. Now the crowd stood bewildered in front of the basement door. "Where should we go?" they asked.

Like a mother hen Frau Zirkelbach tried to drive the residents under the sheltering roof of the air raid shelter. "If the artillery shoots, we'll only be safe down there," she explained again and again in her best High German.

The building superintendent met with strong resistance. No wonder, because the basement, after the big bomb attack patched together with a few wooden beams, had instilled great fear in the residents during later air raids. Even when bombs hit at a distance, the new beams had made suspicious crunching sounds, and no one had failed to notice the sounds that came from the cracked walls and missing bricks.

No, even Ilse had no great desire to go into the basement. But going into her old apartment didn't have much appeal for her either.

Frau Rauscher came to the rescue. Frau Rauscher, the neighborhood delicatessen owner, long without a delicatessen, made the decision that was followed by most of the building residents. "Know what?" she said to her husband, who was so old that he hadn't even joined the "folk storm" of the last "heroic enlistment." "Know what? We'll go to our apartment. And you," she invited Ilse along, "you can come to our place. Everything is still intact in our apartment."

It was true. The Rauscher apartment was in the part of the building that hadn't been hit by the bomb. Ilse accepted the offer gratefully.

"It's the safest in the kitchen," declared Frau Rauscher, and when they arrived there, she spread blankets on the linoleum floor and laid a couple of pillows down as well. "In case you want to get some sleep. You look tired. We'll stay awake."

Of course Ilse wanted to get some sleep. She couldn't imagine anything nicer than finally being allowed to sleep. The wumm — wumm — wumm had let up and could only be heard at intervals; if she wanted to she could even ignore the sounds.

The Rauschers sat down at the kitchen table. The candlelight flickered on the table, and at every movement the warm glow of the light flickered across the faces of the couple.

Ilse, lying between the coal box and the gas stove, went right to sleep. Only once was she torn out of her slumber; it seemed to her as if a great fist had lifted her up from the kitchen floor. At the same time a loud roaring and hacking came up from below, just as she had experienced during the carpet bombing at the Fishermen's Steps.

The Russian artillery seemed to be shooting again, she decided. She threw a short glance at the Rauschers. They weren't sitting in their nightclothes anymore, but were fully clothed, and wearing hats and coats as if about to go out. Herr Rauscher was holding the edge of the table with both hands. Frau Rauscher, murmuring steadily, was turning a rosary in her fingers.

The elderly couple's vigil was so comforting to Ilse that she curled up under the covers again and went right back to sleep.

"How we envied you your healthy sleep," said old Herr Rauscher a few hours later. "We thought the world was coming to an end. We couldn't get a wink of sleep ourselves."

It was quiet outside, completely quiet. No Easter bells. The three ate their breakfast together. The end of the world seemed to have been postponed to another day.

Chapter Ten: The Hiding Place

The hen's name was Susi. She was a truly magnificent specimen with raven black, gleaming feathers, well fed and spoiled, friendly, but proud and fiercely independent, as is expected of a hen raised all by herself. Susi seemed very aware of her special worth in a hungry egg-rationed environment.

Susi belonged to "Aunt" Grete. And Aunt Grete, Ilse's grandmother's sister, rang the bell at Grandmother's early in the morning right after the night of Russian artillery.

"Here I am," announced Grete, a large suitcase in one hand, a roomy leather satchel, fixed up with air holes, in the other. "May I stay with you until it's all over?"

Of course she could. Grandmother was actually very pleased at the appearance of her sister, because she had found it arduous to suffer through the artillery night alone. So arduous, that worry over all her loved ones had caused her to start biting her fingers again, a "bad habit" dating back to her childhood. A bad habit she had never been able to conquer completely, for she had always fallen back to it when something was bothering her. And in her life worries and misfortunes had come along regularly, sometimes without a break between them, so she had never had a long enough interval of calm and serenity to ever conquer her bad habit once and for all.

Grete, her robust, cheerful and uncomplicated sister, who had always been able to face life head-on, she was very welcome indeed.

"I was waiting for you," confessed Grandmother. "Out there, in your settlement on the edge of the water, it must be pretty dangerous."

"I guess so," answered Grete abruptly. "You know, the truth is I'm coming on your account. I don't mind being alone as much as you do. So here I am."

And after this mater-of-fact explanation of her appearance, Grete went directly to the business at hand: she undid the leather bands of the air-hole-satchel and opened her suitcase.

Out of the leather satchel strutted Susi proudly, uttering insulted-sounding cackles — her protest against the presumably constraining and bumpy transport conditions was unmistakably expressed.

"She lays an egg every day!" announced Grete and stroked the hen.

In the suitcase were other necessities of life, all the things that Grete had wisely been saving in anticipation of a coming shortage of groceries: bread, flour, sugar, lard, condensed milk, dried beans, and some canned goods.

Grandmother clapped her hands together, "We won't starve."

"Unless it lasts a really long time, we'll be just fine," Grete stated, "But the suitcase was heavy, especially climbing up three flights to your place."

A few hours later Ilse was standing in front of her grandmother's apartment door, a heavy cloth sack on her shoulders. Heyse's foreign word dictionary had cried out for company, and at the sight of the many beautiful leather volumes in her family book cases, Ilse couldn't bring herself to abandon the collected works of Goethe and Schiller alone in the apartment and leave them to the mercy of bombs, fires, looters, and other horrors. On the long walk to Grandmother's, she had cursed the "heavy" literature several times. "What a stupid idea — carrying a bunch of books halfway across the city," she could hear her mother say; and she came near to agreeing with her.

Aunt Grete, who had installed herself in the kitchen to put the groceries she had brought along into the cupboards, opened the door.

Aunt Grete didn't give the heavy sack a second look, but cried, "How crazy!" when Ilse explained the reason for her return trip to Vienna. "That's just like your mother. A few lousy documents are more important to her than you are."

Her eyes filled with tears, Grandmother embraced Ilse. "It's such a joy that you came back to us safe and sound!" she cried, and another time, "Thank the Lord that He has answered my prayers, but," she suddenly realized, "How will you get back? Should we let you set off again? The Russians are already at the outskirts of the city. It's getting dangerous."

Ilse looked over her grandmother's shoulder at Aunt Grete. Aunt Grete winked at her. Grete couldn't stand Ilse's mother, and she occasionally said so, even vehemently. At this moment, she said, "Of course we won't let Ilse leave again. Even if a good chance to get away came up, I wouldn't let loose of her. That will serve her mother right, the beast. Now she'll have neither a serving maid nor a bomb certificate. Serves her right, it does!"

Grandmother, always opposed to her sister's crude way of speaking, protested strongly, particularly against the word "beast." "Don't be so vulgar, Grete. After all, you are talking about my own daughter!"

How glad Ilse was over their agreement not to send her back to her mother. How lucky that Aunt Grete is here, she thought. Grandmother, who always tried to smooth out even the worst disputes between Ilse and her mother, and always aimed at reconciliation, even when none was possible, might have hesitated. She would have agonized over the decision, wondered if it might have been better to send Ilse and the documents back out of the city. Aunt Grete, however, had always been a rock-solid supporter of Ilse; she always said what she thought, and she never thought anything good about Ilse's mother.

"You'll stay here," said Aunt Grete again, very decisively. "You'll stay here, and that's final."

At that moment, with the decision announced, Aunt Grete turned back to her suitcase and the work she had been doing. "You won't starve with us," she promised and pointed proudly at the treasures she had brought along.

Now Susi, who had just undertaken an inspection tour through the living room, was introduced to Ilse. "Please watch out," requested Aunt Grete. "If she lays an egg, take it away from her immediately. Otherwise she'll peck it apart. The poor creature is starved for calcium."

The three began to discuss their plans. Where would they be able to cook, for example? The gas lines were closed off. Grandmother seized the opportunity to praise the advantages of her old walled-in stove, unused for decades. "And I have wood in the coal box," she explained. "I always keep some in reserve because I need it to heat up the kettle in the laundry room."

"We should cook ahead some every day," suggested Aunt Grete. "We don't know when it will get bad and we'll have to leave the apartment."

"Leave the apartment," that meant move into the cellar because of renewed and stronger artillery attacks. Almost all the residents of the building were already making preparations for such a move — the dragging of mattresses, emergency provisions and other necessities had brought a lot of people into the normally quiet staircase. Those who had decided on cellar life made parts of the cellar liveable. They laid mattresses over the piles of coke and coal, and set candles, petroleum lamps and matches around in easy reach.

"It looks quite cozy down there," reported Grandmother to Aunt Grete when she and Ilse returned from the first mattress cellar tour back up to the third floor.

"Frau Brunnhuber has already taken her pelargonium plants down," reported Ilse. "They are on a little table in the front of the cellar. And there is a pretty tablecloth on the table."

"Some people have to go to extremes," muttered Aunt Grete.

Nevertheless, a little later Ilse discovered that Aunt Grete herself was paying a lot of attention to Grandmother's plants. She finally put Grandmother's favorite, the passion flower, into a remote corner, but next to the objects they had collected to take down to the cellar.

When Ilse went to get the blankets and pillows to take down, Aunt Grete whispered to her as she passed: "Don't say anything to Grandma. This'll be a surprise for her. But when you go down, take the plant, ok? You know, she loves it as much as the *Life of Christ.*"

Only soft, dull rumbles of cannon, far away from the city, were audible during all the preparations for living in the cellar. They got as accustomed to these sounds as to Susi's cackling, as the hen pecked more and more intensively at the wall.

"She'll peck the whole wall away," Grandmother complained.

Aunt Grete explained quietly and firmly: "Susi needs a little of the wall material for the egg shells. She's just taking a little right over the floor. If the bombs or artillery destroy the whole building, this damage to the wall won't amount to much," she added reasonably.

Later, at dusk, after they'd had dinner, the soft, dull rumbles stopped.

Grandmother was the first to notice. "It's quiet all of a sudden," she said. And now the three sat at the table and listened to the silence.

"It's really true; they're not shooting any more," nodded Aunt Grete. "A pause for today." Suddenly she sprang up. "And Susi?

Where is Susi? Listen, can you hear her?" Again they all three listened intently to the silence. It was true: not only was there no air raid alarm, there was no clucking and no cackling to be heard.

A zealous search for Susi began. Where was she? Where could she be? But as hard as they looked, Susi was nowhere to be found. Not under the double bed, not under the cupboard, nowhere in the kitchen.

Aunt Grete opened all the cupboard doors; she even looked in the kitchen credenza. "Sometimes she slips inside somewhere and no one notices," she explained; and after that all the drawers were opened, but still no Susi.

"She can't have disappeared into thin air," cried Aunt Grete. She now looked full of anger and despair.

"Could she have run out into the hall? If old Navratil gets her, we'll never see her again," Grandmother, who in her life had always expected the worst, opened the apartment door and began to call, "Susi, Susi!"

Aunt Grete, made even more upset by Grandmother, wanted to go right over and ring Navratils' doorbell. "Where does the hen poacher live?" she cried.

Ilse paced back and forth in the kitchen. She wasn't so quick to believe that Susi had disappeared, or been stolen, but searching more seemed pointless. There was no place to look that hadn't already been searched. Then she looked at the kitchen stove. Grandmother's old stove had worked flawlessly and without smoke; the supper Grete had prepared had been good, pancakes made from Susi's first — and hopefully not last — egg.

Yes, the old stove, that should have been disposed of long ago, was now giving them the best service. Through the crack in the rusted oven door the last flickering of the glowing pieces of wood could be seen. Ilse opened the oven door to stir up the last life in the dying embers with the poke, and at the same time she looked down to the opening for the ashes. Is there enough room for the ashes? — she wondered.

But — what was that down under? Something dark, black! It looks like Grandmother's kitchen broom, she thought. She'd take it out. If the embers fall through the rust, the bristles will burn up.

Ilse reached into the ash opening to pull out the hand broom.

She took a firm grip of the bristles — and at the same moment the bristles began to cackle, excited and angry, they cackled! Susi! Susi! Covered all over with ashes, Susi, warmed up a little, but still very much alive, emerged.

Right after the first cackle Grandmother and Aunt Grete had hurried into the kitchen. Thank God they hadn't gone over to Navratils' — a false accusation would have started up a neighbors' feud.

But Aunt Grete reproached herself sternly. "The poor critter. She could have been burned alive! Why didn't I think of it? I should have known. She likes to peck in the ashes so much."

Susi was brushed clean, stroked, admired. "Such nice black feathers! The prettiest little hen for miles around, you are!" Aunt Grete praised her darling pet.

And then night fell. Without thundering cannons, without airplanes, only here and there a weather beacon on the horizon. They stayed in the apartment, and they all went calmly and happily to sleep. Susi was back.

Chapter Eleven: Necessity is the Mother of Invention

Retirement does not free you from your profession, and if you also wore a uniform, then you will continue to see that uniform in your environment as well as in your memory.

Herr Vojtisek from the first floor suddenly remembered quite clearly that Herr Pospischil of the third floor had been a policeman a few years ago, a man of authority, committed to "protect and serve" as they say. To ask him for help in a situation that Vojtisek didn't feel adequate to face alone, seemed like a reasonable idea, although Frau Vojtisek was not so sure. "I don't think I'd get involved with Pospischil, the old lunatic," she said, trying to convince her husband to abandon the idea. "What could he do to help you?"

Her discouraging words simply strengthened Vojtisek's resolve to climb up to the third floor and knock on Herr Pospischil's door.

His problem was quickly explained. Vojtisek had been the head salesman of a shoe salon on Kärtner Street for many years, and the boss's right hand. The boss, a high-ranking member of the Nazi party, had, for understandable reasons, fled to the West a few weeks ago and left Vojtisek in charge of the store. Vojtisek took the responsibility for the fashionable shop and the merchandise very seriously, and he also owed his boss, with his good connections with the "higher-ups," his exemption from serving in the Wehrmacht "for reasons of health." Whatever crimes such a man was accused of now, and whatever changes came along, Herr Vojtisek was quite sure that his boss would come back, the shoe salon would keep going, and his job right now was to save the business.

"Yes," Herr Pospischil confirmed his suspicions, "there is a danger of looting now." And Pospischil hastened to add, "But you can't expect any protection from the police. Now, when the Russians are on the march, the police are not even functioning. And everyone has his own worries. Besides, who knows who is responsible for what?"

Herr Vojtisek had made the same assumptions about the coming days. "And so I have thought that the smartest thing to do would be to give out the shoes to people for free," he declared. "News like that would spread around quickly, the store would be cleaned out, and no one would need to storm it or destroy it."

"A reasonable idea," agreed Herr Pospischil. "Your boss would certainly approve of it."

"But there is one catch," sighed Vojtisek.

"When you should begin the distribution?" said Pospischil, trying to guess what the catch was. "Of course, right away. Better today than tomorrow. A few stores on Thalia Street have already been broken into and looted. Whatever we don't take will be taken by the Russians, the people are saying. A conclusion, that certainly makes sense, don't you think?"

"Absolutely! I have to take action right way. But my problem is that I don't have any employees. No one is coming to work. I'm alone! A single person giving out shoes would result in pure chaos! I would be overrun."

"And your wife? Wouldn't she help?"

"She won't set her foot out of the apartment any more. Artillery and air attacks. My wife is one of the most frightened people."

"All right, then you could just recruit some people off the street. Promise them a pair of shoes as extra payment and you should get more people than you need. Just ask passersby to help," suggested Pospischil.

Now Herr Vojtisek got to the point. "I've been thinking of *you*, Herr Pospischil. You were a policeman. You would know the best how to keep control of a crowd of people. And maybe you could suggest someone else who could help us out in the store? We'll need to prepare carefully so that everything will go smoothly. It must all be fast, orderly, and smooth. The people appear — everyone receives one pair of shoes. And the helpers of course a few extra."

Do I need shoes? Herr Pospischil asked himself. Maybe I do; maybe I do; who knows what times we have ahead of us? But do I need them enough to set out into the inner city, face a mob of ruffians and play the role of peace officer once again — no thank you?

Pospischil was about to turn Vojtisek down flat, when he suddenly thought of Ilse. Ilse has been here since yesterday, he didn't want to pass up the opportunity to get her a nice pair of shoes. Besides, Ilse might be able to come along and help Vojtisek out

"All right, I'll help you," Pospischil promised. "And I think Ilse, the girl at Frau Kreidl's, she would be willing to help. The three of us ought to be able to handle the job."

And so it happened that the very next day the merchandise in the shoe salon was distributed to a patiently waiting line of people. Pospischil stood at the entrance of the store and kept order and quiet. "Everyone will get one pair of shoes. Everything in the store will be given away. There is no time to look the shoes over; just tell me your size. As long as they last, we'll give out the right sizes to men and women." Again and again he repeated these sentences, and he said them in the same tone of voice that he had used as a policeman, as, for example, he had said at a traffic accident, "Keep moving, please. Don't stop here. Keep moving!"

Now, however, he asked the people to stop and wait. No more than ten were allowed into the store at a time, then he shut the door, an intelligent method of keeping the work in the store going smoothly and without a commotion.

Posted inside the store were Herr Vojtisek, Ilse, and two other girls who had happened to be walking past and had gladly agreed to help out when asked. They were a good team. With drawn shades they had sorted the shoe boxes into piles, arranged into men's, women's, children's shoes according to sizes, stored the carpets and valuable store furnishings in the back room, and arranged for the entry and exit of the expected storm of "customers," using cushions, chairs and ladders to create aisles. After the agreed-upon signal — "Here we go!" — the avalanche of shoe seekers began, but they met the distributors in a more or less disciplined way. Everything went lightning fast, and luckily, no great uproar ensued.

Vojtisek was satisfied. From the furthest corner of the store he pulled out the hidden reward for his assistants. "Exquisite shoes, peace-time quality," he assured them.

Ilse made her way home in the company of Herr Pospischil, with one brief interruption at the pharmacy near the shoe salon. There was a line of people in front of this store too, and Ilse wanted to know right away what the crowd had and what was being given out.

"We'll be asked where we hurt," joked Herr Pospischil. He was in a good mood after their successful work. He was happy that the shoe distribution had gone so well; actually, he had expected tumult and chaos. Besides, in his backpack he was carrying two pairs of men's shoes for himself and three pairs of ladies' shoes for Ilse. In addition, the praise he had received from Ilse was still ringing in his ears, "You really did a good job, Herr Pospischil," she had said. "The way you controlled those people! And you even brought a backpack along. You think of everything!"

In the pharmacy one shelf after another was being emptied, and each one of the waiting people received whatever happened to fall into the distributors' hands. Ilse and Pospischil each received a bottle of cough syrup, a square little half-liter bottle filled with thick liquid.

"They look disgustingly romantic," said Ilse. The "disgustingly romantic" referred to the color of the syrup: an intense, violet-tinged pink.

Pospischil said that "no cough in the world" would bring him to drink this liquid. Ilse, however, walked a few steps and then opened the bottle and took a taste.

"Well?" asked Pospischil. "How does it taste?"

"Not bad at all," Ilse stated. "Sweet, with a funny aftertaste." She took another sip. "Yes, sweet. Not bad at all."

"But you don't have a cough," Herr Pospischil reminded her, as Ilse started to open the bottle again.

What a homeward journey! Making their way straight through the inner city, past the piles of rubble and bombed-out buildings, they noticed piles of half-charred, glowing paper, with printed words no one wanted to have found in their houses.

Ilse looked at the contents of the piles, the same everywhere: appeals to the folk comrades to offer resistance to the "Bolshevik hordes"; copies of the *Folk Observer*, Hitler's *Mein Kampf*, announcements of the bestowal of the Mothers' Cross, official documents that all had one thing in common: they were decorated with the swastika and they ended with "Heil Hitler!" The swastika had become a dangerous and detested symbol, suitable for burning, although often tenacious enough to resist destruction by flames.

And the many movie programs! Movie programs from films like "Jud Süss," "Grandma Krüger," "Ride for Germany," or "The Wish Concert" program, full of pictures of the most famous actors, such as Ferdinand Marian, Emil Jannings, Willy Birgel, Ilse Werner, Otto

Gebühr. A few of these films Ilse had secretly seen — her mother didn't allow any movies —, but she didn't have the programs because they would have been evidence that she had sneaked out and gone to the movie theater.

On one of the heaps the programs were lying at the side of a fire — undamaged, they looked brand new! Ilse just couldn't bring herself to just walk past them; it was unthinkable for her to just let such treasures lie there. After all, what on earth did "The Golden City" or "The Great Love;" what did Kristina Söderbaum or Zarah Leander have to do with Hitler or the Red Army?

Ilse voiced this question to Herr Pospischil, who began to make objections, "Take things off a pile of refuse — that's not a good idea! Besides, believe me, there must be some reason that no one wants to have these film programs in their homes. Here, look at this picture, for example: Viktor Staal as a pilot in a German officer's uniform! And here, this scene: a swastika and the Reich's eagle on the wall. To some degree all of these films were probably propaganda pieces. Don't touch this stuff. You don't want to bring such things into your grandmother's home! You don't want to do that to her!"

"I'll hide the programs from her," said Ilse defiantly and picked up the whole pile. "I did see these films. The programs telling about them I'll never be able to get again."

Now she seemed like Irene, thought Pospischil. Or did she? No, he couldn't imagine that Irene would have acted like this in the same situation. So childish! But then Pospischil tried to come to a fairer judgment. Irene, who was his age, had been just eighteen when he met her. Ilse is four years younger, a child. Another generation, and what a generation to belong to! Don't make comparisons, Pospischil rebuked himself.

And in the next moment Ilse looked at him and asked him, "Do you like Carl Raddatz? He is a movie actor," she added to be safe, for she wouldn't have been surprised at any ignorance of the world on the part of Herr Pospischil. Pospischil avoided answering directly by saying that he hardly ever went to the movies.

Ilse began to tell about the class field trip, about the errant ball that had soiled the actor's suit and about his letter complete with photograph and dedication.

And yet, thought Pospischil, when she laughs and looks at me sideways she does look a lot like Irene. These eyes, yes. The same eyes; the same way of looking at him.

He told her so. "You remind me of someone," he told her. He was surprised to realize that he was suddenly able to talk quite easily about Irene. Maybe it was because of the film programs with their kitschy pictures? It seemed to him as if he were talking now about film actresses, about the content of a film plot. The title, yes, the title would be "The Great Love." It was nice to be able to talk about it; he almost enjoyed it, suddenly to have such distance from his "youth film." It was a brand new discovery, almost a liberation.

They had a long way to go, and when they reached Thalia Street it was starting to get dark. Here and there a distant weather beacon shone on the horizon and they heard the dull murmur of the Russian artillery. But during the day the weapons had been silent; or had they just gotten used to the artillery rounds and not heard the rumbling?

"Romantic," said Ilse and took another big swallow from the syrup bottle. There wasn't much left of the sweet pink cough medicine. When we turn into Maroltinger Street I'll finish it off, she decided.

"Romantic," she repeated, and Pospischil didn't know what she was applying the word to. Maybe she was still referring to the pink color of the syrup? Or perhaps to the "film story" he had just finished telling? To their walk in the eerie twilight, this trek through the completely deserted streets? Or to everything together?

"You'll probably make yourself sick," Pospischil predicted and pointed to the almost empty bottle.

"I'll never get a cough again," Ilse laughed.

Grandmother received her with nothing but reproaches. Of course she had once again endured "the fear that Ilse was dead," and Ilse's protests that her day had been harmless, even fun, did nothing to calm her down.

"The unsafe streets! And not until now, night time, do you come home. Looters and all kinds of rabble are out there," cried Grandmother. "And you can be sure I'm not letting you go out after dark again. It is really dangerous, especially for a girl of your age."

Aunt Grete intervened and tried, in her resolute way, to put things in perspective. "You heard her say," she said to her sister, "that nothing was going on out there. Herr Pospischil said the same thing. Let the girl have a little freedom and adventure. You don't need to worry about Ilse; she can take care of herself. She's worse off at home with her own mother."

Ilse loved her grandmother, but at this moment she wanted to hug Aunt Grete.

The next day Aunt Grete earned even more hugs. As Grandmother always said, Grete had known how to get her way even as a child. Aunt Grete proved this time that this was still true.

Although several years older than Grandmother, and therefore almost seventy now, Aunt Grete was filled with the initiative to take action, and it seemed to grow in her from one hour to the next. The day before she had already made contacts with people in the building and street, and she meant to use them. Early in the morning she announced her action plan, and she was filled with determination to carry it out. She wouldn't budge from her plan, even though it had put Grandmother in a state of near panic.

"Mitzi," said Aunt Grete to her sister, "Mitzi, in the inner city, in the textile district, everything is being cleared out. Bolts of cloth are just lying around. Ilse and I need to get right over there, and hurry, or we'll get there too late and nothing will be left."

Grandmother protested; she listed all the dangers they might face, beginning with the cannons and dive bombers and ending with the looters' wild massacres and the executions of those who undertook these forbidden activities.

The idea of being executed evoked a scornful laugh from Grete. "Would you please let me know who that has happened to? The government observers are all long gone. And the Russian artillery is so far away that you can barely hear it. And the dive bombers; that is just a rumor."

Grandmother's protest was in vain; it was clear that even she realized it.

"And stop your nail-biting," said Aunt Grete, "Why don't you come long? Do you think that you can accomplish anything staying at home?"

So the three set off together for the textile district. And because it was located right around the corner from the Rudolfsplatz, at least Grandmother had an excuse for going along. "I'm not going to go looting. I will not join you in that. But I can go look at the apartment. There may be things there I can bring home. One must save what can be saved — the plundering has already begun." The word "plundering" Grandmother uttered with as much disapproval in her voice as possible.

Ilse looked forward to the outing. She had nothing at all against another walk into the inner city. The distance there seemed shorter and shorter to her; it seemed as if the first district was getting closer each time she went there. Another adventure awaited her! And if she reached the vicinity of the Rudolfsplatz she might be able to use the opportunity to make inquiries about Robert.

If only he were still home — she wished to herself. He and I, we could walk through the city together and observe people, that teaches a person so much. And, I wish I could ask him, at last, what school he goes to. It occurred to Ilse also that Robert had said, "We have nothing to lose." What a moment, back then! The airplanes high above and he said, "Nothing to lose." And, just like back then, in that moment, it was the same now, and all the time. Robert was right. Today is today — and tomorrow is tomorrow. What is the purpose of thinking beyond that? Ilse also had trouble imagining a later time, a different time — a time in peaceful, orderly circumstances. No, she told herself, for us there is no tomorrow and no day after tomorrow — the only thing that is real is now, the present. And, besides, the way it is now is better for me. Being free! Ilse thought of her mother as permanently away in the West. She could and would not picture to herself these days being over and going back to the way things were before. Back again, home, back in prison? No! Now, this was the endpoint. Somehow a real endpoint. She would stay free.

Aunt Grete would certainly have allowed her to go for a walk with Robert. But Robert was gone. Ilse was told by a lady from the building next to his, "Robert is in the Wienerwald. They took him away to serve the defense. He wanted to hide, but his mother...," the neighbor lady made a disgusted gesture. "She's a Nazi dame, she is. And his big sister, that girl war telegraphist, is even worse. Just served up the boy, they did. It's a crime. Sending half-grown kids off to war!"

So nothing came of the walk through the city. Why hadn't Robert hidden himself somewhere? thought Ilse, disappointed. Like I would have. And then just run away once and for all! Off and away. But Ilse knew that running away wasn't that simple. Not even when one has a good reason; even then running away isn't as simple as it looks.

Aunt Grete urged Ilse to hurry; the streets were full of people running around with fabric and bolts of cloth. The bolts were being thrown out of the windows of the warehouses and stores; from the thick, heavy bolts people were tearing or cutting pieces, as big as they could. When the bolts got smaller and weren't too heavy to carry, then they were shouldered by especially lucky salvagers and carried away.

It was hard to move forward into the crowd around the bolts. Aunt Grete and Ilse tried it a time or two, but then Grete suddenly started to act extremely particular. "I'd like something for a Dirndl costume. Preferably in light blue. Go and look Ilse. See if you see anything suitable," she called out.

No, there was no Dirndl cloth to be found, not even any plain blue cloth, and certainly no light blue cloth that Grete was demanding. But between the legs of the people battling for cloth Ilse spied a white bolt with little, pale red stripes, that apparently no one wanted. "Let's take that," Grete decided. "Better than nothing!"

Together they pulled the bolt along. It was not very wide and not too heavy. On closer inspection, however, they realized why the bolt had been left. It was damaged, burned in two places. The burn holes were not very big on the surface, but they were deep, boring through all the levels of cloth. "Doesn't matter," said Aunt Grete. "There wasn't any Dirndl cloth." And then, suddenly disdainful of all the people scrambling for cloth, she added loudly, "I'm not gonna slug it out like this." She shouldered the bolt and, with a dignified, "Come on, Ilse, we haven't lost anything," she marched away from the fray.

Grandmother was fetched from the apartment. In the meantime she had found "a few things of value," which Grete, unpacking them back at Grandmother's, called, "a bunch of worthless junk." She had brought flatware, clothing and a picture of the Madonna, which Grandmother's pious heart prized as much as the passion flower that was already adorning a table in the cellar.

Surprisingly, Grandmother approved of the salvaged bolt of cloth. "It's so soft. The little burned parts don't matter. The holes are a good distance apart." She took her centimeter ruler and began to measure the cloth from all directions. "It'll be fine," she finally pronounced. "I'll make handkerchiefs for all of us."

There was a knock on the door. Susi cackled and ran excitedly around the room.

"My Susi's like a watchdog!" Aunt Grete cried admiringly. "She announces all the visitors."

Frau Brunnhuber, the neighbor, appeared in the crack of the door.

"I just wanted to tell you that the margarine factory on Lorenz-Mandl Streeet has been opened up," she reported. "Everybody who shows up can get a package of margarine, but you need to come fast, they've already started. Hurry or they won't have anything left."

Lorenz-Mandl Street wasn't too far away. The news had spread like wildfire. People were streaming out of the nearby buildings in the direction of the margarine plant.

A long line of people had already formed along the sidewalk. Aunt Grete and Ilse set off right away, and Grandmother came running along later. She was late because she had taken time to lock up the apartment, and to voice her usual protests about looting.

There was more and more pushing and shoving the nearer they got to the factory entrance. The distribution, however, was carried out without a hitch and in no time everyone had a quarter kilo package of margarine. A few tried to get more by whining, "I got four little kids. They can't come over here to get their share," or, "Our Grandpa is sick and bedridden. Is he supposed to go without?"

"No exceptions are being made," repeated the two factory workers who were directing the crowd, a few at a time, through a narrow door of green iron. Again and again they said, "One package per person. Or we'll lock the doors." Those at the back of the line showed great understanding of the rule. They were afraid that if a more generous policy were adopted there would be no margarine left when their turns came.

"This is well organized," said Ilse to Grandmother. "This is just the way we did it at Vojtisek's store on Kärntner Street. You see, you didn't need to worry."

When they arrived back in the apartment, Grandmother looked at the three packages of margarine on the table and shook her head.

"I wonder if the factory owner knows anything about this. Maybe it was all the employees' idea," she began to grumble.

"Maybe so. It was a reasonable idea in any case. Giving goods away voluntarily is better than . . ." Aunt Grete left the sentence unfinished.

Soon thereafter a lot of goods clearly taken against their owners' will began to be carried through Maroltinger Street.

Ilse, lounging on the window sill, noticed from a distance the moving masses of people. What was going on? A march, she wondered, or a demonstration?

Ilse called Grandmother and Aunt Grete to the window. The three were astonished at the river of people moving past. They all had in common that they were carrying things, in backpacks, bags and suitcases. Or they were pulling heavily laden handcarts. At first the three observers couldn't tell what was being carried, but then they began to identify many of the larger objects. They saw tables, easy chairs and office chairs, floor lamps, beds, chests, shelves, sinks, jugs, brooms, rugs, blankets, boots, boots and more boots, a great many pairs of boots. And typewriters. A cry escaped Ilse, "Typewriters!" If only she could have gotten one. She had wanted one for a long time.

"They must have taken apart a whole house," said Aunt Grete and pointed to the last salvagers who were carrying wooden boards. "That must be the floor," she declared. "Those who didn't get there in time had to take what was left."

"It was the Breitensee barracks," said Grandmother. "All those soldiers' boots — of course, they cleaned out the Breitensee barracks."

Ilse was inconsolable. Once again she had missed out on something special. Shoes, handkerchiefs, margarine — those were not things her heart desired. But a typewriter — that wasn't granted her. That had gone right past her. A lost opportunity! Just like last winter on Wipplinger Street at the Wehrmacht's ski collection point for the soldiers on the Eastern front. People had stood in line to donate pairs of skis. At the sight of the enormous piles of skis already collected and the people bringing still more, Ilse had thought to herself: I could ask some friendly-looking person if he might perhaps give *me* a pair of skis. They were giving them away anyway, so it wouldn't have made much difference. And if I brought home a pair of skis I might have been permitted to take a skiing course. Without skis, no ski course. And my mother would certainly never have bought me any. There was no sense in even asking her.

A good quarter hour Ilse had walked around the collection site, but she never found anyone who looked friendly enough. Besides, the feeling got stronger and stronger in her each minute that maybe her intended question was too bold, maybe even strictly forbidden. She suddenly became afraid of her own daring and ran home.

But I could at least have asked someone, very quietly and discreetly, she reproached herself.

Susi had laid her daily egg. Grandmother was eager to try the oven in the old stove and so that evening they had a poppy seed cake. There was another reason to bake it, however.

Aunt Grete had brought the poppy seed along — to Grandmother's alarm. "Poppy seed," she had cried. "Having poppy seed is strictly forbidden. Surely you know that, Grete. They have severe penalties for that!"

"Yes I know, severe penalties," confirmed Aunt Grete, laughing. "The death penalty, at least."

"We need to get it out of this apartment!" Grandmother, who usually went along with others, spoke this sentence with unusual vehemence. It was clear that they couldn't count on her lenience in this matter. She said it a second time, "We need to get the poppy seed out of this apartment!"

"Okay, then, let's just make ourselves a poppy seed strudel. Or a poppy seed cake," suggested Aunt Grete. And because Aunt Grete, in her practical, common sense way, carried everything out to its logical conclusion, she added, "The toilet is out in the hall — and so the poppy seed really will leave the apartment."

This remark made Grandmother angry. She despised such vulgar thoughts, she said. Besides this was her apartment, and people should ask her what she thought. Her whole life long she had tried never to do anything forbidden, to obey both the Bible and the law.

"It's also against the law to have hens in your apartment," answered Aunt Grete calmly. "And because you are so strict about laws and religion, remember that killing is also forbidden. And what do we have now? War! People are killing each other and the priests on both sides are blessing the weapons. It says 'God With Us' on the soldiers' belt buckles. And in this chaos, when we don't know if we'll still be alive tomorrow, when there is no real order anywhere anymore, and the laws are not functioning, in this environment, you expect me to just throw away this poppy seed I paid a king's ransom for on the black market?"

And so they baked a poppy seed cake. Grandmother couldn't resist Aunt Grete's logical argument. Anyway, Grandmother couldn't be angry for long after the usually reserved Aunt Grete had, for once, spoken her mind and spelled out in detail what she thought — also she was right — and so the poppy seed controversy was settled.

And if Herr Pospischil didn't pop in right when they were cutting the cake! After a brief knock on the door he came right into the kitchen, and Grandmother almost dropped the knife out of her hand from shock. Forbidden poppy seed and a policeman, even a retired one — that was too much for her.

"Mmm," sniffed Herr Pospischil. "It smells really good in here."

"Poppy seed cake," explained Aunt Grete, even though it was clearly visible on the table. "Would you like to have yourself a little piece?"

Of course Pospischil would. He nodded and his eyes took on a dreamy aura. "My favorite dessert," he confessed. "I haven't had it in years. I can hardly remember what it tastes like anymore."

"Me neither," said Ilse.

As Aunt Grete wrapped his piece of cake in paper, Pospischil explained the reason he had come over. Tomorrow morning, he reported, there would be a give-away at the tobacco factory on Thalia Street. He couldn't reveal how he knew that, and they shouldn't spread the news any further; they had to keep it a strict secret. He knew the way to the factory. "I don't smoke myself," he went on, "but tobacco products will certainly be the best currency in the coming times. Maybe you'd like to come along?" he asked and looked first at Aunt Grete, then at Grandmother. "Or you, Ilse?"

Ilse nodded her agreement right away. Grandmother, however, sat down suddenly on the coal box, without intending to, and tried to find words to speak. Poppy seeds, a tobacco factory, and a policeman extending an invitation to go looting! She didn't understand the world anymore.

"Won't it be dangerous?" she finally managed to ask. "It will surely be dangerous?"

"Hardly," answered Pospischil. "As long as there is no shooting, it won't be dangerous. And today we didn't hear a single shot fired."

"And tomorrow?" asked Grandmother.

"If there is shooting, of course we won't go."

On the next morning there was no shooting — and they set off on their way to the tobacco factory, they being only Herr Pospischil and Ilse. Grandmother absolutely refused to come along. She announced that she was not taking part in any plundering. "Even if a policeman goes along — it is just not for me!" And Aunt Grete, who would have loved to go along, had "thrown her back out" during the tussle over the bolts of cloth. "I'm no good no more," she complained. "And my feet hurt. Yesterday's walking and the long wait for the margarine — and after all I'm no spring chicken any more either." But Aunt Grete, nevertheless, had enough strength to convince Grandmother to let Ilse go with Herr Pospischil.

"Your grandmother was a hair away from refusing to let you go," Herr Pospischil told Ilse as they left the building. "I had to promise her to really look after you, and stay right by your side."

He wanted to add something, but didn't. Should he have revealed to Ilse how much he had hoped that she would come along with him? That it was actually all on account of her that he had suggested this "excursion?" That would have sounded a bit strange. "On my account?" she would have asked. "Why on my account?" And at that point he would have had to confess how much he enjoyed her company; that he loved going to these exciting events with her by his side. "It will be exciting." Yes, he could say that to her; that and nothing more.

But he said nothing of the kind. Instead he began to talk about books as they walked. Was Ilse familiar with Büchner's plays? "Leonce and Lena," for example. Or — "Woyzeck?" "Dantons' Death?" In literature class in school, had she perhaps heard of them?

No, she had never heard of Büchner or his plays. But she did like to go to the theater, she told him, although for her she was more often forbidden than allowed. Oh yes, there were wonderful productions in the Burg Theater! Shakespeare, Schiller, and Grillparzer! She began to name the actors: Aslan, Maria Eis, Ewald Balser, Liewehr, Heinz Woester. Woester she especially praised; Else would have been very pleased to hear her.

Yes, the classic playwrights, the classic plays, they provided great experiences; Herr Pospischil hastened to add his agreement. They deal with timeless issues of human life But — he hesitated a moment before he continued — but these classics: didn't they really seem (with some exceptions, such as "Hamlet" for example) to be a little outdated? He couldn't help but have that impression.

Outdated? No, she never had that impression, Ilse said. Classics are classics; one can't expect any more from them.

Büchner, for example, Büchner was quite different, said Pospischil. In his plays the characters are like people who could live today and among us, even though his plays were also written more than a hundred years ago. "By a genius," added Pospischil. "Just imagine! This Büchner died when he was only twenty-three."

"Only twenty-three — and a genius?" repeated Ilse, not without admiration and astonishment. But she was even more astonished at Herr Pospischil. Hadn't Grandmother been shocked yesterday that a policeman had invited them to go "plundering" — as their current expedition proved — and now it was Ilse's turn to be astonished by him, this time by the combination of police career and knowledge of literature. To be sure, the extensive library in Pospischil's room could have given her some idea, along with the books of poems that he had given her — Hölderlin, Rilke, Mörike — it was quite a selection! And it was not the first time that Pospischil had asked, in an offhand manner, what she was being taught in her literature classes in school.

And, as if he had guessed her thoughts and wanted to give them more evidence, he now asked, "And Kafka? Have you read any Kafka?"

"Kafka? Never heard the name. Kafka?" Ilse said the name like a foreign word.

"Dumb of me!" cried Herr Pospischil suddenly and hit his hand against his forehead. "Kafka was a Jew! Of course he couldn't be included in today's lessons at all."

Herr Pospischil began to tell about Kafka and the Prague Circle, about what beautiful German they wrote in. He told her that it was through Kafka that both his love of literature and his first love had been awakened. "I will lend you one of Kafka's novels," he promised. "Specifically, *The Trial*. And his short stories. I'm curious about what you'll say about them."

In the meantime they had reached Hutten Street, more exactly, the point where the connecting streetcar track came to the side of the tobacco factory. The half-meter high brick wall along the bend, which the train track surrounded like a sheltering wall, was protected with barbed wire On the other side of the streetcar line there was a wide open area. The factory storerooms were there, and behind them the buildings of the "tobacco government" as the people called the factory headquarters.

But Herr Pospischil and Ilse were not the first ones there. They could see from afar that behind the wall, bent down, a crowd was already huddled in anticipation.

They had to find a "free" place along the wall, from which the two could observe what was happening down below in the factory yard. Trucks stood ready; boxes were loaded onto them in great haste, and a few soldiers, armed with machine guns, oversaw the loading.

"That's mean," murmured the people crouching behind the wall. "They're snatching it all away right under our noses." "Let's storm the storerooms!" suggested one young fellow. "We're in the majority." "But they'll shoot, they'll shoot!" cried a woman. "They've already shot one man dead." "Yes, they did, I saw it with my own eyes," confirmed another.

"Wait, wait, and keep waiting," whispered Herr Pospischil. "And if it gets bad, we shouldn't under any circumstances run the way the crowd is running. That is always dangerous."

Ilse was prepared to do whatever Herr Pospischil told her to do. After all, back at the shoe store give-away on Kärntner Street he had proven to be very shrewd. He had known how to maintain calm and had started the distribution at exactly the right time. Strange, this Herr Pospischil! When push came to shove he always seemed to be in control of every situation. Strange, strange — she never would have expected that of him. He must have been a good policeman after all. Grandmother had always called him an unworldly oddball, and I always thought of him that way too — but in the future I'll contradict Grandmother on this point.

"Careful," whispered Pospischil. "It's time."

Yes, it was. The trucks started to move, and the soldiers sprang on the running board. A column of trucks left the factory grounds. At the same moment the people waiting behind the wall started to scramble up. A few young fellows worked on the barbed wire with iron bars and tore out an opening in the fencing. Soon thereafter the slope was full of people, all running over the railroad tracks and down toward the factory yard.

Ilse, who jumped up involuntarily, was held back by Herr Pospischil. "Duck down, and stay put!" he ordered — an order that immediately proved to be right, as several shots rang out.

"They're covering the exit," explained Pospischil. "Thank God they shot into the air."

Now Pospischil and Ilse also began to run. From all sides people were streaming toward the hole in the wire covering. There, however, they halted, for the opening wasn't very big.

As Ilse and Pospischil finally reached the steps, they encountered a few of the "successful" ones, loaded down with packages, cartons, and boxes.

"They came from the other side of the factory," murmured those waiting in front of the hole in the wire.

The crowd in front of the stairs started to get angrier, because some of them, like Ilse and Pospischil, wanted to get inside, others out.

Ilse wouldn't forget what happened next for a long time. A woman came out from the factory and started to climb over the wall. She looked harried but satisfied. She was dragging a large carton held together by a steel band. She scrambled up the wall and was poised to jump down — just at that moment the steel band broke and the bottom of the carton gave way, and a flood of cigarettes poured down over the wall. The woman bent down to gather up the packs of cigarettes — red boxes bearing the label "Korso" — but not one box was left. The edge of the wall at her feet was empty; the ground on both sides of the wall was empty. As empty as if no cigarettes had ever showered down in the area. She just stood there, that poor woman, holding the broken steel band and the empty, collapsed box. She stood there a few seconds, like a statue, stiff and full of astonishment. A disappointed statue, marveling over the speed of the many hands that had snatched everything up so quickly.

The ground at the woman's feet looked as if it had been swept clean. It seemed as if all the bystanders had been waiting for a certain signal to grab up everything that came their way; to take what they could before someone else did; and foolish were they who didn't grab what they could. A signal, almost like a command. A command that left no room at all to think things over. To ignore such an order seemed to be quite impossible.

Even Ilse had joined in; she had shoved a box of "Korsos" into her coat pocket. Did she have sympathy with the woman who had lost all her booty? Yes, afterwards, for a moment, when the woman had stood up there on the wall, the empty carton in her hand, as all the cigarette packages had apparently just blown away, but right afterwards Ilse ran next to Pospischil along the slope, toward the factory yard, and her sympathy was forgotten. Then finally, finally, Ilse succeeded in getting through the opening in the wire fence.

Pospischil and Ilse landed in the middle of the crowd, led by the youths armed with iron bars. The group kept running, rattled locked doors, pressed into empty halls, ran in circles without realizing it. Their anger over the idea that they might have come too late and their fear that they might leave empty-handed drove them on, made them keep moving here and there throughout the enormous factory grounds.

On the side of the storage buildings, on a side railroad track, stood a single railroad car. Who was the first to discover it? A woman yelled, "The car there — It could still be full!"

And so everyone ran toward the car, surrounded it, stood in front of it. The heavy iron bars on the car's sliding door were locked with a massive hanging lock. No shaking, pushing or prying could budge it — the lock wouldn't give.

"Go ahead, boys! Bust it open!" cried the people around the car. And the boys didn't need to be asked twice — if they could conquer a barbed wire fence, they could conquer this lock too. They began to pry at it with their iron bars.

The sounds of splintering wood and bursting iron bands drew more and more people. When the lock was finally broken, everyone pressed at the same time against the door of the railroad car. So forceful was the crowd, that the boys had a difficult time finally opening the sliding door.

The car was full, actually filled to the brim with wares from the tobacco company! Now the trick was not to be overwhelmed by the crowd, to try to push forward with it; not to be pushed over to the side, but to reach the door opening and to get to work.

Ilse had lost sight of Pospischil a while ago. His last warning words still rang in her ears: "Run away, if things get too bad!"

Run away— where to? She was stuck in the middle of a moving mob pressing on the train car door. She could only think of one thing: concentrating on not letting herself be pushed to the side.

And then everything happened with lightning speed. A foothold in the car, two long, dark green boxes fell out of a torn-open carton toward her. She grabbed them and pressed them against herself. Okay. Now she had her share! Now it was time to get loose from the crowd and get back outside.

And after that, run away, run away from here as fast as possible. Away from the railroad car. Away from the struggling people there. The woman with the broken steel band, standing like a statue on the wall, had taught Ilse a good, warning lesson. Watch out; whatever you think you have this minute could be taken from you in the next.

On the way back, right next to the train track, Ilse was met by Herr Pospischil. He also had been able to get a few of the green boxes. Side by side they ran toward the wall.

"I have no idea what has fallen into our hands," called Pospischil.

They stopped running for a second and looked at the boxes, reading the inscription, "100 cigarillos."

"Not a bad bargaining chip," stated Pospischil. "This could buy all kinds of groceries. In the coming times money will be hard to come by."

"Grandmother will be happy," cried Ilse, still running. "But it was really exciting at the wall and by the railroad car."

"Yes, but we don't want to tell her everything," suggested Herr Pospischil. "Especially not that shots were fired — that I don't think we should mention to her."

Chapter Twelve: Stories from the Vienna Woods

Twilight creeps along,
Locusts sing their songs,
Evening air caresses all,
Brings a spicy forest smell.

The white street in the sunlight, lonely and deserted, with the dug-out trenches, the street so unassuming, untraveled, so empty, as if it weren't a street at all.

But the machine guns were pointed at everything that could come along this road. And the boys behind the machine guns had not forgotten what they should point them at.

"This is a strategically important street," the non-commissioned officer had said in a hurry at the last military inspection. "Be vigilant! Russian patrols can't be allowed to penetrate our defense belt. It is your mission to discover these patrols and render them harmless. Boys, the fate of our city, the fate of our nation depends on you. The front line around Vienna must be maintained. Prove yourselves, show that you are the manly soldiers of the future! You are the hope of the Führer — prove yourselves worthy of his hope!"

Holding himself tensely, the officer had taken hold of his belt buckle with his left hand — thereby covering up the "God With Us" on the clasp — and raised his right hand in the German salute. After a loud "Sieg Heil" and "Heil Hitler!" he had jumped into the sidecar of his motorcycle.

That had been four days ago, four days since they had gazed after the plume of dust his motorcycle had left behind. Since then they had taken turns standing watch, always in twos, for four hour shifts during the day and for two hours at a time at night. Hans, the squad leader for mission "Viennese Woods," carried out a precise hour-by-hour plan that all his troops had to follow each day: care of weapons and ammunition, scouting forays in the area, kitchen duty, extending and improving the trenches.

Hans knew how to handle the young men. He made it clear to them that they had to stand their ground this time, that it was very important to stick together and just as important to be vigilant. Unfortunately he couldn't tell them what he really wanted to say, here and now, in the Vienna Woods, what he really had in his heart. Because he knew that Bernd, always the strict one, was observing everyone with double vigilance; his eyes and ears were always open. He was always on the alert for anything that sounded the least bit like "betraying the defense effort." Bernd had already gotten credit for reporting "anti-folk" comments made by his comrades. His father, one of the highest ranking SS-men, made it his mission of honor to keep those boys' families under a magnifying glass in the interest of purging the great German Reich of any "subversive elements."

Hans was not the one who had chosen Bernd for his squad. He had been assigned by a decision made "higher-up." This fact warned Hans that he needed to be especially careful. Because he and his "team" were still surrounded by the regular Wehrmacht troops, and there were still the harsh war courts that gave deserters short trials, more precisely *no* trials quickly followed by sentences for which they needed only a street lamp or a tree and a rope. There was certainly a possibility that this Bernd, acting as an informer, could put someone in danger of his life. Hans — once such an obedient, dedicated Nazi Wolf Cub, once so happy about the campfires, the comradeship, and the uniform — had come to realizations during the last four days in the trenches of the Vienna Woods that would certainly have fallen under the rubrik, "betraying the defense effort."

He talked honestly to Robert, his friend, when they were both on night watch. "Go AWOL," whispered Hans — he was using the current phrase used in place of the dangerous, fateful word "desert" — "go AWOL, that's what I would like to advise the boys to do. But we have to watch out for Bernd. If he listened too soon when we are talking — "

"— then he'd betray us in a minute!" Robert finished expressing Hans' greatest fear.

"Yes. So I can't tell the others until the very last minute. Not now — we're still in a jam. Our own troops are quite close, and the Russians, where are they?"

"But when the time comes, in what direction can we run AWOL? Do we even have a chance to get away?" Robert stroked the mouth of his machine gun. "If we run into the Russians they'll shoot at us.

If we leave our posts and run into our own troops, then — " Robert ran his hand along his neck and pointed to the nearest tree.

"We have to find the exact right minute. Be on the lookout for the most favorable opportunity. I'll keep sending the boys on the scouting missions to find out where the Russians are and where our troops are."

Robert suddenly laughed. "Have you taken a good look at our little band, at us? Don't we look pretty funny? I can hardly imagine that anybody will do anything to us, or even shoot at us. Look at our uniforms: they don't fit. Our helmets are all much too big. We look like clowns, like ridiculous toy soldiers, or something out of the comic pages! If I were on the other side and came across us, *I* would be laughing so hard I wouldn't be able to shoot. Of course I probably wouldn't be able to shoot anyway, ever, at anybody. I don't think I'd be capable of it."

"I wouldn't either," admitted Hans. "But the others," he pointed around at the woods opposite, "but the others, they could."

Sleeping on the ground. Pale stars over the dark treetops. Robert heard the woods breathe. Here and there he saw strange, fleeting images pass by. Was this a waking state, sleep, or a brief dream interlude in a twilight land . . . ?

Forms emerged and enlivened the sloping road and the white street with eerie shadows. Strangers, black forms that came nearer and nearer, then were suddenly clearly visible in the moonlight: yellow, frightening Mongolian faces, cruel and ugly, with malicious, evil-glowing slits of eyes, caricatures Robert had seen on posters at an exhibit, "Bolshevism Without Masks" — a required field trip for all school classes. Part of the curriculum, objective: FOLK STUDIES of a very special kind. VIEW: the crooked-legged, primitive *soldateska!* What massacres they carry out! How they stab through the bodies of their defenseless victims with their bayonets! TAKE A LOOK as well at the mass graves full of the bodies of the victims of their executions! GO FURTHER from hall to hall dedicated to the concentration camps of the GPU, the Russian secret police. BE SHOCKED at the slave laborers in the quarries, emaciated to skeletons. BE STUNNED, BEGIN TO FEEL HATRED when you are now shown the end products of the concentration camp factories:

lamp shades made from human skin, soap from human bones, rugs woven out of women's hair. And here, here, STARE IN ASTONISHMENT at the gleaming pile of pure gold from the ripped-out teeth of the murdered — melted down, it will provide welcome capital to finance more weapons of murder.

MOVE FORWARD, MOVE FORWARD, German boys and girls, proceed to the next rooms where more Bolshevism without masks waits there for you. And NEVER FORGET: here you see the true faces of our enemies! However, German boys and girls, be comforted. The Great Germans, the Thousand Year Reich, will know how to save Aryan humanity from the cruel deeds of the Bolsheviks. Mark well these images, children! The nation of poets and thinkers will know how to protect the world from such a bestial reign of terror!

Keep going, Robert, keep going. Well-behaved, following row and order . . . Follow your teacher!

After the exhibit, back on the school ground, eating bread and butter during the long recess. We play catch and soccer. We scuffle and push each other around. Robert, who is the strongest? The most agile?

The next hour we have physics. We have a test. The force of gravity, centrifugal force. Explain centrifugal force to me, Robert. Have you learned the formulae by heart? All right, come on, recite them!

Hans suddenly is sitting high up in a pine tree. He waves and calls, "Come on, Robert! It's magnificent up here!" And then Hans shows that he can fly. He explains how one must start, "It's really easy, Robert, easy as pie. Just try it. You simply jump down from high up, and then, then look; it's just like swimming. You simply swim through the air. It's very easy, the easiest thing in the world."

And he really shows him, very clearly he demonstrates all the arm and leg motions. It's true; Hans can fly! He flies over the street, the meadow, toward the woods opposite them, farther, toward the buildings and towers of the city. He's already at the Votive Church, at St. Stephen's Cathedral, at the Prater Ferris Wheel. Then he rounds the Kahlenberg, glides along the Danube, hovers in the sky.

Now, all of a sudden, Robert can fly too. He doesn't even need to climb a tree; he just pushes himself with a spring up from the ground and makes swimming motions up into the air. He has to pull his legs up high. That is important, that he realizes right away. He pulls his legs up, higher and higher up away from the ground. Continuous swimming motions, that is also important. It works; it goes really well; it is not hard at all. Why didn't he ever discover before how easy it is to fly! And how nice. One must only concentrate on wanting to stay up in the air, and then one can really fly.

"What is going on?" Hans asks in the middle of Robert's flight. "You've been paddling your arms and legs and gasping for air like a fish out of water. Were you dreaming?"

"Today is today — and tomorrow is tomorrow," murmurs Robert, confused and startled. Then suddenly he has landed on the forest floor next to hard metal. His machine gun gleams maliciously at him.

"Nonsense!" Hans is chewing on a blade of grass, his face pale blue in the moonlight; he looks like a ghost, Robert thinks.

"Nonsense," repeats Hans. "It's clear enough that today is today. What do you mean by that?"

"Nothing special. It's just an expression of mine. I said it once to a girl."

"Oh, a girl. And nothing more clever occurred to you to say than that?"

"No, at that moment, nothing else."

"At that moment?" The pale blue ghost named Hans spat the blade of grass out and grinned. "At that moment?" he repeated and now grinned shamelessly. "You were out to impress her?"

Robert saw once again the gleaming silver squadron over the park; all the airplanes, back then, at "that moment." They were flying, high in the sky. Flying is beautiful. He had been able to fly — he still felt the wonderful feeling from the dream in his body.

Fly away, thought Robert, if I could just fly away. He saw the Rudolfsplatz in front of him, the park, his building. The building that was his home. The front door. The stairs leading up to his apartment. How often had he begun to count the steps as he climbed up, somewhere, on his way, begun to count. It was a rule of the game: don't start counting on the first steps, but later on, somewhere, so you won't get the real number. And then, up the steps, one, two, three, four, and so on. If the last step is an even number, then everything is fine, Mother isn't home. But if it's an odd number, then that's bad; she is home. Then, sooner or later, there will be scolding and noise; he'll be reproached with something; have done something wrong, or forgotten, or not told. He'll be reminded that he is the black sheep of the family and belongs in reform school.

Why can't he take his sister as an example? his mother rebukes him. She has made something of herself, she is working as a war telegraphist, sacrificing for Führer and Fatherland, bringing money and groceries home. She knows how to pitch in and help in the household, is always true and at her mother's side. He, on the other hand, amounts to nothing; he hasn't even made it to squad leader in the Hitler Youth. At his age his sister was already leader of the Bund Deutscher Mädchen! You are a disgrace to your father in Yugoslavia! she scolds. Your father, fighting against the partisans and laying his life on the line. And you? What a sissy you are! If your father's SS-comrades knew about you!

Fly away, yes, take off, simply take off, as Hans had suggested. Take off — but in no case go home. No! He was never going back home, even if his mother and sister weren't there any more. And they wouldn't be there; they had been in a hurry to leave. His mother, whom everyone feared as a denouncer of her neighbors; his father an SS-man in the Skull Battalion. And they had taken over a Jewish apartment, besides.

But he would find his own way. He didn't need to worry about where those two had gone. His mother could always take care of herself. And he didn't need to worry about his father any more than his father had worried about him. To his father, the most important things in the world were his comrades in battle, his collection of weapons, his pistols and sabers.

It was a wonderful feeling, to finally be able to go one's own way. "Tomorrow," said Robert to Hans, "tomorrow at dawn, I'm taking off. I can't wait any longer. Are you coming along with the others?"

"Yes," answered Hans. His pale, ghostly face gleamed suddenly more brightly; his whole body was bathed in bright light. "Yes," he repeated in a strange voice.

But no one heard him any more. A wave of fire burst forth over the boys and soon thereafter it was dark and very still.

Chapter Thirteen: The Bliss of Wine

Instead of one egg, on this day Susi laid two eggs. Two eggs — what an event!

"The endless cannon thunder drives the poor Henny to distraction," complained Aunt Grete. "Once before, during a terrible thunderstorm, she laid two eggs." She stroked Susie's beautiful black feathers. "It's okay," she whispered. "You don't need to be scared, Susi."

But Grandmother was scared. Restlessly she paced back and forth, from the kitchen to the main room, the apartment door to the window. She opened the window, looked down into the street, went back to the door, looked out into the hall, all the while casting despairing glances at the picture of the Madonna over the sink, and murmuring things that sometimes sounded like prayers of supplication, other times, however, like impatient, angry curses. "Where do you get your calmness, I wonder?" she finally reproached her sister. "There isn't a single soul on the street. I can't hear a single person from our whole story in the hall. I'm sure they've all packed up everything they have and moved into the cellar. And it's high time, that we also — "

"They're all still in their apartments," interrupted Aunt Grete. "Stop running back and forth and biting your nails. The shooting is a long way off; don't worry, we'll get our chance to enjoy cellar life soon enough." Aunt Grete caught her breath, looked around the kitchen and then cried out, "Two eggs! Go ahead, why don't you make us a couple of pancakes, as long as we still have fire in the stove."

As always Aunt Grete held the upper hand and could give the orders. Grandmother started the assigned task, shaking her head and muttering, laying wooden logs in the still glowing embers in the stove and mixing the dough.

How good it is that Grete is with us, thought Ilse once again. Aunt Grete was so unshakable; in her presence one really wasn't afraid. And it is certainly better for Grandmother to have something to do. Otherwise, she just worked herself up with her constant pacing back and forth.

The wonderful aroma of the cooking pancakes in the pan was also comforting. Grandmother, red-cheeked, busying herself at the stove, seemed to have plunged eagerly into her efforts and thereby forgotten all the air raids of the world.

The decision had been made to share some of this wonderful dish with Herr Pospischil. "After all, Ilse owes him three pairs of brand new shoes. And the cigarillos; I'm sure we'll put those to good use," said Aunt Grete. "They're the best currency to have."

And so, Ilse was sent with a plate of warm pancakes to Herr Pospischil. The short trip over to his place, past the neighbors, was to turn out to be very rewarding — in a strange way.

No, this time she didn't expect any presents of chocolate; no food exchange took place. Something else happened: without wanting to, completely unintentionally, Ilse got a look into Pospischil's greatest and most closely guarded secret.

Herr Pospischil was discovered completely immersed in his favorite pastime. He was concentrating so hard that when the pancakes arrived he just muttered, "Thanks, thanks," in a distracted way and immediately sat back down at his desk and picked up his fountain pen.

"What are you writing there?" asked Ilse. And because she didn't get an answer right away, and because the adventurous outings and events of recent days had built up a kind of comradeship between her and Herr Pospischil, she went ahead, without hesitating, and boldly picked up the top piece of paper covered with Herr Pospischil's handwriting, and began to read:

It was very early in the morning, the streets were clean and empty, I went to the train station. When I compared a clock tower with my watch, I saw that it was already much later than I had thought, I had to hurry, the horror over my discovery left me uncertain. I didn't know my way around this city, so I was glad to encounter a policeman nearby. I ran over to him and asked him, out of breath, for directions. He smiled and said, "You want me to tell you the way?" "Yes," I said, "because I can't find it myself." "Give it up, give it up," he said and turned away with a great swinging motion, as people do who want to be alone with their laughter."

"Suspenseful," praised Ilse and laid the page with the other sheets full of meticulously neat handwriting. "Really suspenseful, and beautiful," she added, embarrassed. No other word occurred to her but "beautiful." "Beautiful," she repeated. "Beautiful to read, and you also have a beautiful handwriting. So, you are a writer. You are really an author!" Full of admiration she took a step back from the desk in order to be able to see what he was doing and assess it at the same time.

Herr Pospischil threw her a glance that she couldn't interpret. Confused, helpless, he looked at her. Then he said aloud — very loudly, it seemed to Ilse — "But no, but no. I didn't write this text. It's a parable by Kafka. By Franz Kafka. I just copy it all down. I copy down everything I really like. I've been doing it for a long time. Do you know, you retain texts so much better, and can understand them better when you write them out. I make them my own this way. Reading alone — it is so fleeting."

He copies down things that have already been written, already printed, just for himself! Ilse was, if possible, even more astonished at Pospischil's writing habits. His copying seemed to her at this moment at least as heroic and original as the creation of a story or novel. And then he told her that he had copied entire plays, "Hamlet" for example. Simply copied them out for his own pleasure. He went on to tell her that he was a regular customer at the stationery store, one of their best customers. To be sure, no one had ever wondered about his regular consumption of large amounts of paper. Thank God! Because he didn't really know what he would have answered if asked. She, Ilse, was the first and only person who knew about this "odd habit." He said "odd habit," as if to mock himself, but the phrase also sounded a bit proud and a bit like a defiant self-assertion.

Now I know Herr Pospischil's secret, thought Ilse on her way back to Grandmother's. He didn't need to tell me to keep it to myself and not tell anyone. Of course not! Such a peculiarity shouldn't be told to others, by no means. The knowledge of such a "secret" was a proud possession that she shouldn't, and didn't want, to share with anyone.

Ilse went through the quiet corridor. The black and white patterned stone tiles clattered as always quite softly at the usual place by the water faucet, where the inhabitants of the third floor gathered daily to fetch water for smaller or larger basin-fillings.

Frau Weissenböck's hall window was, as often, open just a slit.

"So that she won't miss anything," Grandmother always said. "Old lady Weissenböck is such a busybody."

As she went by, Ilse heard the clatter of the Weissenböck sewing machine. Grandmother had a similar, equally ancient one, a large black monstrosity with iron foot peddles that set in motion the driving wheel or the work plate that in the end made the needle go up and down.

Hard-working, thought Ilse, old Weissenböck was hard-working. Even now she is sewing. She had gotten used to the endless shooting.

Just as Ilse reached Grandmother's door there was a noise of another kind. Wasn't someone singing? Yes, several voices were coming up from the mezzanine, louder and louder, coming up the steps and resounding through the whole staircase.

Frau Weissenböck stuck her head through the open slit of the window. "What's going on?" she asked. "Who is singing?" She listened. "Heurigen songs? Is it possible? The taverns have all been closed up for a long time."

She was quite right about that. All the businesses had been closed for days. Closed up tight, with shades drawn, windows and doors crisscrossed with boards and nailed shut.

"I wanna be in Grinzing once again," came the melodious words up from the first floor. But in between there was suddenly a hard knocking and a sharp whispering murmur: "trrokkntokktokkktokk," banged and hammered the sounds down from up above the rooftops.

"Attention! Dive bombers!" The warning came up from the mezzanine. Heindl, the air raid warden, cried with a loud voice up from the staircase door. "Dive bombers! They're shooting. Keep away from the windows!"

The Heurigen song stopped for a few minutes, but the air raid warden's warning had barely died away when the voices began again. "I wanna be in Grinzing once again, drinkin' wine, drinkin" wine, drinkin' wine!"

There were two singers, a man and a woman. They had reached the second floor and their song could be heard in the third.

Everyone was standing there, drawn by all the noise, all the inhabitants of the third floor gathered together around the landing. Even Herr Pospischil, holding his fountain pen, poised to write, in his ink-stained fingers, had come out of his lair.

"Lord God planned so fine for you and me," they sang more loudly, coming nearer and nearer, "after six days of work comes one day free . . ."

"Jeesus!" gasped Frau Navratil. "It's Herr and Frau Brunnhuber! And look at all the stuff they're lugging." She pointed to the two enameled buckets and backpack Herr Brunnhuber was carrying. Frau Brunnhuber also had a backpack strapped on and was carrying a heavy-looking shopping bag in one hand and a water can in the other.

" . . .So we must all be thankful, grateful all — for wine, for wine, for wine!" the couple sang, finishing off their song as they finally reached the third story.

"Hello! Where on earth have you been?" Old Frau Navratil was the one who posed the question, her voice full of envy. The eyes of plump little Frau Brunnhuber were glistening with glee, her full cheeks looked like little red apples, and Herr Brunnhuber's nose was also aglow in a happy shade of red. There was no way these two could be sober; they were not just tipsy, but really drunk.

"Well, where should we have come from, do you think?" asked Herr Brunnhuber and put his two pails down on the floor. "From Grinzing of course. Where elsh?" From the pails a liquid was seeping out of the wrapping paper wrapped with a cord.

"These damn old' three stories," gasped Frau Brunnhuber. She put the watering can and the backpack down in front of her apartment door. "Finally we're home," she sighed. "It's a good far piece, it is, from Grinzing all the way back here to Ottakring."

As if to add acoustic support and proof of the not only far, but also dangerous way, there was a sudden roaring and rumbling added to the hard, sharp sounds already heard from above the rooftops. Everyone ducked involuntarily and pulled in their heads, but the uproar died down as suddenly as it had started. They were used to much worse.

"You Brunnhuber, don't keep us in suspense no more, tell us what's up," demanded old Herr Navratil of his neighbor. "Tell us, have you really been in Grinzing?"

"Well, do you think we're making up stories? We were in Grinzing, without a doubt. And let me tell you, this was one Heurigen party that I won't never forget, as long as I live."

"My soul," agreed Frau Brunnhuber, "such a Grinzing as that —

hard for anyone to imagine, it was."

"Go, on, old gal, fetch the drinking glasses," commanded Herr Brunnhuber. "We all need to drink us a toast, all together. We're not getting no younger."

Frau Brunnhuber disappeared into her apartment and came out with a tray of empty glasses, and Herr Brunnhuber shared the results of their excursion to Grinzing with the whole third floor. There was wine in the water can, enough to fill all their glasses. They told about their experience. They had gone to see their daughter-in-law in Grinzing to see if it was dangerous there. They hadn't had any news from her and their grandchildren for days. Well, everything was fine there; they needn't have been worried. But then, suddenly, the news spread like wild fire through the streets: "All the wine cellars are open to anyone; everyone should come and take whatever they can!"

"Because of the Russians," explained Frau Brunnhuber. "So that the Russians don't get the wine — because when they're drunk — well, you can just imagine, they're likely to get wild, attack the women, rape them, or just start shooting in all directions."

"You can't hardly imagine what it was like," interrupted Herr Brunnhuber. "We were in the first group there. A big cellar, big barrels, monstrous big they were. At first I thought I could pick out what I liked: Nußberger, Sylvaner, Riesling, Veltliner, Müller-Thurgau, and all the finest wines — "

"My God! Too bad I wasn't there," sighed Herr Navratil.

"A lucky thing that you weren't there," corrected Frau Navratil, and gave her view, "You'd have been so smashed, you'd have been lying down and I would have had to carry you out of there."

"I took a taste here and there from the barrels," said Herr Brunnhuber, continuing his report. "But more and more people kept coming, with buckets and shovels and baby bathtubs, with bottles and pots. In the end all hell broke loose. They let out all the stops — and do you think that the people were waiting their turns, one after another? Not hardly! They beat open holes in the barrels, they did, and wine came pouring out like noodle soup, all over everywhere the good wine was running." Herr Brunnhuber lifted his arms up and cried out melodramatically, falling into his best High German, "We were wading in wine!"

Frau Brunnhuber conveyed the further course of events to the rapt listeners in good Ottakringerisch dialect: "An' in all da streets aroun' da wine was aflowin' in li'l brooks."

"It's for the best," remarked Frau Zimmermann. "When the Russians get here, there won't be any left." She spoke in a loud voice as she winked at Frau Navratil, who didn't know what she meant by the wink. Was old lady Navratil for the Red Army or not? — she wondered. She hadn't noticed that her friend had said the phrase "When the Russians get here," very cheerfully, or with special emphasis on "the Russians get here."

"In the bucket is a wine syrup," said Herr Brunnhuber, concluding his report. "I don't have no idea what you're supposed to do with it. Dilute it, I know that! It's real concentrated, they told me."

Grandmother barely sipped at the Grinzing wine; Aunt Grete, however, had emptied her whole glass. Ilse took one last big swallow, then she looked at Herr Pospischil who was standing over to the side. Now he was making a gesture with his glass, a gesture that could have been a wave of greeting, but then again maybe it was a farewell. A farewell: Come on, we don't need to stay here. Probably he had been missing his writing desk and his books for a good while already. My God, he is eccentric, thought Ilse; he can't accept the fact that the group is having a little fun. And he doesn't even know how to raise a toast properly.

Ilse, who had enjoyed the wine, suddenly felt quite bold. And as she looked over at Herr Pospischil, she thought of the cigarette cartons, the red Korsos that the lady on the wall had lost. She hadn't shown her own hard-won carton to Grandmother or Aunt Grete, but kept it hidden, just for fun, to have her own secret, personal souvenir of her adventures at the tobacco factory. What would happen if she decided to taste one of those cigarettes? She had never tried smoking before. Of course she would have to keep such an attempt completely secret; not only Grandmother, but Aunt Grete too would forbid it. But right now would be a good opportunity; no one was in the apartment. She could get the carton without anyone seeing her.

Ilse hadn't quite thought out her idea before she was on her way, to the apartment, then to the hiding place, and right after that she was sitting in the hall toilet closet, armed with a cigarette and matches. Behind her back was a window that went into an air shaft and was always open, so the smoke would dissipate quickly.

She was smoking! It didn't taste especially good; actually she didn't like the taste at all, but everything around her, the whole situation, was exciting; she felt somehow grownup, bold and very independent, special and superior.

Outside, in the hall, there seemed to be a drinking party going on. Herr Brunnhuber went on bragging about his experiences in Grinzing; there was laughter, talking, louder laughter. And she was here, so secret, so completely secret, having her first smoke with cigarettes she had gone out and obtained with her own hands! It was a special experience, she could boast about later, an historical moment, never to be forgotten! A defiant moment!

Satisfaction and pride filled her as she took her next puff on her cigarette — and at this moment of indescribable triumph, it happened: "trrtokktokk trrtokktokktokktokk!" It came directly behind her back into the air shaft; "trrtokktokk trrtokktokktokktokk!" There was a rumble and roar. The machine gun salvo nailed and riveted and echoed so close by as if her little quarter of the toilet closet was the sole and exact target, the only goal that the dive bombers were aiming at.

Ilse stood up, completely convinced by the ear-deafening din that she had been hit, hit, if not shot clear through. Didn't people say that in the moment when you are wounded you don't even feel it? She looked herself up and down, and felt around her back; but no, she was all right; she wasn't wounded. She had been hit, but only by terror, terror that she felt throughout her whole body. The cigarette, her first, secret cigarette, she was still holding in her fingers, in her trembling hand.

"It's God's punishment!" Ilse heard herself say. "God's punishment for your forbidden smoking." And she also heard that she was speaking in Grandmother's voice and tone, although she had no intention of imitating or making fun of her grandmother.

The drinkers in the hall had also been filled with terror by the sounds of the flying plane passing by so close above their heads. There were sounds of hasty footsteps, clearing away glasses, and cries such as, "Now it's getting serious," "We gotta go to the cellar." Then the general retreat began, first to the apartments.

In the kitchen Aunt Grete was busy trying to catch a completely distraught Susi. The "poor henny" had also been affected by the dive bomber, so loud and so close. Susi refused to move from her spot under the coal box. She absolutely refused to be lured into the suitcase with the airholes.

And Grandmother was going around the room again and again packing the "essentials" and asking, "Do I really have everything we need? Have I forgotten anything?" Then there came the anxious inventory, the checking and re-checking: "Our residence papers? Baptismal record? Passport? Rudolf's wedding ring? His death certificate? The Bible? The Mariazell Madonna? The golden necklace?"

The golden necklace! This very necessary piece of jewelry, which had been pawned from time to time, times when Ilse's mother hadn't had enough grocery money, or when she wanted to buy a new dress ("another rag" as Aunt Grete put it).

"Come on," cried Grandmother, and beckoned to Ilse. "Come on."

Grandmother's voice sounded solemn, and her face looked solemn as well. She reached into the "essentials" bag, pulled out a little case, and handed it to Ilse. "This belongs to you from now on," she said. "A family heirloom. Take care of it."

"And don't show it to your mother," added Aunt Grete from the kitchen. "Or she'll take it straight to the pawn shop."

A golden watch! And look at it! Ilse could hardly believe her eyes. The case was decorated with the finest carved leaves and flowers, and there was a border of gleaming gemstones.

"It's worth a fortune," said Grandmother. "Diamonds, real diamonds." She picked up the watch again and opened the smooth polished cover so that the delicate mechanism inside became visible. "The date carved in the cover is the date of my mother's wedding. We were once quite well-to-do, before inflation . . ." With a sigh she laid the watch back in Ilse's hand. "Take good care of it, and don't ever let it go. It will bring you good luck."

"And hide it real well from the Russians," added Aunt Grete.

Grandmother began to chew her nails. "We need to hide *Ilse* real well from the Russians, we do," she called in the direction of the kitchen. "Hide the girl from the Russians, that's the most important thing."

"Would you just tell me *where?*" Aunt Grete appeared in the doorway. "Where can she hide in the cellar? Between the coke and the coal?"

"Stop, don't scare me," said Grandmother. "We'll find some corner for her."

But Ilse wasn't afraid. Or not very. The day before she had been in the attic looking around for a hiding place. The attic, in which she had expected to find all kinds of junk to hide in, had turned out to be the worst place to hide. There were no old trunks or wooden partitions; nothing was as she remembered from her grade school days when she had spent time at her grandmother's. Of course! Because of the danger of fire from bombs everything had long ago been cleared out, and done so in accordance with precise Prussian rules, not in the more relaxed Viennese style. Lonesome, surrounded by no disorder, the wooden support posts loomed up in regularly spaced intervals toward the frame of the roof. Between them was nothing, nothing at all. No old stoves, no rusty ovens, no crates, no trunks — nothing. Nothing but air.

On her tour through the emptiness Ilse did think of a possible place to hide, however — for if there was nowhere inside the attic, why not look for one outside? She opened the eave window, stuck her head out, and looked at the gutter that ran along the edge of the roof, and discovered right next to the window the brick square of the chimney. Could she lift herself up to the attic window, move along the roof, land with her feet on the gutter, then pull herself on her stomach over to the chimney, and then climb up there — wouldn't that be possible?

Would she have the courage to do it? Of course, she would avoid looking down to the street. Just don't look down, no matter what, if it comes to this, she admonished herself. I don't dare even *think* about looking down, she thought; after all, I'm four stories up! It makes me dizzy just to think about having to scramble around out there. But, she comforted herself, if I have a Russian behind me, I won't have time to think about anything.

No, she couldn't be afraid, couldn't show any fear. She didn't dare do that to her grandmother.

"Is the watch running?" asked Ilse and held the wonderful golden object to her ear.

Grandmother looked almost insulted. "Of course it *isn't*

running!" she cried. "It's a very old one."

Ilse shook the watch and fiddled with it, knocked on the housing with her knuckles, shook it again, listened again, and finally, at long last, realized with astonishment that it was ticking!

With a cry, "It's working; it's working!" Ilse held it out for her grandmother to listen to.

For a whole minute Grandmother stood there, pressing the watch almost reverently to her ear. "It's a miracle, a miracle," she cried again and again, looking quite transformed. "It's a miracle. You'll see, everything will turn out all right. God is with us!"

"And Susi is too," reported Aunt Grete from the kitchen. She was waiting at the door of the apartment, all ready to set forth, the satchel with air holes in one hand, a bag full of groceries in the other.

"Well, what is it? Are we going down to the cellar or not?" she asked.

Chapter Fourteen: A Movie Visit in a Red Blouse

"No, she can't be allowed out of the house. It would be too dangerous. The streets are full of Russians!"

Grandmother's strict tone of voice made Ilse fear the worst, that this time she wouldn't give in, even if Aunt Grete stood on her head.

According to a notice on the blackboard in the front hall of the building the Rosegger Theater was playing "The Woman of My Dreams," this Sunday as its "first peace-time show." From the window Ilse could see how Maroltinger Street was beginning to fill up with more and more people. They were all turning onto Rank Street; they all seemed to be going in the direction of the Rosegger, and if Ilse weren't allowed to join the pilgrimage soon the rather small cinema would be sold out before she could get there.

"It is said to be a really fine film," said Ilse, trying to persuade her grandmother. "In color. With Marika Rökk. Please let me go!"

"The war is barely over, and you have nothing else on your mind but this constant movie-going. Just get it out of your head!" Grandmother looked really angry and also really worried.

"Constant movie-going?" murmured Aunt Grete. "What does she mean by *constant movie-going*? We've been sitting in the cellar for days on end. Let the poor gal get a little breath of fresh air!"

"Fresh air — at the movies? Don't make me laugh!" Grandmother actually tried to get a chuckle out, but it didn't sound at all like she was amused. "I don't know why you have to meddle all the time anyway," she rebuked her sister. "Outside the Russians are running around all over the place. And I am the one who is ultimately responsible for this child."

"It is a children's performance," inserted Aunt Grete, putting great emphasis on the word "children's." "Do you understand: a family performance in broad daylight. Don't you see all the people on the street? The Russians can't just do whatever they want; that was only when we were on the front-lines."

"It is still dangerous," said Grandmother, insisting on her opinion.

"It's not enough for you that poor Ilse was forbidden to do

anything by her mother, the beast. Now you are starting up with the restrictions."

These words went unanswered. Grandmother sobbed, chewed her nails and looked even more worried. She didn't really look so angry any more, decided Ilse.

"You want to lock up the girl. Just keep her locked up all the time," added Aunt Grete. "In this cruel time when the young people have nothing to laugh about, especially Ilse. When her mother comes back..." Aunt Grete left this sentence unfinished.

Now it was Ilse's turn to face a bitter truth. "When her mother comes back..." echoed in her mind. Horrible — she hadn't thought that through, hadn't wanted to. She had wished that her mother would stay in the West forever. Wasn't it a lot nicer there? "The land of milk and honey," as people said when they talked about the Salzkammergut and Salzburg.

It was still for a while in the apartment. Then Grandmother suddenly said, "Oh, all right then, she can go to the movies. But, Ilse, only if you wear your red blouse. Your red blouse. Then you'll look like a communist. Better safe than sorry. And I beg you, stay where there are a lot of people."

As an additional safety measure Herr Pospischil was recruited to go along, because neither Grandmother nor Aunt Grete had any desire to go to the movies.

And Herr Pospischil? The very man who had confessed to Ilse that he "had no interest at all in movies;" this same Herr Pospischil agreed gleefully. "Of course, of course. I'll be glad to go along. Everyone says it's a good film."

They managed to get two of the last tickets sold, the worst seats, of course, in the second row, right in front of the screen and clear over on the right side.

In front of the theater, while waiting for the film to start, Ilse would have her third personal encounter with a Russian soldier. Walking back and forth, holding her purse indifferently in her hands behind her back, she was trying to explain to the ignorant Herr Pospischil what a versatile actress Marika Rökk was. "And what a fantastic dancer!" she cried, waxing enthusiastic over her great admiration for the star's fancy footwork. Then, suddenly, behind her, there was a pull, a push — and her purse was gone. Someone had grabbed it in one swift move! Enraged, Ilse turned around, wanting to confront the thief, to speak to him; after all there were enough people around to back her up.

Then, however, she tried to look as friendly as she could. A Russian! A young Russian soldier was standing opposite her; he couldn't have been much older than she was, and his face didn't look like the Mongolian villains she knew from posters and exhibits.

No, this Russian didn't look dangerous or evil; on the contrary, he was grinning with his whole face. He said a few words that Ilse didn't understand, gave her purse back, and disappeared among the crowd of waiting moviegoers.

"He thought that was a joke," said Herr Pospischil. "I'm sure he had his nasty fun over your fear."

The two other encounters Ilse had had with the Red Army had also begun in fear and come to a good end. The very first had been during the period of "cellar life."

"The Russians are here," it was announced, and this information had been supplied by Heindl, the air raid warden, who had gotten it from the warden in the next building. Heindl had been the only one who had dared to come out of the cellar at that time, and the nearer the alarms got, the more seriously he took his duties as protector of the building. Ever since the moment that Frau Resch had called him a "true hero," his zeal had known no bounds. So he had been the one who had hung the new flag on the roof of the building, a huge red flag with the once treacherous dark red circle — the part that was left after the swastika was removed. (He had decided on this solution because no one wanted to dye a white sheet red.) Weeks before that he had put up, in very visible letters, "Civilians Only," on the walls and shades. Not only that, but on the day of the flag hanging he had added "HEIL Red Army," and "Warmest Welcome," in both German and Russian. Frau Brunnhuber had reacted with the words, "This is going way too far," but Frau Zimmermann had broken into loud applause. Herr Navratil had also approved of these actions. After the First World War, he had been a Russian prisoner of war for years in Siberia, and this was his first opportunity to offer the warden use of his knowledge of spoken and written Russian for the good of the building. Now he was enjoying the sight of his Russian knowledge displayed on the wall of the building for all to see.

The small red flag fluttered, the flag that had been adorned with a swastika until it was recently altered by Frau Weissenböck to conform to the current situation. They only hoped that Heindl hadn't gotten false information and jumped the gun, because there were no soldiers anywhere around — neither Russian nor German, and the former, at least most of them, wouldn't have had much appreciation for new flags with Cyrillic letters.

After yet another night in the cellar, spent in uncertainty over the current state of the war, the residents of the building began to get impatient. One at a time they started to pay visits to their apartments, to check them over, look out the windows, fetch more supplies, and try to find some new hope.

Ilse's first encounter with a Russian had occurred during such an interval in the apartment. There had been a short, hard knock on the door. Grandmother, as usual rather distracted, had said "Come in," out of habit. A Russian soldier opened the door — no doubt he would have done so anyway if she hadn't said anything — and strode right into the kitchen.

"Inspection!" he announced, looked around the room and then strode into the other room. Grandmother, Aunt Grete, and Ilse followed him. He looked around again, even under the bed and in the wardrobe, and finally asked, "Hitlerr Soldati chere?"

Aunt Grete was the first to find her voice, although she suddenly spoke quite strangely. She said, "No Hitler Soldati! Njet Soldati. Kommunisti!" She asserted and pointed at herself and Grandmother.

The Russian took off his fur cap with its red star and suddenly began to laugh. He was a young soldier with blonde locks peaking out from under his cap. He was laughing heartily now. The three women didn't know if they were supposed to laugh too, because they had no idea what he found so funny.

"Everybody same, all house, no Hitlerr," he cried. "All house Austria, all Communisti." He laughed again, put his cap back on properly, shook his head over this door by door unified Communist enemy land, and departed to pound on Frau Weissenböck's's door.

"What do you know?" marveled Aunt Grete. "He had blue eyes and blonde hair. I never imagined a Russian would look like that guy there."

Ilse had also imagined Russian soldiers differently. And now she thought of her plans to flee up onto the roof. "Would I have dared to try it if things got serious?" she wondered.

But things weren't so "serious." Maroltinger Street and the streets around it, unlike some other areas, had been spared attacks. The news spread quickly that the feared violence and rapes had happened mostly in the rural villages.

Later, Grandmother insisted that she had lost her fear as soon as the old family watch had started ticking again; it gave her a "good feeling" because it seemed like a sign from her mother, a sign that she was standing by her. In addition, she had faith in the Mariazeller Madonna.

"Go on," said Aunt Grete. It was written on her face that she didn't believe in Grandmother's lack of fear, and she didn't like all this superstitious talk. "And Susi is standing by me," she joked. "Wherever Susi is, nothing bad can happen. We have this wonderful hen to guard over us all."

Ilse's next encounter with a Russian also occurred in their apartment. This time the doorbell rang and Grandmother, now more careful with her "Come in's," tried to look through the milk glass windowpane and see who and how many people were on the other side of the door. She made out a tall figure and heard Russian words. "Well, here goes," she thought. Grandma, Aunt Grete, and Ilse were all afraid, but there was nothing to do but open up.

Behind the tall figure, a Russian officer in dress uniform, decorated with rows of medals, appeared Frau Zimmermann, so dolled up that she was hard to recognize. She was wearing a dark blue, form-fitting suit, a small, perky hat, red lips, and elegant black high heels. She looked young and happy.

"May I introduce my gentleman friend?" she said ceremoniously, and "Come, Igor!" She took Igor by the hand and pulled him into the kitchen.

It turned out that Igor was a member of the "high military ranks." "He is a colonel," said Frau Zimmermann proudly. "And he can even speak German."

Igor smelled like perfume. Frau Zimmermann smelled like the same perfume. They sat down in the living room, but said, "no thank you" to Grandmother's offer of tea.

"Isn't he dashing, my Igor?" asked Frau Zimmermann and stroked Igor's chest of medals, then his smooth-shaven cheek.

Igor really did have an impressive appearance. "A man in his prime," as Aunt Grete put it later. His face tanned, a manly profile, gray eyes. He looked at least as athletic, brave, and loyal as the many cross of honor recipients, submarine captains, and dive bombers of the "glorious German army," whose fine portraits, in the form of color photographs, had not so long ago been passed around by the dozens among schoolgirls. No doubt Igor was also a hero, thought Ilse, and tried to count his medals.

Now, of course, the hero looked embarrassed, for Frau Zimmermann was giving him a loud smack on the cheek.

"Russia, great fatherland," said Igor. "Austria also great fatherland. We love Austria. Good country, beautiful country."

"Well, the main thing is that you love me," laughed Frau Zimmermann, and then she mentioned that she had just been at Frau Navratil's because she wanted to introduce all of her Austrian friends to Igor. At that moment she pulled a package of genuine bean coffee out of her purse and gave it to Grandmother. "This is for you," she said. "Appropriated from the Russian army."

The couple stayed only a few minutes, and in this interval the conversation turned to Susi. Igor spoke Russian to the hen, petted her, and then said to the others in German that Susi was the most beautiful of all the hens in Austria. As the pair were leaving, just as they reached the door, Frau Zimmermann tugged on Igor's uniform sleeve and whispered, "Don't forget, Igor. You'll say something."

Igor cleared his throat. "The Red Army is a disciplined army," he began. He continued solemnly, "We want everything in order. If a problem arises, if soldiers are impudent, then please come to Igor. We have stringent penalties for soldiers who do not behave correctly."

"Just come over to my place if something comes up," said Frau Zimmermann. "Igor belongs to the city command. One word from him and —." Frau Zimmermann made a motion with her hand signaling a beheading.

Grandmother stayed at the half-opened door and stared at the pair as they left. "I can't help it," she said. "But every time I see a

Russian I feel scared all over, I do."

"I thought you said you'd lost all your fear," Aunt Grete reminded her. "And now that we have this Igor you can forget it. He'll look after us." She laughed maliciously and began to count up their good luck charms. "Igor protects us, and the family watch, and . . ."

Ilse finished her sentence, "And Susi, and the. . ."

Aunt Grete threw her a warning look, and so Ilse didn't add the word "Madonna."

No, Ilse didn't feel comfortable in her red blouse. She had never liked her showy red blouse anyway, and now, as she went into the movie theater it seemed to her as if everyone was staring at it. Soon, however, she realized that quite a few women were wearing red blouses. She didn't stand out after all! Red had become all the fashion, she realized, relieved.

"When does the show start anyway?" she asked Herr Pospischil, for the theater had been full to capacity for several minutes. No one else was being admitted, but the lights were still on.

Finally the ticket-taker appeared with his big sprayer. As always, he walked along the walls and sprayed pine scent high into the air. The spray descended on the moviegoers in visible and aromatic clouds; all were enveloped together in the sweet, unavoidable scent.

Herr Pospischil bent over from his neighboring seat to Isle and whispered into her ear, "Is that a treatment for lice?"

"Lice?" Ilse looked at him, upset. Was he trying to be funny? Or was he serious? He wasn't laughing. He probably went to the movies only rarely; maybe the fact was that he had never been before? Here the spray of scent was always part of the program, although that wasn't the case in every theater.

Ilse didn't have a chance to find out if Herr Pospischil's question was in earnest or not. At that moment the lights went out. Ilse straightened up in her chair, full of anticipation. She looked forward to the film and to seeing Marika Rökk.

But no! The dark red curtain was not, as it usually was, pulled to the side to reveal the screen, but it stayed in place. Instead, a glaring spotlight lit up the podium in front of the screen, and an older man climbed up onto the stage with the help of a ladder. The small man was wearing a shabby tuxedo that was much too large for him. If he had been wearing make-up he would have looked like a clown.

Now the ticket-taker came over to the ladder. With a flourish he held up an accordion. After the man in the tuxedo had strapped it on, he greeted the audience, and, with many bows, introduced the "song artist and Heurigen singer." He had the honor of introducing a short quarter-hour program that would be their first peace-time performance, he declared. And now, he continued, now that the Austrians had been liberated, although not yet entirely from hunger, the theater management wanted to give the honored public a few hours of entertainment. And, with a swinging hand motion, gesturing toward the hall, now shrouded in semi-darkness, he asked the audience to greet the guests of honor with special applause.

The audience, used to obedience, looked around for honored guests and didn't see any, so there was only a little applause, scattered and hesitant.

"But please, ladies and gentlemen, what kind of special applause was that?" reprimanded the man in the tuxedo. And then, trying to give an indication of who the "guests of honor" were, he gestured with a sweeping motion of his arm toward the box seats and the Russian soldiers sitting there. He cried out, "Please, give a real greeting to our liberators! Our liberators, the representatives of the Red Army present here in the theater!"

Everyone there looked up to the box seats, and the newly instructed audience now gave a much louder burst of applause.

"A Heuriger wine garden singer," moaned Ilse under her breath. Had she come to the movies to hear corny wine songs?

But it was no Heuriger song that the tuxedo-clad man now sang his best, with a deep bow toward the box seats, but a popular hit song. In fact, it was not only a Zarah Leander hit, but one that Ilse had often played on Else's gramophone in the studio on Wiedner Main Street. "On the Volga, glides Olga, on a ship to the ocean, great tide . . ." The singer tried to imitate Zarah's voice, successfully for a while, especially as he sang, " . . . and Ivan, her Ivan, dear Cossack in flight, rode after her truly, as day follows night." It almost sounded as if Zarah herself were singing. And at the refrain, "Ride on, little rider, ride on, love may reward you, maybe it might . . . " his fingers moved with agile skill over the keyboard, playing with wilder and wilder rhythm.

The hall erupted in enthusiasm, as Viennese and Russian spectators joined each other in hearty applause.

Ilse was appeased. Now some Viennese folk songs did follow. Ilse could tolerate the song, "Goethe didn't write this song, nor Schiller neither," but she hated the next number, "My Ma, she is a Viennese, that's why I love the place," with her whole heart. After all, she had suffered a great deal here! She had suffered here in so many ways, but in the end she did love Vienna and wanted to continue to do so. But when she thought about her mother, and took the words of the song literally, it seemed to her a paradox, illogical and impossible, that she should love the city. Ilse fidgeted uneasily back and forth on her wooden chair. Why was the theater still lit? Wasn't the movie *ever* going to start?

Finally, it seemed to be time. The singer finished his last song. Now, to conclude this show he had something special to present. A song that fit the times and was close to his heart. "Take it home with you!" he instructed them. Then, with a wink of his eye, he said under his breath, so only the first rows could hear him, "What am I taking on?" and he began to sing;

> He's lived through it all,
> old Saint Stephen's so tall
> saw Turks invade, and French,
> looked down on storm and stress.

The little man paused, looked up at the box seat area, then at the rest of the audience, the Viennese who already knew every word of his song. It was completely still in the hall as the added the second stanza, singing with a serious face.

> Looked down on all the happ'nings there
> that put us near despair,
> But some comfort a little song brings,
> that everyone in Vienna sings.

There was another short pause, and then, singing the refrain, the clown that was not a clown, but acting more like a benevolent Santa

Claus giving out gifts, continued:

> Good old Steffel smiles down from the cloud,
> and the cathedral is thinking so proud,
> Here is my Vienna, Vienna so true,
> Vienna, the city of songs
> on the beautiful Danube so blue.

Applause, applause. In the hall and in the boxes, the applause thundered on, and the Heuriger singer was forced to sing the refrain again. Only then did he climb down from the stage, taking many bows.

Now, at last! The curtain moved back to the side, the light in the hall was extinguished. Ilse sat upright in her seat, full of expectation. She moved back so she could lean her head on the back of the seat and get a good view of the screen, which was very near and very high. Now, finally, Marika Rökk would appear, singing and dancing.

But no — they still weren't showing the feature film, because the flickering on the screen was in black and white! And "The Woman of My Dreams" was definitely in color!

All right, a short subject was being shown before the feature. Some short film, probably on a cultural subject, she would have to tolerate, like it or not. They could be very useful and informative sometimes. She had learned a lot from them, such as what it was like in a pot factory, what effort the farmers in the mountains had to expend to harvest their crops, or how the Eskimos managed to survive in the Arctic regions.

This one had a grim title, as she now saw flickering on the screen, a title that confused her, "The Death Mills in Mauthausen." Death mills — what was that supposed to mean? And — Mauthausen? That had to be a place name, but it meant nothing to her. A place she had never heard of. Had she slept through that lesson in geography, or not paid attention? And now, instead of a culture film, this was turning out to be a horror film, a horror film in short subject form? The unwelcome idea crossed her mind that maybe a different film was being substituted for "The Woman of my Dreams."

Strange, strange. Ilse looked questioningly at Herr Pospischil. He shrugged his shoulders and looked at her, just as confused. And their neighbors around them also looked confused and shuffled uneasily back and forth in their seats.

Next, after the first introductory scenes, sweeping shots of barbed wire and dilapidated wooden barracks, came the close-up scenes. Merciless, ever clearer, bigger and sharper, terrible images dominated the screen. A mountain of human bones. A mass grave, full of piles of corpses. Skeletons and more skeletons.

As the camera showed the places of death, the announcer reported that this documentary film conveying the atrocities of the Hitler regime had been made when the American troops marched in. Mauthausen had been one of many concentration camps in which the "cleansing" of the German folk of "undesirable elements" had been carried out, in cold blood and with factory-like precision. In extermination camps like the one at Mauthausen, hundreds of thousands, even millions of people had been sacrificed to the "final solution," in order to remove the "ancestral enemies" of the "pure German race" — Jews, Gypsies, criminal enemies of the German nation and homosexuals — once and for all from the face of the earth.

The murders, reported the announcer, were well-organized and committed with German thoroughness. As seen also in documentary footage of the concentration camp in Ausschwitz, the prisoners were first transported in cattle wagons to labor in rock quarries. Those who were no longer able to work, because of weakness and malnourishment, had their necks broken on the "death stairs" and fell into mass graves dug by the prisoners themselves.

The fate of all the others — the announcer paused as the camera showed a large hall with blank, somber walls outfitted with showers — was to perish in the enormous "washrooms," hermetically sealed rooms in which poisonous gas was introduced to send the prisoners of the concentration camps quickly to their deaths. Under the pretext of "washing" and "delousing," the prisoners had to enter the hall naked — a practical measure that enhanced the efficiency of the slaughter, together with the "reclaiming" of body parts: soap was made from the victims' bones, lampshades from their skin, and carpets were woven from the women's hair.

All of this, continued the speaker, was, as mentioned, very well-organized, purposeful, and rationally planned and carried out. The inventors and administrators of the murder factories had shown devilish cleverness in their orderly, organized functioning, down to the smallest detail. For example, the personnel were spared work by having the prisoners themselves sort their own clothing and possessions into separate piles in a designated room before they entered the "washroom."

The film camera showed the result: mountains of shoes, briefcases, eyeglasses, watches, hats, purses, and garments — every category meticulously separated from the others. In addition there was another round of harvesting after the gassing: the large pile of gold teeth that had been broken out of the victims' jaws had a special place of honor.

Image after image accompanied the announcer's words. The last survivors who had escaped the "washroom" gas chambers were shown: walking skeletons with sunken cheeks, apathetic, hardly able to express any joy over their liberation. Photographs and films from the archives of the camp directors gave more insight into "camp life," the horrible, finely-tuned functioning of the "death mills."

Should she believe it? Was what she had just seen real? Ilse had seen a similar presentation before, almost the same thing, in school at a required field trip to the display "Bolshevism Without Masks:" the same mass graves, skeletons, barracks, the same information about lampshades, soap, gold teeth! At that time she had been accustomed to encounter horrible images of the enemy, from "degenerate art" to the "authentic Talmudic texts" detailing the slaughter of Aryan children in Jewish ritual killings.

"Nazi propaganda," her stepfather used to say when she told about the "Bolshevism Without Masks" display and similar information. "Nothing but slander and lies," he said. "These things are just trick photographs pasted together: pictures of lamps and soap, how can you tell what they're made of?"

And so, now, Ilse wanted to believe that the films were just another instance of "propaganda" and "lies," and not something that had really happened. Besides, her stepfather, who never tired of running down and cursing the Hitler regime, never mentioned German concentration camps after her report about the Russian camps. He would have said, "The Nazi swine took these pictures in their own camps and fabricated all this!" No, he had never said anything of the kind.

No, there couldn't have been such horrifying atrocities on either side, such bestial behavior could never have occurred; it's impossible, Ilse told herself again and again. There simply couldn't be people like that, capable of such cruelty, of planning and carrying out such mass murders.

Ilse sneaked a look at Herr Pospischil. She looked at the other spectators in her row to observe their reactions. It seemed to her that all the film-goers were being lifted away from the screen; it seemed as if all the people in the hall were suddenly numb, as if they were lifeless and turned into stone. Were they still breathing or had they stopped? Was she still breathing herself? Because if it were possible that what they were seeing had actually happened, was it still possible to keep breathing the air of this world without smothering?

Film music, main feature, Marika Rökk. Hits, swinging hits: "Every evening I stand on the bridge . . ." crooned Rökk, and "At night no one likes to be alone . . ." She danced, she stepped, she let her partner twirl her high in the air; she sulked, she smiled, she sang, she comforted, "Don't look forward, don't look back, just look straight ahead, and whatever comes, comes, so don't worry."

Had the Heuriger singer promised the audience "a few pleasant hours?" Now, enjoy the film! Be grateful for the program shown. Relax, laugh! Laugh when Rökk laughs — because up until now you've had little reason to laugh. But now, dear people, the war is over, and you are among those who have survived. So laugh and enjoy yourselves!

Yes, the war was over. And Marika Rökk comforted the audience at the end, singing once again with her familiar Hungarian accent and in her thin singing voice: "Don't look back; don't look to the sides; just keep looking straight ahead . . ."

Chapter Fifteen: Flight

"You need to look old, old und ugly!" As she said these words, Grandmother looked so sternly at Ilse that Aunt Grete once again felt compelled to intervene in this family issue.

"No matter how sternly you look at Ilse, she can't, I can't, you can't, nobody can transform her into an old lady!" she said in an exceptionally soft voice.

"That's why I'm looking for a shabby smock and a faded head-scarf," explained Grandmother curtly, as she began to rummage around in the furthest corners of the clothes cabinet.

"Head-scarf?" Ilse sighed. She hated head-scarves.

"Yes, head scarf. Your pretty black hair is dangerous, and the Russians are still very much a danger. Anything at all could happen to a young girl. You have to look old!" Grandmother asserted again. "Old and ugly."

Old and ugly — if only Grandmother knew! Ilse felt old and ugly through and through, even without any disguises. And unhappy, for several days now very unhappy, ever since her stepfather had turned up. He was wearing civilian clothing, having thrown away his German uniform and deserted at just the right moment, as he told it. He was unshaven, dirty, thin; he looked half-starved. Grandmother had immediately given him some food and drink. He had been at Maroltinger Street barely an hour, when he began to say how much he wanted to go to the West right away, to join his wife and children. "And then we'll come back to Vienna as soon as we can!" he announced. "Soon, very soon. Everything is orderly now wherever the Russians are." After that remark he suddenly began to sing the praises of winter, to say how beautiful the Rudolfsplatz was when it was full of snow and everything was white, the streets, the park. "And with red flags waving from the rooftops!"

Ilse couldn't share his enthusiasm for the future. All she heard were the words, "back to Vienna" and "Rudolfsplatz." Her prison — her prison was nearing her! Everything would be as unbearable as before.

"How soon?" she asked in as neutral a tone as she could muster, hoping that dread couldn't be heard in her question.

"I would like to stay with your mother and the boys in the Salzburg area for about two weeks. I think they have plenty of food there. But then life has to begin again as before!" He laughed. "Now that the Russians are here, we Communists will be just fine!"

"And where will you live?" asked Grandmother. "Your apartment was bombed out."

"I know, I know. Well, for a Communist like myself there must be an empty Nazi apartment available somewhere."

From a "Jewish apartment" to a "Nazi apartment," thought Ilse. Practical, practical! Her mother had gotten a "Jewish apartment," and now her stepfather was in line for a "Nazi apartment." We're a fine family!

As soon as her stepfather left the apartment, Ilse got sick to her stomach. Thank God the pail of mop water was still in the kitchen, because she never would have made it to the bathroom out in the hall.

"What's the matter?" Grandmother asked. "I wonder why you took sick so suddenly. We didn't eat anything bad, did we? Or maybe you're anxious because of those documents? You don't need to have them. I spelled all of that out for him. And he'll tell that to your mother. She'll understand exactly why I wouldn't let you leave here to get them. Me, send you right into a war zone?"

How could she explain it to her grandmother? It's all so horrible. I'm filled with horror over everything, she admitted to herself. Starting with the "death mills" and the trucks loaded with mutilated bomb victims to the changeable apartment vacancies; to the image of flags in white snow. I'm filled with horror by all the flags in the world; and being thrown back into the lap of my "happy family" makes me throw up.

"Happy family" — yes, that was the expression. She could hardly believe that her own mother, of all people, had been able to say these two words without embarrassment. She thought of her family portraits. Her mother, her two half-brothers, and Ilse, all decked out in their finest, straining to deliver the photographer the nice smiles he wanted. The photograph had been taken during one of her stepfather's leaves. Before and after the photograph the parents had been fighting, verbally and physically; the boys had been crying, Ilse had received an ear-boxing, (why she couldn't remember; they had been so frequent. Any reason was enough, a "sloppy" job washing a dish, or forgetting to dust some place). But every time her mother had showed someone the photograph, she had nevertheless, full of emotion, declared, "Here we all are together, a happy family."

It all made her sick, and not only when she was vomiting into the mop pail; she continued to feel sick after that. She felt sick, sick and afraid, full of dread of her mother's hard hands and angry blows. She was afraid and disgusted, not so much in dread of the physical pain, as of the indignity, the physical insult the blows inflicted. She would no longer be able to tolerate such insults, such violations, anymore, Ilse realized for the first time. In the meantime, during the "front time" away from her mother, she had changed. Something in her had changed — what was it? Had she gotten used to being herself, being self-reliant, being allowed to have her own opinions and wishes without being punished for them?

In addition, she had experienced and seen so much, and she no longer found it necessary to write everything that happened to her down in her notebook, because she now could keep all her thoughts and experiences in herself. There was nothing to hinder her or set up barriers between her and her own life. She had — what had Else's beloved hero Don Carlos said in those declamations? — she had, "freedom of thought." Freedom of thought!

All at once Ilse realized that thoughts are just as vulnerable to threat and oppression as words, words themselves! Those quiet thoughts, whose existence can't be proven, even those inaudible, invisible thoughts; they can be strangled, killed, annihilated — by merciless enemies when they hold the power.

No, she didn't need to write anything down anymore. In the meantime, her own thoughts and experiences had gathered themselves inside her, had formed without words; no family fights could drive them away as long as she could escape her "happy family."

But how much longer did she have? Two or three weeks? What do two or three weeks amount to? A short grace period! And then back to misery? How she had dreamed of a future time when her mother would stay permanently in the "Golden West!" Dreamed that the end of the war would signify a demarcation between East and West and a permanent separation from her mother! What had she been imagining? That her desires for the future, desires she scarcely dared to have, would be fulfilled by external events, by developments in the war? What a delusion! Events were running their course, and soon everything would be completely back to normal, as if this violent interruption, this great upheaval, had never happened at all.

Events were running their course, and would keep doing so — in general things were coming back to what they were before. For those who couldn't face the situation there was only one way to bring about a real ending, and that was by seeking the great finality of death.

Ilse knew a few people who had chosen this option. Trude's father, for example (little, pale Trude, from the second row of school benches on the left in her old class) had taken his family of four with him in death. Or Uncle Otto, a distant relative of Grandmother's, who, together with his wife, had committed suicide before the Russian invasion.

All of these people had also been unable to imagine the course that events would take. They couldn't imagine enduring the victory of the Russians; they feared a future that, as they had heard again and again, would amount to "the end of all culture," even "the end of the world." Neither Uncle Otto nor Trude's family had been politically active during the Hitler era. They hadn't received any advantage from their faith in his ideology. Uncle Otto, the old nature boy, had a Boy Scout mentality and a desire to be a leader of boys. He was almost seventy, with his tanned skin and corduroy pants, still dancing around the campfire with the young Wolf Cubs. He couldn't imagine any little Mongolian boys taking their place; only the eternally prophesied "end of all culture" and "end of the world" that would be brought about by the victory of "Bolshevik barbarism."

Many of these suicides were victims of the Hitler propaganda, a propaganda of hatred and fear. But *she*, Ilse, intended to keep holding onto one particular slogan of the propaganda, namely, "NEVER FORGET!" She remembered that the words "never forget" had been drummed into her in school and in the "home evenings" of the Jungmädchen club. "Never forget," they had all been told, "never forget all the humiliation that has been forced on the German people again and again from the peace accords at Versailles on, up until the oppression and terror that would break out if Germany were defeated by the "American capitalist Jews" and the "Bolshevik sub-humans."

From now on, she, Ilse, would "NEVER FORGET" what words can do, what inflammatory propaganda can cause; she would never forget that and always hold it in mind! Always, that meant for the rest of her life, she would keep alive in her memory what destruction, what fanaticism can be brought into the world by slogans. Whatever words were uttered by authorities, whoever used such slogans to promote political ideas, she would not listen, no matter how well-reasoned and illuminating the supporting arguments sounded!

What had it been like back in 1939? When she, like all other ten-year-olds, had joined the JM, the "Jungmädchen?" So nice, so wonderfully lyrical and moving the song words had sounded that the girls had sung together during the club "home evenings:" "Every birch tree turns green on moor and heath, every broom-bush gleams like gold . . .;" "In the springtime, in the mountains, off we go, vallera . . ." "Wild geese rustle through the night, with wild cries, toward the North . . . ." As they sang it had always been such images of the beauties of nature that Ilse had seen in her mind's eye.

But, thought Ilse, that should also be something I learn. No matter how beautiful the songs were that we were asked to sing, that harmonious music didn't stimulate in us children just an appreciation of nature. It was only a small step from us singing, "You'll find no nicer land than our own, no matter how far and wide you roam . . ." to us developing the proud notion that ours was the best, most beautiful country among all on earth. And the next step then, the step to battle songs, was just a small one, so small, that we didn't even notice it, but kept singing cheerfully, "A young folk stands up, ready for the storm! Hoist the flags higher, comrades! We feel our time draw near, the time of the young soldiers!" And that was long before the war, and we sang war songs and didn't think anything of it.

But she could at least excuse herself for her naive singing with the "ignorance of youth!" What do ten- and eleven-year-old children think about as they sing the songs they are taught? And then when they sing them again a few years later, they still have no intention of evil-doing through such songs.

The current situation was worse for Grandmother! She hadn't been able to say no to her friend, Frau Mandl, who had asked her to help knit socks for the soldiers on the Eastern front. It was bad for Grandmother now. Those evening knitting sessions after hours at the

Wilhelminen Hospital had been sponsored by a chapter of he National Socialist Frauenschaft, and Frau Mandl had been the chapter head. And Grandmother saw herself, a few days after the invasion of the Russian troops, labeled an active member of the NS-Frauenschaft. A Nazi! "Bumstinazel," as the Viennese said when any misfortune struck. "Bumstinazel!" Now Grandmother was in a jam. Two men with red armbands — the adornment of many of the occupiers that were rushing busily about the city — knocked on the apartment door and displayed a document giving them the right to confiscate Grandmother's small "folk receiver." In black and white it was stated there that it was "unlawful and forbidden" for her to possess a radio due to National Socialist party membership and the likelihood she would undertake "additional hostile agitation."

Grandmother was sad; Grandmother was enraged (after the men who took the radio were gone); Grandmother was a walking question mark. She had knitted socks, socks to guard against the Russian cold. That was her "Nazi activity" and that was the extent of it. Hostile agitation? With the help of a small, scratchy radio? Ilse had been able to hear a few foreign-sounding voices out of it only a few times, and had immediately turned the dial out of fear, because receiving foreign broadcasts had been a capital crime. And, if you please, where, on what radio station, were they supposed to pick up these "hostile" transmissions now? The war was over; Hitler was dead. Who was left who would even want to establish radio connections with him and his kind?

Grandmother didn't understand the world anymore. Aunt Grete tried to comfort her ("Damn the radio! I'll buy you a new one when there's one to buy!"). Susi cackled, and Ilse thought to herself, "It's even dangerous to knit socks! Something else to make a mental note of!" To be honest, however, there was no likelihood that she would ever endanger herself by involvement in such an activity because she hated everything to do with handcrafts.

It was a confusing, disturbing time, confusing and disturbing on all sides. And suddenly, mysteriously but unavoidably, the black and white images of horror from the "Death Mills" film would come back to Ilse. Now, in the background at first, those terrible images would insistently appear. Again and again they came to her, as if illuminated by a flash of lightning, suddenly, and seemingly very near, they appeared before her eyes. They were clearer and sharper than they had been on the screen. She could no longer push them away as if they had been something unreal.

And they had played a Marika-Rökk film right afterwards! "What an outrage!" Ilse told herself. Whenever she had, without thinking, started to sing the Rökk hit, "At night a person doesn't like to be alone," this mindless singing came to a quick end. Scenes of the Mauthausen camp appeared; the "Death Mills" began to roll!

"At night a person doesn't like to be alone." Ilse was certain that the hit would always be associated with horrible murders for her.

On one of the following days, while waiting in line to buy a loaf of bread, Ilse ran into Herr Pospischil. He looked exhausted; his face was ash-gray. He told her that he had been up writing the whole night. At this time he couldn't shake the feeling that all the literature the great writers had produced, and everything he himself had copied out so reverently, had never had the slightest effect. And, he continued, the same was true of the most beautiful and the deepest thoughts that human beings had ever put into words, had ever transmitted to other human beings as a sign of their humanity.

"Not the slightest effect?" asked Ilse, who at first hadn't been listening closely and hadn't been prepared to encounter such a serious and exhausted Herr Pospischil.

"Is creative writing, is poetry capable of changing the course of the world, or the way people live their lives?" he asked in reply. "I don't believe so anymore," he said, immediately answering his own question. "Not like I used to," he added.

The baker hadn't opened up yet. They were standing rather far back in line. It could take another hour or longer before they got any bread. Too much time to stand silently next to each other. At the moment nothing occurred to Ilse with which she could comfort or cheer up Herr Pospischil. And she didn't want to tell of her own suffering and dark thoughts. That wouldn't help either of them.

But then she began telling about her grandmother's confiscated radio, and the unjust treatment she had suffered. At the hospital she had also been told that her job sewing for the institution was in jeopardy, at least until "De-nazification." Grandmother had no idea what that meant or when it would happen.

"My God!" cried Herr Pospischil, suddenly irate. "The little people always get it. Your grandmother certainly had no insight. She never had any interest in politics. Knitted socks! Who would think there was anything in that?"

"Did you have any *insight* yourself? Did you know about the concentration camps?" Only now did Ilse dare pose this question. After the movie visit, on the way home, she had talked about Marika Rökk. That afternoon, she had wanted the film not to be true, and so she acted as if she hadn't seen it. "If I imagine that there is no truth to it, I can make the truth unreal," she had thought, fleetingly, and tried to do so.

"I didn't know a thing!" cried Herr Pospischil. He looked despairingly at Ilse. "I really knew nothing about it," he repeated. "You must believe me, Ilse."

"And yet you spoke just before the Mauthausen Camp film about de-lousing," Ilse reminded him.

Herr Pospischil looked questioningly at her. "I spoke about de-lousing?"

"Yes. You asked if the ticket-taker was going around with a de-lousing chemical. And then, then we saw the gas chambers. The *washrooms*!" she reminded him.

"Yes, that's right." Completely confused, Pospischil shook his head. "That's right. The ticket-taker with that oppressive scented spray! It reminded me of an insect spray . . . an extermination spray, yes."

At the word "extermination," Pospischil suddenly clutched his chest and looked like he couldn't catch his breath. With wide open eyes he stared at Ilse. "Terrible," he finally said softly. "Terrible. Was that perhaps a premonition?" Now Pospischil became quite upset. "As if I had had an inkling of what we were going to see," he said. "As if I had known! But really, Ilse, I really knew nothing about these ghastly things!"

Ilse had no reason not to believe him. Naive to the core, as this Pospischil has always been! Ilse thought of her stepfather. Even he, in general not at all naive, and a Communist, had never said a single word about the extermination camps. Undoubtedly he would have if he had known about them! And, it also occurred to Ilse, back then, when she told him about the "Bolshevism Without Masks" exhibit, it would have been an especially good opportunity to talk about concentration camps in their own country. Her stepfather had never held back when there was a chance to say something against Hitler. Everything bad he knew about the Nazis he was in the habit of talking about. And now a joke popped up in Ilse's memory, one of the many "Hitler-jokes," that her stepfather had brought home on one of his leaves.

She wanted to tell this pale, completely nonplused Herr Pospischil the joke. A little laughter certainly wouldn't hurt him. In addition, Ilse could create suspense with an introduction. She had heard the joke during the time of the victorious special announcements, and as a matter of fact at Hansi's parents', who didn't laugh at the punch line at all. No, they acted as if they hadn't understood the joke or hadn't heard it. Ilse had wondered about that at the time, although now, as of a few days ago, she understood why they hadn't been amused. Namely, when she went to ask at Hansi's parents' delicatessen whether Hansi was still evacuated, she learned from the new owners of the business, strangers to her, that the previous owners — who would have been Hansi's parents — had been "Nazis," and therefore the store no longer belonged to them.

The joke went as follows: One day Hitler learned that he had a double who looked exactly like him, and people couldn't tell them apart. "I absolutely must see this man!" Hitler declared, and the objection that the man was a dangerous psychopath confined to a mental institution could not dissuade him. He had himself driven to the institution, and in spite of strong warnings that the patient was dangerous, he insisted on going alone to the man's cell to talk to him privately. Orders are orders, and so no one could stop Hitler from entering the cell alone and locking the door behind him. Full of fear for the life of the "Führer," the hospital director and Hitler's entourage waited behind the door. For a good while it was silent in the cell, but then, suddenly, there was a noisy commotion, and then rapid footsteps. The cell door was torn open and a man stormed out. ... And yes, since that point in time no one has any idea, *which* of the two came out.

"And you told that to your classmate's parents?" asked Herr Pospischil angrily. "You told what your father said at home to outsiders?"

"Only occasionally. I liked the joke so much. And Hansi was my best girlfriend."

"At risk of your life," cried Pospischil. "Jokes like that could have put your life at risk. If those parents had reported you at that time . . . *And* it was their duty to do so! It was everyone's duty to report the spreaders of such *enemy propaganda*. He who didn't do so was punishable by law."

"Hansi's parents? Do someone in? Of course they didn't do that. They were harmless, kind people. They just believed in Hitler and all his beautiful speeches. At least at first. But they were certainly not evil people."

"But there were a lot of evil people, as we now know," stated Pospischil softly. "Evil people who issued evil orders. And evil people who were capable of carrying those orders out. Can you understand that, Ilse? I can't! I don't understand my own times anymore."

For a while they stood silently next to each other. The bakers had rolled up the shades; the line of people was moving; the bread distribution, the clamor for loaves of bread had begun.

"The endless waiting," complained the lady behind them. "But you have to be grateful if you actually get something."

"I'm glad to wait in line," said Ilse to Pospischil. "As long as I can stay with my grandmother, I'm glad to do it. But in a few days . . . in a few days my *happy family* will be re-united."

"Your mother is coming back?" Pospischil looked at Ilse with such a frightened expression that they both would have broken out in laughter if they had been in the mood.

"Yes, the three weeks are up. I can't imagine it, that everything will be like it was before. No, I just can't."

"It will all pass. Don't forget, in a few years you'll be an adult," said Pospischil consolingly.

"In a few years?" cried Ilse. "That is an eternity to me."

Some people pushed between her and Herr Pospischil, and they lost each other in the shuffle. When she was standing next to him again, Ilse said, "I really can't endure a few more years."

"Yes, you can. You can make it through. There are so many chances to flee, Ilse."

"Chances to flee?"

"Yes, yes!" Pospischil, who used every free moment for his own special escape into the world of books, nodded vehemently. "Yes, yes," he repeated. "That is the only way out. I have to endure what comes too, for better or worse."

If Pospischil only knew! Without realizing it and meaning something quite different, he had confirmed and suggested approval of what Ilse had for days been regarding as the last and only way out for her — flight! In fact, she had a very literal flight in mind; a flight away from her mother, away from the Rudolfsplatz.

Why did she have a father in Italy anyway? A real life, flesh and blood father! A father who had never paid any attention to her, true, but the separation between him and her mother was surely to blame for that. She didn't actually know where he lived, but Ilse did have the address of his mother and grandmother. She would ask her "Italian grandmother" about his whereabouts. She will surely know where he is! And "Omi," her great-grandmother, she'll have a chance to see her again; old "Omi" is still alive. Their last Christmas card to Maroltinger Street had borne her very shaky signature. Ilse began to calculate: Omi, born in 1848 . . . now ninety-seven years old. Ninety-seven! It was high time to visit her! No one could have a better mother than Omi. Long-ago images, laden with love and tenderness, popped up in her memory. Playing "Ride-a-cock-horse," on Omi's lap, and when she came to "fall down in the swamp, that makes the rider go bump!" Omi let her almost fall, but only . . . almost. At the last minute Omi held her tight and lifted her up again. And then she sang, "Let's copy the swallows, and build us a nest . . ."

Italy! With Omi on the balcony. The sea in front of them, the fishing boats with their lanterns, above them the sky all full of stars, and Omi pointing out the constellations, Ursa Major, Ursa Minor, the Cassiopeia.

Italy — that was the way out! The "chance to flee!" Hadn't she already dreamed of Italy during her Easter trip to Vienna? It was no coincidence: the little flight from Salzburg had made the greater flight seem like a real possibility.

Of course there was a lot for her to think over, such as leaving Maroltinger Street and Grandmother in the lurch, secretly, without a word? How Grandmother would worry! But yes, she had to leave without farewell, quite secretly, for Grandmother wouldn't just let her go! Without farewell — that would be cold, quite unkind to Grandmother. But, Ilse tried to comfort herself: in a way my going would at least spare Grandmother one worry, being caught between two fronts, between her daughter and granddaughter, buffeted back and forth. If I disappear, if I'm not there anymore, at least that battle will stop.

The only other problem is losing my school class, Ilse thought. Her girlfriends, her teachers. My God, I'll be going to a completely new environment, a foreign country with a foreign language — I forgot my Italian long ago. I'll be landing suddenly in a completely new world among completely unknown people. But, should I be afraid of that? Must I be afraid?

And, what would she do if her father didn't want her? If this other grandmother with whom she had never had a warm relationship as she had with her great-grandmother, if this Italian grandmother didn't want to take her in either? Well, then I'll just get a job, Ilse decided. I don't have much chance of keeping up with the material in an Italian school anyway.

But she won't send me back; she couldn't do that to me. The world right now is full of refugees. Fine, I'll be one of them. Things can't be worse for me than they have been up to now. I just have to get away, away from home! To be free! And anyway, why am I worrying so much? Today is today — and tomorrow is tomorrow: Robert was right when he said that. It just depends on what you do with your tomorrows, what you really want for your future. And what had happened to Robert? Had he survived the "final victory?"

The last time, the walk to the Rudolfsplatz. Although she was standing quite near her bombed-out building she saw it as if from a great distance, as if countries, seas, years, were already between her and the house. It is decided, thought Ilse. Yes, it is decided. Actually I am already underway. I will have nothing more to do with this building, these ruins.

As she came diagonally across the square, Ilse stopped a lady from the neighboring building. Had she heard anything about Robert? No, nothing, was the answer. Robert hadn't come back. "Lucky for him," the neighbor lady reported. "His mother and sister moved to the West. We're finally rid of those two Nazi dames. They put the whole building in danger."

"If Robert should turn up, then greet him from me," requested Ilse. "Tell him I'm on the road, and I'm doing fine."

She would never see Robert again. Too bad. She would have liked to have told him about her plan to flee. What would he have said? Maybe he would have even gone with her. His mother and sister wouldn't stay in the West forever. So, he also had to find his own way, to find a way to escape. Or has he already done so? At this time there are many ways to escape.

Ilse couldn't know that he had already taken the most final escape of all.

Ilse is intensely involved in her secret preparations for flight. She has saved a little allied money. What else does she need? Her green knit vest, in case it gets cold. Her windbreaker, in case it rains. Her notebook, even though it has been ages since she has written anything "personal" in it. But it has to come along as a memento, just as it always accompanied her down into the air raid shelter. In the meantime she has copied out a few nice poems in it that she wants to take along, for example, this one by Martin Greif:

> Now there stir the ears in the field
> moved by a soft breath.
> If one bends over, the next
> trembles as well.
> It is, as if all can feel
> the sickle's coming slice.
> The flowers and strange stalks
> tremble together.

As far as the Semmering, up to the border of the Russian zone, she will be able to hitchhike. Crossing the border will be difficult; according to rumor, the Russians guard their zone very closely and shoot immediately if they suspect border-jumping. But once she has the Semmering behind her, then she should be able to keep going somehow. Semmering! Ilse has to laugh. There she had been conceived, and from there she would have her rebirth in freedom.

She does suffer pangs of conscience when she thinks of

Grandmother! She will have to take off without farewell, secretly, while her Grandmother is working at the hospital. And then her grandmother will be all alone, for Aunt Grete has moved back into her own apartment. The weeks here were pleasant, she thinks, pleasant weeks with Grandmother, Aunt Grete, Susi and me. Pleasant weeks even though everything was in chaos.

No, don't think, and above all, don't think about what it will be like when Grandmother comes home and discovers your flight. It occurs to Ilse that she can leave a note. A note saying, "Don't worry about me. I have to go. I don't want to move back in with Mother." She won't say any more than that. Just these two sentences; one word more might give away her plan, her goal.

It is terrible to have to depart without saying good-bye, without a good-bye hug, or a single farewell word. And she doesn't dare act any more friendly or loving than usual this morning when her grandmother leaves — she could awake suspicion that something was wrong, could cause Grandmother to ask questions. Then she might start to cry. No, Ilse decides not to think about the next day. If I don't succeed in doing it tomorrow, then I may never make it! And I want to *get away*. I *must* get away.

It has to be tomorrow.

"Steinhaus, Semmering, hitchhiking going well," writes Ilse in her notebook. "We're waiting for the man who'll bring us out of the Russian zone. By 'we,' I mean a group that now numbers eleven."

Of course the man wants money to lead the group. He points out that it's a dangerous trip, a dangerous trip for everyone. They are very near the minefields, and no one knows exactly where their borders are. And he has to be in the front.

Ilse has only part of the sum that he asks. But he puts together the money he has collected from everyone, and there is enough. He lets her come along.

What good fortune — she is allowed to come along! Through a minefield? No one in the group hesitates.

"Anti-personnel bomb, fire bomb, dive bombers, artillery — mines are the only thing missing in our collection so far," murmurs an older man in German with a Hungarian accent.

What was a Hungarian doing here, in Lower Austria? In Semmering? That's not the way home for him. Is he perhaps going to Italy?

Ilse would have liked to ask him, but they can't talk while walking. They have to be quiet, very quiet, to step carefully, not to make cracking sounds in the bushes, and above all, to walk as fast as possible. Hardly any one of them knows where any of the others come from or where they are going, but they can't think about getting acquainted, or even exchanging names. Why should they? Everyone has enough to think of, just concentrating on trying to get over this damned border!

A minefield? It doesn't matter. Ilse would rather go over the minefield into the unknown than back home. The whole world was turned upside down; why should she, Ilse, remain in her "normal" environment, an environment she hated? Where nothing was right! And it was no better because someone like Pospischil tried so hard to convince her that there were "values of eternal worth." If that was true, then why had he copied out the whole play "Hamlet?" Only by writing it out in his own hand could he at least be sure that Shakespeare's wisdom would last, could be preserved for the moment and for the future, engraved by *him*, Herr Pospischil himself. He had not only read "Hamlet," not only heard it and seen it in the theater, but he had pinned it down in a very personal way, and so given it a certain definite reality. The whole truth of the play, letter for letter, symbols from the book, scratches in the paper: the result will perhaps remain a little longer and better with Herr Pospischil than the rest of the chaotic world.

"The times are out of joint . . ." Yes! The times are out of joint, and she, Ilse, wanted to make use of this "out-of-joint" condition. It's now or never! The opportunity is offering itself right now.

She moves forward with the little group over the possibly mined area. Their leader points to a steep incline, to a meadow right next to it, and whispers, "Be careful! Over there someone stumbled over a mine a few days ago. They say several border-jumpers have already been killed there. But the wind is favorable. Today you can't smell anything." He laughs as he utters these words, his wrinkled, tanned bearded face creased into a friendly grin, and no one knows if he has just tried to make a bad joke with his macabre comment or if he is actually warning them of real dangers.

"He just says that because he wants more money from us," murmurs the woman behind Ilse. "They always talk like that; it's an old trick."

They keep going, more and more uphill, and only after a long silent march does the leader stop and point again to the cliff, "Keep going up here. I have to go back. The next group is already waiting for me."

"You promised to lead us the *whole* way," protest a few in the group. "As far as the border of the zone."

"This is the whole way. On the little way to the road up ahead nothing is going to happen." The leader says this in a very vague tone, then points at the road high above them. "Simply go up the mountain, then over the road. On the other side of the road the English zone begins. After that it's child's play, no matter where you're headed."

"Who guarantees that that's the right way? That the English zone begins there? Or that we really can get over the border?" says the woman next to Ilse doubtfully.

The leader of the group grins again. "We are all in God's hands," he says and stretches out his hand, as if his words suddenly reminded him to make this unambiguous gesture to the border-jumpers. "If I go further my next group will be delayed, so I need an extra fee," he says, clarifying his gesture.

Ilse has no more money but the others pay, murmuring or in silence. God's hands, thinks Ilse, God's hands, extended through human action.... She joins the group, ashamed that she is the only one who hasn't paid again. Is the meadow really mined? Does anyone want to have that confirmed? If someone finds out, the knowledge will come too late.

After the meadow come bushes, the cliff, the slope, above the slope, the road. They're on their bellies now, crawling, next to each other, between stalks of grass, flowers and plants. The leader lifts his hand in warning. There above a Russian soldier is patrolling back and forth, carrying a machine gun on his shoulder.

They lie pressed to the ground; the soldier passes close to them. Whoever dares look up can see his dusty boots.

Ilse looks at the leader. Now he points upward again, to show that the soldier has disappeared behind the curve of the road. The leader gives a sign, NOW! But, no, only one, two at a time, can go over — he points with his finger, indicating the two people lying next to Ilse.

The first two run, bent over, quietly, quietly over the road. Then the group waits again, waits for the soldier to march by again, for the boots to move past, to come back, waits for the soldier to disappear again behind the curve in the road.

My turn is coming, Ilse prepares herself. No, her heart isn't beating in her throat, although at such a moment it should be. During the walk through the possibly mined field she was still full of fear, also when the soldier appeared and then, when the first people ran over the road. Now, however, she lies there calmly, pressed to the ground, as if carrying out a mechanical routine. She has to wait, and then she has to run when she receives the sign. And it almost seems as if someone else will do it for her, as if she weren't the one who would begin to run — she is so calm and quiet and so free of fear.

Would she find her father? Certainly she would find her other grandmother. And Omi . . . Ride-a-cock-horse . . . but she will be saved; she won't fall in the swamp. She will be saved; she is protected.

Now! The Russian disappears behind the bend in the road, the leader raises his hand, nods to her, gives the sign, NOW! Now!

Yes, yes, she will reach Italy. Italy, her father, the other country. Yes, nothing can happen to her, nothing will happen to her.

Ilse runs, runs over the road, the "Stoj! Stoj!," the "Halt! Halt!" of the soldier doesn't stop her. She runs on and on, toward freedom. Nothing can stop her, nothing can hold her back. Today is today — but tomorrow is tomorrow.

She will be free. She will finally be free.

Afterword

By Rainer Lendl

Sixty years ago, on September 10, 1944, the skies over Vienna were full of bombs. The people of Vienna were experiencing the beginning of the dramatic end of the Second World War. For the first time, civilian Vienna, especially the city center with its historical buildings, was being bombed by Allied forces. The Viennese, along with the inhabitants of the other districts of the "Ostmark," had falsely assumed, until the summer of 1943, that they would be spared bomb attacks. Only after the landing of the Allies in Sicily and on the Italian mainland could Allied bombers reach as far as the "Ostmark" and Bavaria. In July 1943, the 15th division of the U.S. Air Force began to fly over the main ridge of the Alps to reach Southern Germany and Austria. Until the summer of 1944 they had targeted only strategic military sights such as munition factories, railroad lines, and oil installations. In Austria they had concentrated on the regions of Wiener Neustadt, Graz, and Linz. Before 1941 Austria had suffered no air raids. There were only two in 1942, but in 1943, the number climbed to 25. By 1944 the people's false assumption that they would be spared was completely gone. Sirens howled in Vienna on sixty days and during seven nights, and the populace had to spend 118 hours in air raid shelters. During the four months from January 1945 until the end of the war in April the people of Vienna were in fear for their lives for a total of sixty-nine hours of bombing. Unrelenting, the threat from the air continued to grow right up until the bitter end. On March 12, 1945, the heaviest air attack on Vienna began: 747 bombers, accompanied by 200 fighter planes, dropped their deadly cargo onto the city, hitting such major buildings as St. Stephen's Cathedral, the State Opera House, the Albertina art gallery, the Art History Museum, the Burgtheater; in short, the entire inner city. A total of five hundred buildings, approximately two thirds of the structures in the city center, were destroyed. One month later, on April 13, 1945, the Red Army liberated the city of Vienna. Between August 13, 1945, and May of that year the American and British Air

Forces dropped between 70,000 and 120,00 tons of bombs. An estimated 26,000 civilians were killed and 40,000 wounded.

Because the German army was already weakened and unprepared for such an attack, it was unable to mount any real defense from the air or the ground. Some anti-aircraft FLAK guns were stationed in Vienna and Linz, manned by a small number of soldiers. Older men and teenagers were hastily recruited and assigned to newly formed air defense units. Boys and girls fifteen to seventeen years old were recruited as so-called "air raid helpers." After school and between classes they manned the searchlights and performed other duties.

As the front drew nearer and the air raids became more and more frequent, a partially organized, partially spontaneous flight out of the city began. There was a hasty migration of women and children. Those who could sought refuge with friends or family in the provinces where the chances of survival were much higher.

Some Viennese were sent by the authorities to Salzburg or the Tyrol. For many women and children, such a move meant an escape from likely death, but they were fearful for the others left behind and for the property they had to abandon. The powerful figures of the Third Reich had already protected themselves by retreating to the inaccessible mountains and hidden valleys of the Alps.

Graziella Hlawaty describes in minute detail the dramatic final months of the war from a child's viewpoint, initially naive, over time more insightful, experienced beyond her years. The children of this time were raised under an iron authority that could not be questioned. Even minor freedoms were severely restricted. School was a place of fear, intimidation, and discipline, although now and then an individual teacher's own pedagogical mission might reflect glimpses of a different world with other values. Likewise, relationships among pupils, with few exceptions, generally were based on the same prejudices and role models. Graziella Hlawaty clearly demonstrates that school was a place of rebellion and conspiracy expressing childlike dissatisfaction.

Life at home often was the same kind of existence. Anxious silence and resulting fear governed daily life. The logical consequence was the repression of the individual through severe conformity that led to a state of complete voicelessness. The obvious correspondence between reality and literary creation is essential in Hlawaty's work.

The foundation and driving force of all of her books is the evocation of real life. She is a reporter of happiness and suffering, of the heights and depths of human experience, which she relates empathetically, with nothing covered up or held back. To be sure, she refrains for the most part from direct autobiographical writing: "I prefer to keep some distance. It seems too egotistical to me to write about myself." Fortunately for the reader, she has not always held strictly to this principle.

The novel *Broken Songs* is a notable exception. In order to be able to preserve the exact details of her experiences in the last years of the war, she wrote this book soon afterwards, namely in the years 1956-1957. However, it was not actually published until 1995, after all of the individuals from her immediate circle had passed away. "In recording these experiences of wartime I didn't want any gaps in memory to occur, gaps that would need to be replaced later on by vague recollections. I wanted to avoid any flight into the unreal – reality was absurd enough. This was an historical subject that I didn't want to distort by any embellishment that would seem like a lie to me."

Although some of the book's minor characters appear to be composites of various people and their fates, the young Graziella is easy to recognize in the character of Ilse. The author, too, had a mother who exposed her to dangerous situations in Vienna during the bombings. After a happy childhood in Italy, her adolescent years in Vienna were quite the contrary. Hlawaty characterizes these years as the hardest of her life, ones spent in a domestic climate of strife caused by her mother's tragic inability to love, which the daughter and grandmother can do nothing about. Coldness and withholding of love were the signatures of the time as well as of the people around her. *Broken Songs* is a moving document of one oppressed life from an oppressive historical epoch.

Graziella Hlawaty was born on February 2, 1929, in Vienna. She spent her early childhood in Triest with her grandparents, where she formed an especially close bond with her great-grandmother, who was already 83 when the little girl arrived. Again and again in Hlawaty's stories, the reader encounters characters based on this beloved old woman: wise companions and guides along life's journey. In 1936 Hlawaty started school, completing her education in Vienna and Lower Austria, then enrolling in the university in the city of her birth. In 1956 she moved to Sweden, worked as a dishwasher, and then as a cashier and manager in a restaurant to support herself as a writer. Fearing that she was in danger of losing her native language, she returned to Vienna after nine years abroad. From 1965 on, she has maintained two residences, spending half the year on an island near Stockholm and the other half in Vienna. Her writing reflects all the experiences of her self-imposed exile in a foreign land, including brutal demands of the workplace there, interactions with unusual people, and living in isolation on a lonely island. In 1977 her first book appeared, a collection of stories, *Endpunktgeschichten* [End Point Stories]. A mere two years later the renowned Zsolnay Publishers brought out Hlawaty's first novel, *Bosch oder Die Verwunderung der Hohltierchen* (published in English translation as *Bosch* by Ariadne Press in 1995) which established her name in the literary world. Additional novels, volumes of short stories, poems, radio plays and translations of Swedish works followed. She has been recognized with numerous awards and prizes.

Granziella Hlawaty always tells real, not "invented" stories, stories of people with their hardships and triumphs, their questions and their attempts to answer them. In her writing Hlawaty always attempts to forge a courageous path in a confused and confusing world. In the Afterword to her book *Der schwedische Bumerang* [The Swedish Boomerang] (1999), Alexander Giese wrote insightfully: "Whatever we wish for and imagine, somehow, at some time, in a way we cannot determine ourselves, becomes real. Yearnings and premonitions almost always acquire their own reality in our lives, although usually only in highly unexpected transformations." This passage describes how Hlawaty's distinctive voice assumes its rightful place within the continuity of Austrian literature. She avoided the pitfalls of language experimentation; her course has always been straight and direct, one that fully and open-heartedly embraces the human condition with all of its trauma and its underlying significance.

Vienna